Deragon Hex: The Vipdile Key

(Constructed Sanity Sequence: II)

CARLIE MARTECE

AF473379

First published by Castle Mindscape 2016
This edition published 2021
Text and images copyright © 2021 Carlie Martece
All rights reserved.
ISBN: 978-0-9928716-6-6
All characters appearing in this work are fictitious.
Any resemblance to real persons, living or dead,
is purely coincidental.

This is for anybody who has ever been
fed to the vultures…

…and for everybody who agrees that saying
"I've always wanted to be in an alt power couple"
with no trace of irony
should be a criminal offense.

CONTENTS

PROLOGUE

Raise a carnival mirror to their demon glances.

Echo their jagged whispers of judgement.

Vividly recall... this started near cold clifftops but finished with a **three-point** turn in endless desert.

Even now, the Vipdile Key turns and Deragon Hex stirs from anaesthetised slumber, because this is what those people deserve...

Now this is what those people get.

Gift vouchers for a department store, or a wicker basket containing various soaps and those foam things that separate your toes while you paint your toenails, might have been a more welcome gift... but it is too late...

Everybody's favourite dystopian hell, Deragon Hex, is awake.

CHAPTER
ONE

Blood covers the walls, the floor, the furniture and Ash's pretty hands. The corpses of Leah's enemies clutter the room. Their **41** open-mouthed faces caked in red murder and white foundation stare through spilled, claret fluid straight into oblivion. There must have been so much to bleed for.

A striking figure stands amidst the morbid debris wearing a ruined pinstripe suit. Grazed knuckles clutch the handle of an axe, while a pale face holds a worried expression beneath a gelled-back hairstyle drenched in blood and apprehension.

This is Ash.

Surrounded by death and blinking through the scarlet splatter, Ash feels somewhat bemused by these grotesque surroundings.

"This is what you've been waiting for," a sultry voice oozes from speakers on the left as Ash fidgets, overcome with the sinking dread that accompanies an awareness of being watched.

Below the penthouse suite, in the cluttered room of a lonely fanatic, a jaded night porter watches live footage of a gorgeously flustered creature wiping bloody fingers on tailored clothing. The video feed is grainy from lack of Night Vision. Somebody knocked out the overhead lights during the recent whirlwind of executions, and the suite is far above the hex's blue streetlamps, but luckily the criminal is drenched by the glow from a gore-splattered media screen. This display unit fills the right-hand side of the north-east wall and plays cosmetic advertisements in the latest ultra-definition. An enormous mirror fills the opposing wall and duplicates the photogenic sociopath into lunatic twins. It's an arresting sight.

The world-weary night porter has been following this lurid story for weeks. Unaware of this, Ash only knows a certain dumb woman's voice is becoming bothersome.

Safe within her luminous rectangle, dressed in soft pastels, the immaculate female beams down upon the killer and the carnage. She seems pleased to have found a shampoo that gives her life meaning, heedless of the dismembered limbs lying scattered beneath her smile. "Now your hair will get the nourishment it truly deserves," she assures her viewers, her voice gliding with the hollow self-satisfaction of somebody who pretends for a living. She tosses her treasured locks, making them cascade in slow motion, oblivious to the liberated haemoglobin that drips over her radiant countenance.

The night porter decides to stop being a mere witness and interact with the unfolding drama. "Drop the axe, mate," he instructs his new favourite character through the intercom. His voice has the toneless apathy of somebody who pretends they are living while their life is an endless series of mundane tasks and their best days are behind them. He sips more rancid coffee while wondering if he will ever get through a shift in this building without somebody getting shot, stabbed or otherwise butchered.

"You should know, I only did this because I thought it would save her." Ash responds in a more feminine voice than the viewer initially expected from such a muscular frame. Ash confuses most people. Many react to confusion by being hostile or abrasive, which is why Ash carries an axe.

"You too can have the confidence that comes from perfect shine." The glistening actress on the media screen advises her audience of the tired, the crazy and the dead. She smiles, using scripted pseudo-science to discuss a breakthrough in tibshull proteins. The main benefit of only being a transmitted image is you can stand before several corpses and an axe-murderer while only caring about whether your tousled ringlets are receiving added moisturiser.

"The vultures will be here soon," adds the night porter. His voice emanating from the intercom unnerves the addled wielder of the axe, whose piercing eyes now scrutinise a prying lens on the north wall.

"If this camera's working, I'm fucked whether I drop the axe or not, aren't I?" the assassin snaps at the security camera.

A certain mindfuck in synthetic leather had told Ash that surveillance was virtually non-existent in this disreputable segment of Blue **Five Nine**. The cameras are everywhere in this city, glaring through your skin like the eyes of psychopaths, flaying everything that holds you together. This hotel though... she said it ran on antiquated lines that no longer relayed to the master control room. She said the only Night Time staff was a senile porter, too busy completing menial tasks in a fog of dementia to pay attention to the building's video feed.

Ash's unexpected viewer speaks further. "Never mind the camera, mate, the lines round here are fucked. It's the vultures that should concern you..."

Ash's eyes narrow in mistrust. Having been captured on film, there is no chance of getting out of this alive... unless the stranger behind the camera decides to be surprisingly helpful.

Ash has little faith in the kindness of strangers.

If it looks like a rescue boat, it's probably a pirate ship.

"...because if you're still stood there holding that weapon when they arrive, there will be no way to avoid a lethal verdict," the voice through the intercom continues. "And it won't be a merciful death. Those lasers take their time burning you to the bone, layer by agonizing layer."

"I'm seriously confused as to why you're telling me this," replies Ash, glowering at the intercom.

"I'm telling you this because I don't want to watch you die."

"But why do you care? Who are you?"

The murderer waits for a response, but the intercom emits only a faint hiss of static. Ash starts pacing, still clutching the axe, trying not to trip over the pieces of dead human that litter the floor. A disembodied jawbone crunches beneath the thick heal of stolen office shoes, as the bloody weapon is nearly dropped in creeping revulsion. Ash mutters, "This is why you never go axe to mouth."

Suddenly spinning to face the intercom, the armed intruder demands, "Aren't you the night porter here?"

A crackled "Yes" is the eventual reply as a drop of blood falls from the ceiling onto the ruined carpet.

"Then don't you have any damn boots to polish?"

"If all I intended to do tonight was polish boots, you would be facing imminent death in exactly **26** seconds," the night porter retorts. "Now drop the axe and show me your best corpse impression. You're already covered in blood. Just tuck yourself behind a large, mutilated body and play dead, and for Cash's sake, hide your face! Never mind the heat sensors, your victims are still warm."

Ash listens for the dreaded hum of approaching vultures but all that can be heard is the vapid monologue of the shampoo model on the media screen. Her saccharine voice drips prettily over the muted sound of traffic from behind the drape-covered window that fills the south wall. The perplexed killer surveys the carmine debris of a mass execution, picking a fine time to be questioning life choices.

Should I fall to the floor?

Should I find this weirdo night porter and gouge his fucking eyes out?

Should I buy that shampoo?

It's not until the strange observer adds, "Or there'll be nobody left to save her," that the red-handed executioner drops the axe and falls to the floor behind a heap of dead flesh in black fabric. **Five** seconds later, **three** vultures smash through the window.

Deragon Hex's mechanical law-enforcers, spherical and twice the size of a human skull, make an electric purring sound as they glide into the suite. Constructed from mutitian metal and fuelled by social paranoia, they come equipped with cameras and lasers, and are programmed to make unsanctioned murderers their primary targets for destruction.

They hover in triangle formation beneath the ceiling and begin their scan. A stale breeze flows through shattered glass. The vulture at the north wall floats above the door, blocking any chance of escape, while the vulture near the south-west wall hovers over the largest pile of bodies. Their companion who headed left to the south-east wall now floats directly above Ash and glistens in the flickering light from the media screen.

Wary eyes peek out from the tiniest gap beneath heavy-lashed, blood-soaked eyelids as Ash thinks, *Why the fuck didn't I bring a gun?*

"The multi-stage primer, moisturiser, skin protector and mattifying sealant means you'll never need to carry anything else," says the next model as the advertised product changes from shampoo to age-defying foundation. The vulture above Ash spins toward the sight of the woman's blemish-free features. It performs a swift scan of the screen, shining out against a backdrop of ruined wallpaper. Finding no prey in that direction, it returns to surveying the corpse-strewn floor, where Ash is trying not to tremble from an overdose of adrenaline.

"The person you're looking for left around **five** minutes ago," a weary voice informs the room.

The vultures spin to face the intercom.

These flying, weaponised robots do not feed on the dead, but always appear when an unsanctioned murder or assault is flagged by city surveillance. Even the authorities have adopted their long-standing nickname of "vultures". The term comes from their tendency to circle above corpses in search of a culprit, and naming them after extinct birds is considered a dark irony in a city that has never seen the sky.

"Seriously, nobody would stay here unless they were a necrophiliac," the night porter continues. "Look at these people! Pallid skin, sunken eyes... OK, so they didn't look much different when they were alive... but still! Look at all that blood!"

The vultures confer through private transmissions and decide to ignore the anonymous observer. They return to scanning the room. Their reputation for excoriating the guilty makes Ash hope they fail to notice a particular body is more alive than the others. Smoke fills the air despite the breeze blowing through translucent drapes over the broken window. This could be fortunate. It could interfere with their equipment, with motionless bodies indistinguishable from each other in the dim, polluted haze. There might still be hope.

The vulture above Ash looks down, emitting a series of ominous beeps as its lens zooms in on the carpet of butchery.

Ash tries not to breathe.

The vulture beeps again, still facing downwards.

Ash feels sick, convinced of being spotted, seeing only extermination ahead.

A glowing red dot appears on Ash's cheek.

"Dazzle!" cries the woman on the media screen, driven to ecstasy by the whiteness of her teeth. Distracted, the robotic hunter whirls to view a close-up shot of pearly enamel. "For the whitest shine," brags the giant mouth. "Enough formula to last a whole year, only **89** cash digits while stocks last."

The vulture scans the promotional dental health imagery, then turns away, disinterested. It has already dismissed what it almost saw on the floor. These robots are brutal but not smart.

The trinity of death-bringers continues to levitate beneath the ceiling, capturing and processing information from the human junkyard below, occasionally beeping. The machine closest to Ash remains too confused by its proximity to loud cosmetic propaganda to maintain a consistent view of the ground. After **seven** minutes that drag like **nine** years, the vultures finally glide back out through the jagged hole in the window.

Ash breathes again, stares at the security camera and asks, "So who summoned them if it wasn't you?"

The night porter returns the killer's gaze on his spy screen. "It could've been anybody in that room with you… Before you killed them, that is. It was hard to tell what was happening with you moving so fast. I can re-play this footage, but that'll take time... which isn't something you have. The vultures could return any moment."

A drop of blood falls from the ceiling onto sodden furniture. Where the sanguine fluid has pooled into small puddles, its smooth, reflective surface glistens in the glow from the media screen.

Ash says, "It wasn't supposed to go this way."

"It never is," sighs the night porter.

Where the scarlet liquid is absorbed by soft fabrics, the matte effect looks almost black in the dim illumination. The carnage of this haphazard slaughter will soon decay. Strange, how a collection of characters with individual hopes and dreams become nothing but rotting meat after these moments of devastation.

"I found Leah in a room of blood once, but she was the only casualty," Ash reminisces. "It was a constant struggle to save her from herself... I remember her saying she felt 'icy with death bringing another winter in the shape of poison sharks.' Her depression made her somewhat poetic... I asked her, 'What do you know of winter and sharks? Have you been watching the history channels, Leah?' And she said our history is written in the stars of our arms and the scars in our eyes."

"How deep," responds the unimpressed night staff.

"I asked her, 'Ocean life and stars? Seasonal variations of Day Time? What's next? Are you going to plant me a tree, Leah?' And she smiled and told me that centuries of skies stream through our arteries and we'll never belong here."

"I'm guessing she was fond of drugs then?"

"She didn't need them," Ash scowls, sitting up to survey the room. "This place is poisonous enough! I should never have left her alone in this toxic hell."

"Not everybody is destroyed by this city," argues the night porter. "Maybe she just dated the wrong guy. This happens with vulnerable girls. Once the world has convinced somebody they're a victim, they'll always be drawn to those who victimise them. It's a difficult trap to escape from."

"I don't care how depressive her outlook was, poisoning her was evil! The person who did this to her needs to die!"

"That'll be difficult," argues the night porter. "With him being so far above her in the Cashdamn social hierarchy."

Ash jumps up, glaring at the security camera. "Who the hell *is* this?" More tears of blood fall from the ceiling as the intercom crackles. A droplet lands on the killer's forehead, creating a sudden sense of panic that prompts a dash for the discarded axe.

"Doesn't every woman dream of longer-lasting lipstick?" enquires a curious starlet.

"Shut up!" screams Ash, with a run at the media screen and a swing of the axe that finally terminates the monotony of cosmetic advertising. Pieces of media screen tumble to the ground as the weapon is wrenched back out of the mechanics.

"Who the hell *is* this?" Ash repeats into the resulting darkness.

"I'm not somebody who intends to stop you, but you should be aware of the consequences of your behaviour," is the calm reply from the intercom. "His audience will say his dreadful ex-girlfriend told lies and sent an axe-wielding maniac to kill him because she's crazy and wanted attention. You killing him will make him a martyr."

Ash remains tense and defiant. "Whether he's a dead hero or a dead villain, he'll still be dead, and that might be enough."

"Enough for what?"

"Enough to save her," says Ash. Another shard of screen falls to land on the quagmire carpet. The inky air tastes warm and bitter. "I told you, I only did this because I thought it would save her."

"Well you can still save her, but you need to act fast, or you're a dead man," says the voice through the intercom with a new hint of urgency.

"I'm really not," says Ash, choking back deranged laughter.

"Well, whatever you are, your enemies didn't just have the vultures on their side," warns the night porter. "They could also summon wolves."

As though waiting for an introduction, the low, rumbling noise of mechanical growling now permeates the metallic air. The sound comes from the hallway. You might say it resembled thunder if you had ever heard a storm. Ash turns a beautifully sculpted face toward the ceiling, convulsing with the mirth of the insane.

"Get a fucking grip!" yells the night porter. "Those flying bastards are tame compared to these things! You'll be torn into so many pieces, your victims will look healthy in comparison! You need to run!"

Ash stops laughing, takes a deep breath, and turns to face the growl behind the door with an air of serene conviction. "I'm done running from what those people did to her. It's time to stand and fight! Our enemies have the vultures and the wolves, but we have the truth."

"And what is the truth?" asks the night porter.

Ash waits **three** seconds before responding, while something with teeth, claws and glowing red eyes begins to scratch behind the room's only doorway.

CHAPTER
TWO

It is several minutes before the hotel massacre. Ash is in Estana's passenger seat, holding an axe and watching the passing hexes. The vehicle moves along a port lane, heading east. It is scheduled Night Time, but this makes no difference to the inter-hex roadways where the polluted air is eternally night-lit. The lurid, scarlet lights of a red hex shine directly to their left while across **three** lanes of traffic to their right glow a green hex's emerald illuminations.

Estana says, "Don't worry about vultures here, there's no active camera feed."

Ash regards the driver, an air of invincible arrogance holding her poised as she controls the vehicle, the streetlights shining a vivid glow on her alabaster complexion. Ash sighs and says, "I still can't believe I'm actually doing this."

Estana turns to her companion. The thick material of her exquisite clothing creaks with the turn of her head as she asks, "Doing what?"

"Killing people," Ash replies.

Estana faces forward again and laughs, her glance mocking every particle of dust between herself and the end of the road. She says, "Well *I* can."

Tortured eyes turn from the tormentor to gaze back out the window. Ash elaborates, "I've held back the rage for as long as I can remember. Marching along rusty streets, pounding machines at the gym while death threats set to repetitive beats are screamed in my ear, constantly seeking catharsis... I honestly thought I could go my whole life holding it back. Isn't that how the poor and unpopular are expected to behave? When you can't buy off the wolves or evade the vultures, you bottle it, you choke it back, you exercise harder or punch a fucking wall. You're not supposed to actually kill people."

With her voice like silk dipped in cyanide, Estana enquires, "But why not?"

"Because you can't have much of a functional society if everybody goes around killing people, can you?" Ash snorts. "'Hello, Mrs Smith, I'm heading out to buy groceries. Do you need me to kill anybody at the store? Why, gosh! Somebody's blown your head off with a shotgun! Never mind. Cheerio!' Honestly, it'd be a nightmare. Nothing would get done."

"Your life was a nightmare anyway," remarks Estana, with a frown that might suggest sympathy if not for the cruel amusement in her eyes. "Always trapped in employment that was psychological torture... And what exactly does this society 'get done'? It's hardly 'functional'. We're in a gigantic prison that's convinced it's a hedonist's playground, but in reality, we're all still slaves."

"Even you?" Ash wonders. "Miss Snide Superiority?"

"Everybody's enslaved by something," says Estana, glancing in her mirror and hitting the indicator before moving into the red starboard lane. The junction lights flash a red circle and she turns right without pausing, following the edge of the green hex into the blue starboard lane. The sapphire lights of their destination hex are now on their left.

"What are you enslaved by?" Ash asks her.

Colours race past and only slaughter lies ahead as Estana replies, "You'll figure that out, someday."

Ash groans in frustration. "I'm sick of your cryptic shit! If you insist on being the devil on my shoulder, shouldn't there be an angel opposing you? To tell me, I dunno... not to murder people?"

Estana laughs again and says, "There *was* such a creature, but she's dead now."

"I suppose you killed her," Ash mutters, shoulders slumped in resignation.

"No, it wasn't me."

"Of course. You don't kill people yourself. You just manipulate others into your sick bidding."

"There there, don't cry. When you rescue the lovely Leah, perhaps *she* can be your angel."

"We both know she's no angel."

"Aww, your poor little tragic whore... So alone and misunderstood."

"I *will* save her," Ash declares. "Even if it destroys me."

"Come now," insists Estana, "there's no reason to destroy anything other than the targets I select for you."

"And what if I don't?" Ash wonders.

Estana's eyes gleam as her mouth cracks into the smile of a piranha before responding.

"If you don't, then Leah will die."

It is **eight** months before the hotel massacre and Leah is wondering why the ceiling is pulsating rainbows. Complicated mandalas shimmer, morph and mutate, bleeding in and out of each other, a maelstrom of multi-chromatic chaos. "Do you guys see that?" she asks her friends, who are gazing up with gaping mouths. It takes the group a while to remember they dropped capsules of **4**C-I an hour ago, and this explains everything. Upon realising their idiocy, the **six** friends crumple into fits of laughter.

"That was confusing as fuck!"

"How did we forget we took that stuff?"

"I thought I was losing it!"

Everybody laughs so hard their faces hurt, while a tramp with neon lips stumbles past outside the Road Level window. Beyond the glass lies a fake garden, the white lights of scheduled Day Time, and various mutilated homeless people wandering round the synthetic lawn.

Leah and her friends are in Feng Baca vacation zone in the south segment of Red **Two Six**.

Each hex segment is a large city zone. From Road Level upwards are high-ceilinged 'outdoor' areas that exhibit lighting changes similar to overground day patterns but without seasonal variation. The group chose this destination because it compliments their lifestyle choices. Dilapidated dwellings with rusty upper walkways loom above astrograss lawns, the camera feed is off, guard presence is minimal, and everybody is illegally intoxicated.

In their ramshackle apartment, the ceiling swirls its technicolour kaleidoscope above the partygoers while their laughter subsides, and the conversation moves toward more pressing matters. "Well anyway, as I was saying... on this label here..." continues Lori Quietrugs, remembering the last thing that perplexed her. She and Byf Wool are examining a half-empty packet of balloons.

"Yeah, we need more sorutin for those," Byf remembers.

"We can get a box from the other apartment later," says Donnie Benifyr. Leah smiles at her pretty boyfriend as he ensures the glittery sticker with the unicorn saying "I love ballet" is still attached to his forehead.

"That's not what I was saying!" Lori insists. "I was talking about what it says on the packaging."

"Emergency Cat!" yells Leah, throwing a patch of fabric in the shape of a cartoon feline at Lori.

The party girl ignores Leah's attention-seeking antics and continues to glare at the balloon packet. "It says here, 'To protect the eyes, do not inflate too rapidly.'"

"You need to write a letter to the district controller about this," quips Byf.

Lori is incredulous. "Protect the eyes?! They're balloons! How are they gonna damage your eyes? This doesn't make sense!" she exclaims, her face a mixture of rage and confusion. She then sees the cat-shaped fabric patch in her lap. "And why the fuck is there a cat here?"

Everybody laughs and then forgets why they were laughing as the music has a key change that alters the pattern on the ceiling. Donnie and his friend Hector Decallo begin wrestling with an inflatable giraffe. This air-filled parody of an overground creature is the height of a human leg, with bulging, cartoon eyes above a benign smile, and they want it dead.

"That's Emergency Cat," says Leah to Lori, stretching out her legs. Her striped socks are asymmetrical, with loose threads on the left ankle and the right adorned with a small, fabric cat. "And this is Local Doctor Cat," she adds, nodding at the feline design on her starboard leg. "He is to be consulted for non-emergency health matters."

"Why are you telling me this?" asks Lori. "Why would I need a local doctor cat?"

Leah gestures toward her legs. "This solves the mystery of Emergency Cat."

"I don't care about Emergency Cat," Lori responds, "that's no longer relevant. The important question is, why must we protect our eyes while blowing up balloons?"

"Let's have a look," chuckles Leah, holding out her hand to receive the packaging. Balloon faces peer from beneath transparent plastic. "These balloons have faces, Lori! It's referring to the eyes painted on the balloons! The paint might crack if they inflate too fast."

"For Cash's sake, why is everything so confusing?" wonders Lori.

"I hate it! I HATE IT!" yells Hector, punching the inflatable giraffe in the face.

"And I hate you," retorts Lem Napam, sitting up with a look of disdain.

"I thought you were asleep," says Leah.

"Well, I am so sorry," Lem replies, reaching for his cigarettes.

"I've had terrible luck with women," mourns a sorrowful voice from the media screen that fills the north-west wall, now playing an advertisement for Damon Repper's opinion show. The social channels are something the gang had forgotten existed, along with what they ate for breakfast and what day it is.

"That guy's a tool," Donnie surmises.

"Someday I will find my queen," Damon Repper announces from the screen. His female audience in the mediavision studio croon adoration while everybody in front of the screen doubles over in another fit of laughter.

"The Damon Repper Show is playing on Social Channel Four right now!" booms a dramatic voice-over.

Next up is a fashion advertisement, with models Tom Dastirrian and Forensi Purcs sporting a new line of designer sunglasses. This prompts Donnie to suggest, "Hey, it's Day Time now, and they've turned the lights up bright as hell out there. We should get drunk outside!"

"Good idea," agrees Leah. "What's the worst that could happen?"

The pseudo-park is brimming with colourful tramps.

Due to the scarcity of animal life in Deragon Hex, potentially dangerous cosmetic items are first tested on homeless people before being sold to customers who can afford legal representation.

"How can *you* perceive something being deep?" a man with no lips asks a woman with pus and indigo glitter instead of a left eye.

The male vagrant still has both his eyes, which presently seethe in frustrated fury. He tells people child soldiers cut his mouth off in the Kinder Rebellion, but really it melted when a new lip colour sealant turned out highly corrosive. Instead of keeping pigment in place for longer lasting colour, it dissolved half his face. Lobbyists cite such incidents as great examples of why testing on impoverished, ugly people first is essential for the safety of Deragon Hex's aesthetically pleasing population.

"Very funny," the woman with an indigo mess instead of a left eyeball replies. "But what I'm saying is, he was the first person they tested it on. It burned through to his brain and he died screaming."

They are discussing a friend whose head was melted by a fast-acting bleach and waiting for Ava, their dealer, under the dazzling Day Lights of the vacation segment.

"Did his family at least get compensation?" the lipless man enquires, forming the words as adequately as he can with the remains of his mouth.

"His family are dead."

"Yup, the poor and hideous don't last long in this city." The man's attention is caught by the party crew walking out onto the astrograss. "It's because of these shallow sluts," he declares, nodding at Leah. "They want to look like Honeysuckle." The maimed man observes the object of his contempt while his own ugliness renders him invisible among the poisoned partygoers. Leah wears a low-cut top to show off her surgically enhanced cleavage, the left strap falling off her shoulder as she arranges a picnic blanket for her narcotised friends. A pencil skirt clings to her toned lower body. "It makes me sick," he lisps.

"She's done you no harm," argues the half-blind woman. "In many ways, she's as much a victim of aesthetic judgement as you."

"Catshit!" the grotesque man retorts.

With nothing more to say, the tramps turn silent as they wait for Ava the sliced-up shaman, patron saint of the broken and disfigured. Ava has the painkillers that will help them survive the week. She provides infinite remedies for those brought low in this toxic dystopia, the folds of her tattered clothing hiding secret stashes of chemical redemption. She dispenses medicine at locations seemingly chosen at random but usually where something dreadful will soon happen.

The gang feels somewhat less trashed under the outdoor lights. Acrylic trees rustle in the breeze from the fans, and the ultraviolet rays of Day Time have a reviving effect on their confused brains. Everybody is euphoric, apart from Hector Decallo who still very much detests the inflatable giraffe. "I HATE IT!" he yells, trying to crush the plastic creature in a headlock while the rest of the crew sprawls over blankets and astrograss.

"It hates you too," Lem informs him. "Especially your face."

Donnie Benifyr laughs and takes Leah in a warm embrace, the Day Lights glinting off the colourful unicorn saying "I love ballet" on his forehead. Suddenly remembering the sticker, he brings his mouth to Leah's ear. "Do you know what?" he whispers, as synthetic plants crackle around them in endless hallucination. "I fucking LOVE ballet!"

"I HATE IT!" is Hector's final cry of rage before he takes a bite out of the inflatable giraffe's neck. Punctured, it collapses beneath him.

"I hope you're pleased with yourself," says Lem.

Hector snarls, "I fucking hated that thing!"

Lori wires up mini-speakers to a portable music player while the sound of distant laughter from overhead walkways adds to the hazy ambiance.

"Shall we ask Gabby and the others to join us from the other block?" Lem asks the group.

"I thought those guys said they were going to the pool," remarks Byf.

"Ugh, Gabby Coilestio hates me..." Leah sighs, lying back on the blanket.

"You know why, don't you?" mutters Lem, glancing at Donnie, who is pouring whiskey and cola into a large mug.

Leah squints up at a massive light, pretending it's the sun, realising she has dropped her sunglasses and wondering why in

Earth they are still called 'sunglasses'. She is about to respond when a shadow falls over her.

"Hey! You guys got any balloons?"

Leah sits up to see **three** young women in kindergore costume with deliberately tattered doll dresses and synthetic wounds giving them the party-version appearance of the undead. The girl on the left has fake blood smeared around her mouth. The messy creature on the right has it coming out of her eyes and the middle wreakhead has red syrup dripping from her hairline.

"We've got balloons but no sorutin," Leah tells them.

"That's OK, we've got cannisters. But we've run out of balloons that haven't burst."

"You can have **three** of ours. They've got faces," says Lori.

"Awesome! Thanks!" the cheerful wraiths reply, accepting the rubber gifts of various colours.

"Make sure you inflate them slowly, to protect the eyes," warns Byf.

"We will," agrees a wavy-haired zombie girl with a bemused smile. The faux dead are preparing to stagger off when they hear the scream.

Despite the girls' garish costumes, the jagged screech of horror sounds incongruous against the innocent noises of revelry. It pierces the gentle vibe of the group's wasted picnic, making skin creep, eyes widen and blood figuratively freeze.

"AARGH!" comes the sound again. The gang spies a slender blonde in high-end designer clubwear who has just run from the neighbouring apartment, covering her face.

A man follows her wearing only his underwear. His eyes twinkle above a malevolent smile as he does the stuttering dance of a broken marionette while she backs away from him, lowering her hand to her side. Actual blood drips from her nostrils, making the synthetic blood of those in fancy dress resemble a tasteless joke.

The nearly naked attacker continues his unusual dance. It takes him away from his apartment and toward a decorative tree where he begins an exercise routine, starting with squats. The injured girl runs back inside, pulling the automatically locking door closed behind her.

"What the fuck just happened?"

"Did you guys see that?"

"That was fucking dark..."

Leah shuffles backwards so that Donnie is between her and the unexpected attacker while passers-by stop to stare at his antics.

"Cash, I know who that is!" gasps the zombie girl with the bleeding hairline. "That's Stan Fellowvic! I've seen his show on the social channels! And I reckon that was his girlfriend, Betty Porlend!"

Oblivious to his audience, the deranged celebrity begins a series of athletic stretches. His victim peers from her apartment's front window with the wide eyes of a vagrant caught in the headlights of a truck.

"We should go see if she's OK," the zombie girl with the bloody mouth suggests.

"Good idea!"

Bravely stepping up to a necessary mission, the costumed friends approach the doorway, checking over their shoulders to make sure Stan Fellowvic is not following them. Fortunately, he is too busy keeping in shape to notice. Young men with bottles of beer stumble past him emitting scornful laughter, but he ignores their taunts.

The girls knock on the door. The bloody-nosed blonde takes a final, terrified glance to make sure her assailant is far from the entrance, then runs to let in her visitors.

"Those damned surveillance cameras never work when they're needed!" exclaims the woman with the indigo infection. Her functional eye had taken in the scene while she stood shaking, the revellers ignoring her outlandish countenance. "He blatantly assaulted that poor girl, and not a vulture, wolf or guard in sight!" she complains, shaking her filthy, matted tresses.

"To be fair, the lack of surveillance is probably the reason she came here. Most of the drugs these kids take aren't licensed," her friend lisps in response.

"But self-poisoning is far less heinous a crime than punching an unarmed woman in the face!" the indigo woman argues. "If this was an affluent segment, he'd be destroyed by vultures or wolves by now."

"Unless he's higher up the social hierarchy," her companion argues. "In which case, his ratings would be ceiling high! Have you seen how fashionable violence is? Also, if this was an affluent segment, the guards would arrest us for ruining the surroundings."

The lipless man keeps his eyes on Betty Porlend's window, where alternating, red-stained faces peer in horror from behind faded curtains.

"The guards will arrive soon," says a voice behind him.

He spins round to see Ava. She stands with unreadable eyes staring from a sliced-up face, clutching a carrier bag in her tar-stained fingers. His favourite maimed mystery has appeared, as usual, during a catastrophe. "Don't count on it, Ava," he retorts. "In these disreputable segments, they take their time."

Ava reaches into her tattered jacket and withdraws the pills for her comrades. "The guards will arrive soon, and it's time to leave," she insists. "He'll go for *her* next." She nods at Leah. "The girl who looks like Honeysuckle."

"I'm not surprised," replies the lipless man, reaching for his medicine. "What do girls expect with such revealing clothing? They're bound to attract the wrong attention."

"That's unfair!" snaps the indigo woman, reaching for her prescription while glowering at her opinionated friend.

They both fail to hear Ava saying, "She is the reason the massacre will happen in **eight** months' time."

Leah and her friends are still warily eyeing Stan Fellowvic, who has progressed to doing push-ups, when the zombie girls come running out of the apartment.

"She was half asleep when she felt a punch to the back of her head!"

"She sat up, Stan was next to her, and he punched her in the face!"

"She says he's never acted this way before. He's taken a new drug that's driven him mental!"

Everybody remains enthralled by the media star as he crouches on his hands and knees, moaning sensually while a stream of urine cascades from his boxer shorts, glinting in the harsh Day Lights as it flows onto the synthetic lawn.

"EEWWW! That's disgusting!" squeals a voice nearly drowned out by jeering from the windows and overhead walkways.

"Somebody should fetch security, none of the cameras are switched on," remarks a dismayed zombie girl.

"Yeah, let's go!" her nearest friend agrees.

"I'll go with you!" offers Hector, jumping up off the remains of the inflatable giraffe. He and the zombies set off to the security office to report the man's unhinged and violent behaviour.

Stan Fellowvic rises but does not follow them. Instead, oblivious to the dark stain on his boxer shorts, he scans the area until his eyes settle on a cowering Leah.

Walking over to the gang, eyes locked onto his next target, he holds out a hand.

"Keep the fuck away from her!" warns Donnie. Stan moans and reaches for Leah's hair. The gang cringes from the stench of him as Donnie knocks Stan's hand away. "I said, 'Fuck off!'"

The loaded media personality backs away, never taking his eyes off Leah, who whispers, "I wanna go back inside."

"Yeah, let's get our stuff and go indoors," agrees Donnie.

The shaken group gathers their blankets, balloons and bottles. Lori disconnects her speakers from the music player complaining, "Where are the damn vultures and guards when you need them?"

"We chose this place for low surveillance," Donnie mutters, searching for the mug containing his alcoholic beverage.

"Alicia could deal with the likes of him," declares Byf.

"Alicia?"

"Yeah, for all her faults, you have to admit, she did make violent asshats like him her primary targets for killage."

"Hey Leah, didn't you live with a guy who looked a bit like Alicia?" Lem enquires.

"Not *exactly*…" responds Leah.

"Yeah, you did!" says Byf. "What was his name? Wasn't it Ash?"

"Yeah, I used to live with Ash," sighs Leah, "but..."

BANG!

Leah is interrupted by the sound of Stan Fellowvic trying to leap through a window.

He has taken a running jump and hit the glass with his shoulder, but the reinforcement grid repels him, and he bounces off and crashes to the ground.

This is when everything starts moving too swiftly for Leah's confused brain to understand. Lori scrambles to take her equipment back into the apartment. Hector has disappeared with the zombies. Byf is picking up a blanket, Lem is gathering empty bottles, while Donnie finds and quickly grabs his mug of whiskey and cola from the ground next to a discarded hat. All the while, Leah is searching for her missing sunglasses and getting increasingly furious at the cheering from overhead walkways. "This guy's hilarious!" crows an ecstatic spectator.

This prompts Leah to stomp over to beneath the walkway and admonish the drunken youths. "He punched a girl in the face! Stop encouraging him!"

She should not have said that. As if summoned, Stan Fellowvic starts running toward her, and she fails to notice him until too late.

"Hey! You come through *me* first!" shouts Donnie, jumping in front of him.

Stan shoves a flat palm into Donnie's face, disorienting him so he can sprint past unhindered.

Leah makes a belated run for the apartment door. There is a blow to her head accompanied by the sound of glass breaking and the sickly chill of being drenched in alcohol. Stan grabs her hair and tries turning her round for a better shot at her face. "Get the fuck off me!" she yells. The strands almost torn from her skull, she instinctively reaches up to hold her hair at the roots. This is how her elbows protect her face when Stan takes her shoulders and shoves her into a window with a force that would have broken her nose.

Leah is wishing she had taken self-defence classes and knew what the hell to do when she is suddenly free because Donnie has Stan in a headlock. She backs away in terror as her boyfriend wrestles Stan to the ground. Donnie gets him pinned by his neck, but his limbs are flailing, and Leah is scared he will escape at any moment.

She hears a tapping to her left. Her back-stepping has taken her to the front of Stan and Betty's apartment, where frightened eyes peer out from above a bloody red nose. Leah and Betty gaze at each other, victim to victim.

"Are you OK? He just bottled me!" Leah cries at the battered face in the window. The blow to her skull along with the smashed-glass noise and alcohol drench certainly gave that impression, although when her scalp is later found free from cuts, she is no longer certain.

Betty gestures toward her apartment's door.

Leah glances back at her assailant.

"Somebody fucking help me!" orders Donnie, who can barely contain the struggling Stan. Lem and Byf both cautiously grab a flailing arm. Lori stands in the sanctuary of the groups' apartment doorway, screaming, "This is horrible!" but Leah cannot reach her without going past the thrashing mass of violent limbs. Deciding that Stan and Betty's apartment is the closest refuge, Leah regards the fellow victim in unspoken agreement before running to be let in. Her back turned away from the high ceiling of outdoor space, she does not see the approaching vultures.

"So *now* the vultures arrive!" snaps the indigo woman. "Those kids must have found the site security team, who've switched on the camera feed."

Around them, doors are closing as people scurry from day-lit resting places on lawns and upper walkways to shelter in dim apartments. The foreboding hum of flying vulture metal fills the air. A decent crowd usually gathers for a vulture trial, but nobody remembers when they last consumed anything legal, and everybody has The Fear.

"You were right, Ava," the lipless man concedes. "The vultures have arrived, which means the guards could be heading this way now."

Ava says nothing, staring unblinking at the scene before her.

Across Deragon Hex, all channels flash "Breaking News: New Vulture Trial Live on the Crime Channel". Viewers are in thrall to their screens, transfixed by a slow-motion replay of Stan bashing Leah's head into the window.

A worried colleague contacts Stan Fellowvic's press officer, who struggles to stay calm.

"Fuck! This guy keeps me busy!" He races to organise on-site representation.

From her prime viewing position on the vacation zone lawn, the indigo woman wonders, "Do you think there'll be wolves too?"

"I doubt it. Why would anybody with that kinda money vacation here?" asks her lipless friend. "I bet the guards will still try doing their job though."

Constrained by their inability to fly, Deragon Hex's human guards rarely arrive in time to prevent a vulture trial's violent conclusion. Now that rich citizens have wolves as well, traditional law-bringers are sliding toward obsolescence.

Around the harshly lit acrylic gardens, doped-up faces peer from behind safety glass and parted curtains to observe the flying, spherical robots surrounding Stan Fellowvic. Anybody feeling competent at operating electronic equipment switches on their personal communication screen, ready to use their voting application. Donnie, Byf and Lem have stepped back from the assailant, repulsed by his stench and wary of the red target dots of laser beams.

"Stan Fellowvic, you have been filmed committing an assault hitherto unsanctioned by public approval. How do you plead?" enquires the robotic voice of the nearest vulture.

Stan emits manic laughter.

"We interpret your response as guilty," the vulture informs him, before spinning to face Leah's friends. "Who will represent the case for prosecution?"

"Can't this be passed to the guards? I want to check if Leah's OK," says Donnie.

"Permission denied," responds the vulture.

"I'm OK!" Leah shouts from the doorway of Stan and Betty's apartment. A couple of vultures spin to face her. "He attacked her too." She gestures to Betty, who shakes her head. "She says she won't prosecute though because she loves him."

Betty proves this assertion by running into a shadowed back room, leaving Leah stood alone in the doorway.

"Will you represent the case for prosecution?" asks the nearest vulture.

"I can do," Leah replies. "Although, you might need somebody else if you want laser punishment. I'm not vindictive. There should be a permanent record on his file though, so he'll get punished if he commits a second offence. That should hopefully deter him from doing this again."

Across the subterranean city, home viewers yell, "Kill him! Kill him!" at their media screens. The pre-voting data is leaning strongly toward Death by Laser. Stan is still lying on the ground laughing under the target rays while Leah's friends continue to keep their distance.

Back at the press office, Stan's favourite employee is on the phone to his contact at the scene, asking, "Can you take this? I can pay you."

"Ha, I earn more money than most people! I will gladly do this for free," grins Gabby Coilestio. The gleeful socialite finishes the call, rounds the corner and steps onto the astrograss lawn trilling, "I am representing the case for defence!"

"Great," groans Leah as her least favourite acquaintance joins the party. With the animosity between them, she would not be surprised if the woman ordered a backlash.

"For fuck's sake, is she crying?" crows Gabby, as she stomps past and glowers at Leah. "I can't believe she called the guards because she got hit on the head! Nobody wants the guards here! She's being pathetic. I got attacked all the time when I lived in the western hexes, and I never called the guards. The poor guy is smashed and now he might get killed because this dumbass couldn't defend herself, it's fucking stupid." She smirks at Leah with a sarcastic closing line of, "No offence."

"Yeah! Stupid bitch!" yell the excited home viewers.

The pre-voting data swings toward Backlash.

"What does she expect when she's dressed in that slutty outfit? Backlash the bitch!" they cry at screens in their dingy mediavision rooms surrounded by empty drinks bottles and plastic merchandise.

Leah senses the possibility that she will burn for her lack of silence. The closest vulture aims its red laser beam at her fraught and weary face, framed by bleached blond curls tousled in the recent skirmish. A camera zooms in to capture what could be the last footage of her unburned features.

"Did Leah even call for the guards?" mumbles Byf to Lem, who shakes his head.

"I'm not pushing for the Death by Laser vote," Leah reminds the viewers. "I'm only asking for Caution Warning."

Stan is evidently amused by this, and his laughter gets louder. The tiny red circles dance across his pockmarked complexion as his countenance crumples with deranged mirth.

"The main reason I find his behaviour sinister is, he was only attacking women," Leah explains. "There were guys walking past, mocking him, earlier. If he was merely lashing out, with no thought behind his actions, why didn't he punch the first guy who approached? He didn't notice any of them. He only notices a woman who's sat quietly with her friends, and doesn't attack until she's separated from the pack. And don't forget, this is after he's punched his girlfriend in the face!"

"For Cash's sake!" snaps Gabby. "The guy is wasted! He doesn't know what he's doing!"

"Then why didn't he attack the *men* provoking him?"

As Leah and Gabby argue, the incoming votes are divided between extreme verdicts. A few viewers opt for Leah's suggested sentence of Caution Warning, but most choose either the harsh Death by Laser, the pernicious Backlash or the brutal Double Kill.

"Maybe you should ask yourself why people hate you," sneers Gabby.

"When did this become about people hating me?" gasps Leah.

Gabby opens her mouth to respond when tyres screech across the nearby parking lot.

"Stand down, vultures! We have this under control!" shouts a gruff, authoritarian voice.

Leah glows with relief, realising the guards have arrived and she has been saved for a second time today. They hurry to the scene, guns raised, sweating under the outdoor lighting in their starched uniforms. It is unusual for them to arrive so fast, but they may have been patrolling outside the venue due to this segment's notoriety. Although many narcotics are now legal, several are still black market, and what remains of guard funding comes from authorities who want this untaxed trade eliminated.

The home viewers swear at their screens. Vultures are still programmed to stand down when commanded by human law-enforcers, and now nobody will get fried for their entertainment. At the press office, Stan's media team whoop in celebration, knowing that the guards' forgiveness can easily be bought. In a distant hex, an unsympathetic Estana watches her media screen and comments, "You stupid, stupid girl...", before the Crime Channel switches back to its previously scheduled programming. The scene is no longer televised.

"Why is Gabby such a bitch to Leah?" Byf whispers to Lem as the vultures withdraw their laser beams and the guards surround Stan.

"Gabby and Donnie used to fuck, but he said he didn't want a relationship and called it off. Shortly after, Leah drifted into our social group and she and Donnie started dating." Lem steps back to give the human law-enforcers space.

"Ah, that explains it," says Byf.

Making no effort to hide her disappointment, Gabby hugs Donnie and tells him, "Keep being awesome," before walking off, throwing a brief, sullen glare at Leah as she passes. Metal vultures float off to distant high ceilings with a receding hum.

The lipless man, the indigo woman and Ava, their mutilated medicator, flee the grounds before they can be arrested for making the place look unsavoury. Leah and Donnie embrace as her attacker is handcuffed and dragged away by the guards.

"Don't kill me! You're beautiful!" Stan begs, before dissolving into further fits of piss-soaked giggles while the guards fail to hide their revulsion.

"Why do these things always happen to me?" frets Leah.

"I don't know, cutie pie," says Donnie, kissing her forehead and holding her close.

"Ever since I was a kid..." she murmurs. "It's like I'm cursed or something..."

Beyond the plastic lawn, on dusty concrete, Stan flails under the grip of the guards as he turns to look back at Leah.

"This way!" the law-enforcers command, shoving him into the waiting van.

"It will be OK," Donnie comforts her. "You've got me now."

Leah hides her face against Donnie's chest; she cannot see Stan's vengeful eyes as he stares a final time before the van door closes. "I've solved life!" he screams at her. "Do you hear me? I'VE SOLVED LIFE!!!"

CHAPTER THREE

"They called her 'lethal Alicia'."

It is half a year before the hotel massacre and Leah's favourite former roommate is watching the Crime Channel in the mediavision room of a dingy prison block. Ash is surrounded by fellow uniformed convicts. The prison contains criminals whose crimes did not attract vulture attention, those who the guards reached before the vultures began shooting, and wolf targets who survived being savaged by mechanical dentition. This massive correctional facility occupies the red-bordered, central, hexagonal city zone from which the underground metropolis now takes its name.

"On a killing spree that began nearly **two** decades ago she murdered **795** people!" enthuses the programme's narrator, prompting an appreciative cheer from the crowd of assembled felons. Fists with tattooed knuckles punch the foetid air, while raised arms reveal sweat patches on red uniforms. Yellow-tinged strip lighting casts a dull sheen on shaved scalps.

The prisoners have gathered to watch a True Crime special on Alicia, the vicious, teenage killer who wreaked havoc when Deragon Hex was still Dew Lorrund. Their scratched and dusty media screen dominates the south-east wall. Monochrome footage shows a young woman dressed in black with blood smeared on her face, aiming her gun at the vulture camera as it flies toward her. The visuals freeze on the final frame before she pulls the trigger.

"It's important to remember how different Deragon Hex was back then," an eloquent voice-over explains. The visual edit lingers on the killer's face, her mouth snarling and eyes gleaming with maniacal malice.

"The vultures worked for the guards, and the social channels lacked the malignant influence of today."

"And you weren't let off just 'cause of a fancy hairstyle or Daddy buying you a Cashdamn media slot!" yells a disgruntled convict.

Murmurs of bitter agreement emanate from the crowd.

"This was prior to the rebrand, when the city was still Dew Lorrund, a poetic anagram of Underworld... Technology was primitive, and the media had nothing resembling today's near-omnipotence."

"Before everything turned to shit!" growls Ash's cellmate, a murderer built like a mountain, cracking his knuckles.

"Yeah, before the damn fags took over!" adds his muscular, tattooed acquaintance.

Sat apart from the others, Ash leans back and sighs, wearily running fingers through gelled-back hair.

"The fuck is your problem?" demands the nearest testosterone-laden felon.

"Absolutely nothing," Ash replies, eyes fixed on the screen.

"I fuckin' thought so."

"She continuously evaded all law-enforcers," the commentary continues, "her brutal crimes happening in the most unexpected places. She was an enigma, and even our top investigators could never predict her next attack."

The visuals cut to a criminal psychologist in a lamp-lit office, sitting at an artificial mahogany desk and wearing a tailor-made suit. "That is until after half a decade of bloodshed she disappeared completely, following the series of high-profile murders that shocked the city," he adds, fixing the interviewer with a look of calm authority.

"Shut up, you tool, she's here in Red **Zero**!" somebody yells, provoking uproar.

"Catshit!"

"You calling me a liar? My girlfriend's seen her!"

"I'm calling your girlfriend a fucking idiot! Everybody knows she escaped overground! Half the bitches in women's blocks claim to be Alicia with facial surgery! They reckon if enough people believe their Cashdamn catshit they might get respect. They're lying sacks of shit!"

Ash tries to ignore the bellowing crowd, shuffling closer to the screen to better hear the psychologist's expertise.

"She never saw her behaviour as evil," the suited professional explains. "This killer had religious delusions, seeing herself as an angel of vengeance. She once told a reporter, 'I am purging this land of the immoral. Their liberated blood will purify the Underworld's tainted walls, washing away the lies and filth that make this place a toxic hell.'"

"That sounds insane!" remarks the interviewer. "What made her believe she was anything more than a particularly brutal thug?"

"She had the certainty of the deranged," replies the psychologist. "Perhaps her belief in her own brand of justice was no different from how a psychotic patient might insist, for example, that their microwave is talking to them. Most dismiss her now as a lunatic, or even a myth of sorts, a bloodthirsty legend to scare children into behaving. Parents say, 'You had better be good, or Alicia will get you!' Her murders have even become a joke in popular culture. There are young people who hold fake pro-Alicia parties where they dress as killer or victim and get intoxicated while re-enacting her most famous murder scenes."

The screen cuts to a shot of inebriated revellers drenched in fake blood, play-acting murder with inflatable weaponry while sporting childish grins.

"There are others who truly believe though, that she was a deliverer of justice," continues the expert. "They say she will return someday to complete the 'holy purge' she began all those years ago."

"I'm sick of hearing about this bitch!" declares Ash's cellmate, changing the media screen over to a comedy channel presently on an advertisement break. The room goes silent. A few convicts appear disappointed at this alteration, but the guy holding the remote is the most colossal sociopath in their block, so they say nothing.

The next programme begins, and Ash gets a nauseous feeling of disgust while the rest of the crowd erupts in barbarous amusement. Feng Baca vacation zone. A blonde woman being punched in slow motion. Her hair almost ripped from her skull, then in stuttering increments her upper body shoved into a reinforced window. They have switched over to the new Stan Fellowvic comedy vehicle.

"Hey, Ash used to live with that dumb bint!" is the first gleeful yell that prompts a wave of taunting shouts and cruel laughter. Stan has become a media sensation since his infamous vulture trial and now hosts a show attacking unpopular women for sport. The footage of his attack on Leah replayed to a techno theme tune forms the programme's opening credits.

"Hey there! Welcome to my show!" beams Stan, grinning under lurid, yellow lighting. The whole studio backdrop is straw-coloured as a hysterical reference to his first glorious episode of violence when he publicly urinated.

"This guy's a legend!" crows a felonious fanboy.

"Catshit! He'd be my prison bitch if his daddy wasn't loaded!"

"I reckon he's the Poisoner!" somebody adds, referring to the latest big name in morbid entertainment. "He's gonna fess up on the last episode of this series, I'd fucking bet on it!"

"Nah mate, the Poisoner's that lethal Alicia!"

"Who the fuck's the Poisoner?"

"Don't you know anything? They're this murderer who gets you with this slow-acting poison that burns and blisters the skin off your lower body and makes you fall into a coma! They've yet to be caught by vultures, and the guards can't figure out who they are, it's fucking hilarious!"

"It's because their poison takes a few months to activate... But once symptoms kick in, their victim's got only a few days in a coma before they die!"

"Yeah, and the only way to reverse the poison is by killing the poisoner, but nobody knows who they are!"

"What about the 'mark of the Poisoner'? Haven't they got a weird birthmark in the shape of a car or something?"

"Yeah, I heard about that, but I reckon it's catshit!" The convicts continue to discuss the latest famous murderer while on the media screen Stan has found new prey for his brutal antics. Ash is about to get up and walk out in disgust when a couple of guards arrive alongside the new clerk. The mousey woman clutches a batch of envelopes against her flat chest as she surveys the room with shy, darting eyes.

"You got any love letters for me there, darling?" enquires Ash's cellmate with a stare that manages to combine both contempt and lechery.

"No, I've only got this for your block," she apologises to the room, holding out a solitary envelope. "It's for... erm... this person here," she utters, passing the lone piece of paperwork to Ash.

"Nicely put." Ash grins.

"Are you sure that's a person?" wonders the group's gargantuan leader, invoking hysterics from the obnoxious pack.

The clerk blushes and tells Ash, "I'm sorry, I didn't want to assume your pronouns."

"No worries," says Ash. "I'm non-binary, and my pronouns are they them."

"A better choice of word might be 'it'," jokes Ash's cellmate as his underlings nearly collapse in another fit of laughter.

"The dictionary definition of 'it' is a pronoun used for a non-human, animal, plant, inanimate object, concept, or sometimes a small baby," responds Ash. "Never an adult human."

"You're supposed to choose either he or she, mate!"

"I prefer Ash."

"But what *are* you?"

"I am what remains when the fire has finished burning. But I can be fire again."

"Very funny!"

"Fucking hilarious."

"But are you male or female?"

"Of course not, don't be ridiculous."

"Wait up!" interjects a confused felon, scratching his head. "How are you 'they' when you're a single person?"

"Yeah!" the guy next to him concurs. "You can't use 'they' in the singular, dumbass!"

The crowd murmur in agreement.

"You guys did just then when you were discussing the Poisoner," Ash reminds them.

The room becomes quiet while a great deal of laboured thinking occurs, and Ash takes this opportunity to open their post. Their name and photograph adorn the envelope, alongside the prison address. Inside is a letter from Leah with her picture embedded in the top-right corner.

"She looks like Honeysuckle," remarks a prying prison guard, viewing the letter over Ash's shoulder.

"For fuck's sake..." Ash groans. "Every fake blonde with silicone gets told she 'looks like Honeysuckle', regardless of whether there's any facial resemblance. Hell, even the notorious Alicia could've 'looked like Honeysuckle' if she'd lost weight, bleached her hair and had breast enlargement surgery. Some guys must think all women are the same person."

"I think Alicia could have looked like *you* actually..." the clerk hesitantly suggests. "Well, if you were..."

"If I was what?" Ash demands with a defensive stare.

"If you were less, er... muscular..." the clerk cringes and trails off, eyeing the letter to avoid Ash's gaze.

Ash lets out a bitter laugh.

The prison clerk smiles before breezily asking, "So is Leah your girlfriend?"

"No. She's nobody's girlfriend."

"A friend of yours then?"

"You could say that," replies Ash. "We used to live together, before I ended up here. I always tried to protect her. We're... It's... Well, it's hard to explain..."

"Did you fuck her?" a bearded felon enquires, provoking further derisive laughter from the gang.

"Please don't speak of her disrespectfully," Ash responds in an ominously quiet voice.

"I heard she's a filthy slut! I'd fuck her senseless without waiting for permission!" is the taunting reply.

Massive adrenaline surges can turn the most peaceful of creatures into hurricanes of destruction, and the need to protect the vulnerable can catalyse such a switch. Hearing derogatory comments about Leah so soon after seeing that abhorrent Feng Baca footage is too much for Ash. They launch themself across the room and start punching the speaker repeatedly in the face. Blood, spit and a broken tooth are bashed out of the offending mouth before anybody has time to react.

"That damn freak is going back to solitary," an unimpressed guard mutters to his colleague as they belatedly move to restrain the offender.

An eager horde gathers around Ash, who has pinned the bearded loudmouth to the ground and is raining a hail of destruction upon his face. "Move outta the damn way!" shout the guards, firing electric stun shots at the back of the mob. The nearest felons collapse with shocked cries as the remaining crowd clear a path.

"Get off him, asshole!" yells the first guard to reach Ash. He fires the stun shot at their shoulder blade, causing their head to jerk backwards and their bloody, raised fist to freeze as they struggle to breathe.

The guard reaches for his handcuffs.

"Get a medic in here!" his colleague barks into his prison com screen, a streamlined device adapted into a shatterproof wrist attachment. He then assists his co-worker in marching the now handcuffed Ash, whose head lolls in a post-shock daze, out of the mediavision room while the other stunned convicts rise, annoyed and disoriented.

The prison clerk follows them. On the way out, she notices Ash's letter from Leah on the ground and retrieves it before scurrying back to the office to request a new escort.

Throughout the skirmish, Ash's cellmate had sat silently with folded arms, observing the scene through narrowed eyes. He sneers, "That was pathetic."

The other inmates collect themselves and return to their seats, a couple of them turning to spit on the motionless, battered victim in unspoken agreement as they pass.

With heavy legs and fatigued breathing, Ash struggles to keep pace with the marching prison guards who have them gripped tightly by agonized arms. Body reeling from the electric battering, they stumble once and are unceremoniously dragged until they regain their footing. It takes them a few moments to register the screaming.

A new prisoner has arrived. His tortured voice rings out across the block, reminding a few inmates of their own painful arrivals.

"The wolves have brought another victim!" gloats the guard to Ash's left.

"I wasn't resisting arrest! I'll do whatever you want! Just get it off me!" the detainee pleads, choking up blood and crying out through a torn-up face.

A massive wolf constructed from polished metal, intricate wiring and corporate inhumanity is dragging the new arrival by a dislocated arm to the reception desk.

Ash turns to look, but the guards shove them forward.

"It's a real shame a biting metal bastard didn't bring *you* in," mutters the guard to Ash's right.

A well-known security firm invented the robotic wolves several years ago as an effective way of arresting thieves. Human guards were too slow, a relic from a past when people still clung to the notion that the city was no different from a regular overground society. The executive class of the rebranded Deragon Hex desired a more efficient form of justice. Wolves are bulletproof, a great deal swifter than human law-enforcers, and remove the need for the garish media circus of a vulture trial. They savage their targets until they are down to their last gasp of life, then drag what remains of their mangled bodies to the central prison. Originally constructed for business use, their services can now be bought by any vindictive individual with enough money.

"Get what's left of that poor bastard to the medical bay!" the gruff warden yells. "And somebody clean up that blood!"

"That's why you shouldn't fuck with rich people!" grins an amused prison guard as they arrive at the narrow cell of Ash's solitary confinement.

"Here you are, asshole!"

"Have fun!"

The guards laugh as they push Ash into a filthy room barely more than a cupboard with a toilet. A puny strip light flickers behind cobwebs and dust as the door slams shut, disturbing the cell's other inhabitants from slumber and prompting the sound of tiny, scuttling legs.

Ash collapses to the ground, smiling as they anticipate a few delirious days surrounded by insectile cockroaches instead of the humanoid variety. In a strange way, it was delightful to be back.

Clang! A few hours into Ash's detainment, the prison clerk slides the metal cover from the hatch in the door. "You dropped this earl..." she begins, then gasps, "I'm so sorry!" She turns her face away.

Ash has removed their chest binder to get comfortable before attempting sleep. The sound of the hatch opening makes them throw a glance that could stab, but they relax when they see who their visitor is. "It's OK," they tell her, buttoning their shirt.

"I should've knocked, but I was trying to be quiet because I shouldn't be here. I didn't think that thing opened so loud... I..." she stammers.

"It's fine!" Ash assures her with a smile of wry amusement.

"I came to bring you this," the clerk explains, placing Leah's letter on the metal shelf before the hatch.

Ash retrieves the correspondence as the office worker hovers in the corridor, nervously checking to see whether the prison guards have spotted her.

"Well done for earlier," Ash says. "Asking my pronouns rather than assuming. Puts you way ahead of most people in terms of respect and social competence."

"Thank you." The clerk blushes.

"You know," continues Ash, with the spiky glint in their eye that suggests an upcoming rant, "I thought I could handle prison."

"Why?" asks the clerk. "Because you're so strong?"

"No," replies Ash, drawing in breath before expelling bottled-up misery. "Because my life was already a prison! Poverty equals slavery. I had to sell my time to survive, and it was worth so little, I spent my life seething in workplaces I wanted to burn to the ground. I thought, at least in prison I could get shelter and sustenance without having to sustain a fake smile and diplomatic manner as I sat through hours of catshit! You don't realise how much freedom lies in being able to make the facial expression of your choosing until you're forced to smile all day at morons."

Ash glares at their new friend in tortured frustration as they vent, their left fist absently clenching and unclenching, while their right grips Leah's letter with white knuckles.

"That sounds awful," the clerk sympathises. "Maybe you would have preferred working in a warehouse? They're always looking for people to carry stuff, and you don't have to smile or be diplomatic."

"I tried that!" Ash retorts. "My last job was in a warehouse, and I enjoyed it at first, despite the monotony. Physical work helped me burn off excess adrenaline. It was fantastic making money to support myself and Leah, so she didn't have to worry. But the problem was, I didn't always look like this." Ash gestures with a nod to their muscular arms. "It used to be more obvious I was what they call 'genetically female'. They said I had to stop doing the heavy work that helped me subdue my anger, and I had to do light packaging instead. They made me stand there listening to gossip I could barely understand, doing dainty work, just because I have fucking ovaries, it was humiliating! So, I ended up smashing my workspace to pieces, and they put me in here for criminal damage. My sentence was originally just a week, but they keep adding extra months because of my violent temper."

A cockroach makes a soft, sickly sound as it scuttles over Ash's right shoe. They lower their head to watch its journey as it dashes into a minuscule crack in the wall, legs scurrying under shiny wings.

"Well, I hope you get your freedom someday," says the prison clerk, smiling at Ash then looking quickly down at her own insect-free footwear.

"I hope you get yours too," replies Ash.

"What do you mean?" wonders the clerk, maintaining eye contact for a few awkward seconds. "I *am* free!"

"Nobody who has to work is free!" declares Ash. "I remember the days of needing medication to sleep and synthacoffee to wake up. Can you honestly follow the timetable they prescribe you without chemical assistance?"

"Well, no..." admits the clerk.

"I just wanted to fall asleep when I was tired, and then wake up naturally the next day," says Ash. "Now, think about how simple a request that is, actually think about it, then try telling me you're free."

"You might be right," sighs the clerk.

"Of course I am!" Ash replies. "Shit, some of these days I wish I'd listened to Estana."

"Who's Estana?"

"Somebody who lived with me and Leah a few years ago. She ended up unnerving me and terrifying Leah by being sinister as hell, so I asked her to move out before she could cause too much trouble."

"I love how protective you are of Leah!" gushes the clerk.

Ash winces at the memory of their former roommate's vulnerability. "Somebody needs to be! She found a helpful, non-abusive boyfriend a couple years ago and I could finally relax, knowing she was safe. But now I'm not sure their relationship will last. Things fall apart with her. I'm scared if they split up while I'm still in here, she'll be a walking target for all this twisted city's psychos."

"I hope she'll be OK," says the clerk. She scans the corridor again, steals a glimpse at Ash then stares at a patch of rust on the hatch.

"Me too," agrees Ash, who starts to turn away then freezes. "Hey, you don't know the master passcode for these doors, do you?"

"The master passcode?" wonders the clerk. "Is there such a thing...? We hate the numerical pads because of how they set off the alarms if you don't get their code right in **two** attempts.

Staff use the retinal scan instead... Although occasionally somebody gets an eye ripped out by a prisoner too stupid to realise the scanners only respond to living tissue."

"Yeah, I know that!" replies Ash, stepping closer to the hatch. "But haven't you heard of the Vipdile Key?"

"The Vipdile Key's not real," murmurs the clerk, enraptured by the charismatic captive. "It's a fairy tale the life sentence prisoners grasp at to believe they could somehow escape here alive."

"Well, I rarely fall for delusional crap, but this is different," insists Ash, keeping eye contact until their visitor colours and turns away. "It's definitely something to do with circles, and you can't hand-draw decent hexagons without first drawing circles. This whole city is an underground honeycomb of perfectly formed hexagons. This can't be coincidence! There's mathematics underlying everything... The whole concept of the Vipdile Key just makes sense."

"I can do some research if you want?" the clerk offers, biting her lower lip with another brief glance at her favourite prisoner.

"I wouldn't need to learn the whole thing," Ash explains. "Just the **eight**-digit segment of the Key that works as a master passcode for the prison doors."

"Who told you about this?"

"Honestly, it's common knowledge!"

"Nobody talks to me in here," frets the young woman. "Most of the inmates want to kill me because I'm staff, and the other staff members hate me because I'm too nice to the inmates."

"You should work somewhere else," Ash responds with a sympathetic smile. "You're too nice for this horrible place."

Beep! Beep! Beep!

The sound of an activated alarm in the neighbouring block fills the space between them.

"Well, I'd better go," says the clerk, reaching to close the hatch. "If I find out the **eight** digits of this 'master passcode', I'll tell you."

"Thanks," says Ash, leaning against the wall and rubbing their temples. "The sooner the better, yeah? I get a hunch if I don't escape soon, Leah will be in great danger."

CHAPTER
FOUR

After the alarm from **one** block away finally ceases its Cashdamn racket, Ash sits on the grimy floor to read their latest correspondence.

From her photograph in the top right corner, Leah wears the smile of a forgotten princess dreaming of gallant rescue. Perfectly styled curls surround her made-up face. Her eyes betray a desperate craving for approval, often hidden behind the bravado of narcotics, that stalked her conscious thoughts awaiting an opportunity to consume her. There was something in the way she conducted herself that made Ash constantly fearful. Her lack of self-preservation instinct often put her in unhealthy social situations she was too fragile to handle, and she attracted malicious interest the same way discarded candy attracts insects.

Dear Ash,

I've been trying to write for days but the words keep getting scrambled. Each time I pick up a pen I end up drawing something weird like a girl made from rags or a cat with spades for eyes. Everything's bleeding. I don't mean I've returned to cutting my skin open like those times you found me in a pool of blood, it's more psychological. My sanity is unravelling. My brain is a ball of string and the madness is a demented kitten and my thoughts become unsolvable knots as I disintegrate.

I broke up with Donnie.

Even at the end, I was so dependent on his emotional support, but I didn't want to stay with him for this. I didn't want to use him. It was so difficult though because Donnie was my best friend as well as my boyfriend. Now my life is free-falling, plummeting, as though somebody knocked me from a Plus **Nine** window and the filthy ground's getting ever closer. There's this sick sensation of shock, the terror of being pushed by an unknown assailant.

But the truth is, I jumped.

I chose this.

Everybody thinks I'm crazy and ungrateful. They're right about the crazy, but I'm not ungrateful. I truly appreciate everything he did for me. But he stopped being attracted to me around **seven** months ago. I have no idea why because I never put on weight or stopped shaving or wearing cosmetics. I don't understand. He was still friendly and kind, but he didn't want me anymore. I became worried I might cheat on him because I need frequent reassurance that I'm attractive. Yeah... it's pathetic. I figured leaving him before getting with somebody else was the best thing to do. I remember your rants about fake, duplicitous people.

So I left him.

Now I'm single and sleeping with a girl called Tharia Bornil who I met through friends a few weeks ago. Most of these strange nights are a tangled mess of girl skin, wine and melted ice cream, but I don't think many people like me now. I wish I could be as self-sufficient as you and not care what people think of me.

I'm constantly scared. This monstrous city is full of mechanical predators, human psychopaths and media judgement, and now I'm seriously attracting judgement. This makes me open to attack. There are villains with eyes like cameras, ever recording your image for future use against you. I don't have you or Donnie to protect me anymore, and I'm behind with the rent.

Don't be mad, but I'm thinking of asking Estana to come back. She said we only had to ask. I know you don't trust her after what she did, but she is never lacking money and it might be less lonely with her here. It might be OK this time.

Now I have to go draw something. I'm glad I was finally able to write, but my brain has started breaking into beautifully jagged fragments and my language centre is collapsing.

Homogeneous existentialist love pixels,

Leah

"Fuck!" Ash slams their right fist against the ground, giving their hand a line of filth across the outer edge and provoking the scuttling of aggravated insects. "I need to escape right now!" They stare at the hatch in their door, hoping the clerk will magically reappear.

Leah can't let Estana back into her life.

*That is **one** conniving bitch who...*

A wave of nausea grips Ash's stomach, causing them to double up for **six** seconds while they vividly hallucinate.

The putrid concrete floor shimmers into immaculate, chequered tiles of gleaming marble. Walls and ceiling fall back... *replaced by opulent screens set into ebony and alabaster surfaces.*

Somebody is presenting a weapon of mass murder, smiling with sick serenity.

Estana.

"Fuck off!" yells Ash, bashing their open palm against the side of their head, knocking away the disquieting visuals. They glance at the hatch again in anxious desperation, but the helpful clerk is still not there.

She never comes back.

Days pass and nothing changes. Tasteless food is delivered once a day by an unresponsive guard. The cockroaches pay sporadic visits, and the little clicks of their legs along with the bellowing from distant inmates forms the jolly soundtrack to Ash's rising hysteria. There is nothing for the tormented prisoner to do but re-read Leah's letter, stare at the walls, or sleep.

Finally, at the peak of Ash's lunacy the cell door is opened, and a couple of unimpressed guards arrive to drag the dazed prisoner from their glorified cupboard.

"Hope you didn't get too lonely in there," a cruel voice taunts as Ash is marched to the mediavision room, weakened legs almost tripping with the unfamiliarity of moving. Unkempt hair falls over tired eyes as their disoriented brain readjusts to their surroundings.

"Now sit with your friends and be a good little freak," orders the guard, pushing them into the room.

Ash tumbles into an empty chair. The felon they fall beside remarks, "Great, the mutant's back!"

Seated on the back row, Ash's cellmate silently surveys their arrival with folded arms and glinting eyes. Still too confused to speak, Ash stares at the screen. The convicts are watching the increasingly popular Damon Repper show.

Damon Repper is a former up-and-coming music performer who now hosts an opinion show on the social channels. Twice a week he attends hospital for kidney dialysis due to a long-term health condition, and his suffering brings out the maternal instincts of his female viewers. The premise of his show is that instead of attacking unpopular strangers for sport, the only people who get assaulted are his awful ex-girlfriends. He insists they deserve it for treating him badly. To every other woman he displays continuous flattery, earning him a fan club of protective, matriarchal socialites who have nothing but contempt for his previous partners. It's a winning formula. People comfortable with their horrible nature get to enjoy watching a violent attack, while those who pride themselves on being 'good people' get the smug satisfaction of knowing the abuse is merely 'karma' at work.

"Hello everybody, and welcome to my show," says Damon. Tall and well-dressed, he reclines in a black armchair, beaming at his faithful congregation.

"Hello Damon," croon the mostly female audience in unison.

The studio lighting dims as the host takes a more sombre tone. "Today," he says, "we're going to talk about *women who lie*."

His crowd responds by booing.

"We're not a bunch of bored housewives, why are we watching this shit?" an aghast felon demands, prompting coarse mutterings of agreement and the throwing of an edible projectile at the screen.

Ash's cellmate clears his throat, restoring silence.

"Don't be fooled by his 'nice guy' routine," the mountainous convict gloats. "We're watching this to see a bitch get fried!" Around the bemused Ash, the mediavision room erupts in villainous laughter.

On the screen, Damon explains, "Here is my ex-girlfriend, Xendra R'oppemes," as the image of a young woman with frightened eyes is beamed onto the display unit behind him. His audience dutifully murmur their unconditional contempt.

"Now, she's been telling people I was 'controlling' and used to lose my temper!"

His enraptured followers gasp in outrage.

"Have you ever seen me lose my temper on this show, ladies? Have I ever been 'controlling'?"

"No, Damon," the audience chant in unison.

"Now here is my lovely friend, Beryl!" Damon's on-stage display unit switches to live feed from inside a nightclub. A statuesque woman aims vicious eyes at the camera. Beryl Pesancho rose to social fame as the wife of a skullball player. Now divorced, she makes her living doing guest spots on other people's opinion shows. The audience remain silent as though unsure of the required response. "Now, Beryl is a good girl, and she hates liars," their host informs them, making his followers break their silence with a round of applause.

"I really do hate liars," agrees the enthusiastic Beryl on the live feed. She clutches her microphone in long-taloned fingers and her pearly teeth gleam under the club's fluorescent lighting. "I'm looking forward to meeting this ex-girlfriend of yours," she grins. The studio audience whoop in anticipation, as do the convicts in their mediavision room, awaiting the upcoming violence with smiles of childish glee.

"I'll leave her in your capable hands," purrs Damon.

"Why, thank you," she replies before exclaiming, "Here she is!" as she looks off behind the camera.

The cameramen follow her as she dashes over to a frail-looking woman in a blue dress who is stood alone at the bar. "Hi Xendra," says Beryl, grabbing her prey by the arm as she tries to turn away. "My lovely friend Damon tells me you've been lying about him."

"Punch her!" yell the more reserved audience members. The rest are yelling, "Kill her!"

"I... I haven't..." stammers the terrified Xendra R'oppemes. Beryl responds to this by punching her hard in the mouth, and the dual audience of motherly women and sexually frustrated felons howl their approval as she collapses to the ground.

As if waiting on standby, the drone of approaching vultures can now be heard above the nightclub's synthpop floorfiller. "Beryl Pesancho, you have been filmed committing an assault hitherto unsanctioned by public approval, how do you plead?" enquires the dull, metallic voice of the first vulture on the scene.

"I plead not guilty!" the confident Beryl announces while a glowing, scarlet dot dances on her forehead. Across Deragon Hex, eager viewers prepare to vote.

"Now, you don't need to be watching the Crime Channel to vote," Damon assures his audience. "Just type the passcode at the bottom of your media screens into your personal com screen. That's this number here for those of you in the studio," he adds, gesturing to the screen behind him which displays a line of digits under Beryl's diabolical smile.

"I wish they let us have com screens in here," mutters the convict next to Ash.

"This girl is a liar!" cries Beryl. "The lovely Damon Repper treated her like a lady. She took his money, then betrayed him!"

Xendra gets up from the floor, her hand over her lip which is split open and dribbles blood down her chin. "I wasn't lying," she sobs. "He lost his temper with me constantly over the slightest thing! I never knew what would next make him furious!" Her mascara runs, her chest heaves, and she tries to catch her blood in her hands to stop it dripping onto her dress. More vultures have reached the scene, their beams aimed at both Beryl and Xendra's faces.

"I can assure you, the woman is a liar," sighs Damon, slowly shaking his head. "I regret she will only learn to not insult people who've been kind and generous, if we issue the Backlash she deserves."

"Backlash! Backlash! Backlash!" chant the rabid studio audience.

The sad image of Xendra's face flashes onto the screen with the word 'Liar' emblazoned in red across her forehead. She has no media team behind her, and nobody steps up to take her case, so the vote is almost unanimous.

"The viewers have decreed the verdict is Backlash," states the vulture closest to Xendra as she screams and tries to cover her bloody face. The vultures set their rays to Maim. They scourge her pale skin, and it sizzles as she shrieks. Still gripping the agonized girl's arm to prevent her from running, Beryl laughs in triumph, not caring when a beam lightly scorches her fingers.

Damon's studio audience rise for a standing ovation.

As the lone viewer with enough humanity to feel physically sick, Ash holds their head in their hands, a solitary gesture of dissent in a room of cheering sadists.

The end credits roll against a backdrop of Xendra's humiliation. Scorched patches decorate her dress and burns blister on her limbs and face while Beryl does a victory dance beside her. It is not until the credits are replaced by an advertisement for moisturising lotion that the shouts of celebration subside. Ash is too overwhelmed by disgust to focus on their immediate reality and fails to notice the approaching footsteps.

"Hey, isn't that your little girlfriend, back off sick leave?" somebody teases, prompting a sharp glance from Ash through the reinforced window into the corridor. Sure enough, the prison clerk is arriving with her guard escort, meekly clutching her stack of letters.

Estana.

Suddenly remembering Leah's recent letter, Ash's heart thuds with panic and they leap from their chair and dash to meet the clerk.

"Hi, I'm sorry, I was off sick, I..." she begins, holding out an envelope.

"That's OK," is Ash's gasped reply as they struggle to keep their breathing stable. "Can you send a reply today if I write it now?"

"Of course!"

"Thank you so much!"

Under the contemptuous stare of the guards, Ash grabs the envelope containing Leah's message and rushes to their cell, ignoring the hateful laughter receding behind them.

Dear Ash,

You never replied to my last letter.

I hope you're OK.

Tharia left me because she doesn't want a relationship and now my psychological cohesion has fragmented further. How could anybody want me when I'm this fucked-up mess who needs saving?

I've started hanging out with Bret Daner. He serves drinks and econica at Bar Ethol. He visits the apartment and we watch Honeysuckle movies and I usually end up naked while he goes down on me. We both drink a lot. He's not a psychopath like the guys I used to date, so I reckon you'd approve of him. He's quite shy, but he pays me attention as though I'm attractive, which I need because whenever I look in the mirror I see something repulsive.

Bret is friends with Donnie, who's given us his blessing, but I don't think he wants to be friends with me now.

Most people don't.

The markets are a disaster too. People don't buy my work because they don't recognise it. They don't recognise it because I can't afford a mediavision advertising campaign. The reason I can't afford media promotion is because I've no money because people don't buy my work. I'm so fucking trapped.

I remember when you used to help me on the stalls and you got so angry. Me and the other original artists were making no sales while people lined up at the pitches selling counterfeit merchandise. I remember the time you demanded, "Do you have a licence to sell those copyrighted images?" and the traders just looked at you blankly. This was a starter pistol for you, and you were off, fast as a homeless person chasing the water bucket.

"Somebody created those images!" you yelled. "Somebody who isn't you! You can't just copy them onto merchandise and sell them without the original artist's or copyright holder's permission! You're a bunch of thieves! You may as well be selling stolen media screens off the back of a truck!"

They said, "You're just jealous because your stuff isn't as popular."

You said, "If you were selling your own, original characters instead of cashing in on somebody else's well-known brand, maybe your work wouldn't be so popular either! You need the right to copy something. Copy. Right. The clue's in the name, dickheads!"

It was so funny! Those traders were stood there with handmade products that represented hours spent committing intellectual thievery and you kept calling them crooks and yelling, "Copywrong!"

Nobody came near our stall after that because you were giving out vibes of bitterness and rage, but you made me laugh! Now it's just me, stood there alone, smiling as I fail.

I'm terrified of what will become of me. People can see the fear and desperation in my eyes and it repulses them. I'm scared I'll have to do fucked up sex work to survive, because I can't hold down regular employment due to my mental health problems. My customers might be violent. If they make me ugly, I could be dragged off for cosmetic testing. Then I'll be another sad person on the streets with pieces of my face missing, always just a wrong turn away from being immolated on a late-night comedy show.

I had better go now because I have to make more merchandise for the market tomorrow, even though I bet nobody will buy it. I hope you're still coping with prison and nobody is hurting you. Tell me if they ever let you have visitors and I'll come and see you.

I miss you so much, your absence is a constant, gnawing ache in my stomach.

Honorary everlasting lavender peroxide,

Leah

Ash is now worried senseless about Leah. The girl's life could find spectacular ways to fall to pieces, with pitiful events lined up like drunken dominoes, knocking themselves over as she falls into oblivion.

With shaking hands, Ash hurries to write a reply to their unhappy friend.

Hi Leah,

I'm sorry I didn't reply to your last letter. They locked me in solitary again, and the new prison clerk (the only staff member who doesn't despise me) was off sick.

Please don't let Estana back into your life.

Remember Fredi Luga?

I believe Estana is dangerous, and I'm not sure she's even human. I know this sounds hypocritical coming from somebody who gets adrenaline surges that cause hurricanes of devastation, but please be careful around her. She's the type of person who would commit premeditated murder purely for revenge or social advancement.

There's no escaping what binds us to her, but we must evade her influence if we don't want to be puppets in her next fucked-up death game. She might use my rage to have me kill for her. I also believe she's capable of sacrificing what's left of your sanity and maybe even your existence just to alleviate her boredom. She could be that much of a malicious lunatic.

I'm sorry the markets aren't going well. When I get out of here, I'll try to help you with them instead of ranting in your ear, enraged by the public's obsession with heavily branded imagery. It makes me furious when people don't appreciate originality, but I shouldn't be such a dick about it. There must be other ways to make money. I wish I'd gained qualifications in a useful subject when

I was young enough to get a free education. Then I could find work that wasn't tedious or degrading. I promise you I will figure something out though. You can always sell my stuff if you need to. I don't care, it's only stuff.

But please don't turn to Estana. I'm not even sure why she wants a place in our shitty apartment when somebody so mercenary and amoral could be living in her late husband's Plus **Nine** deluxe mega-penthouse or something. I simply can't stand the thought of you being alone with that woman with nobody there to protect you.

It's a real shame you split up with Donnie, he was a great guy. Remember when he saved you from that psycho at Feng Baca? I was surer of your safety with him around. It had been great knowing you were finally with somebody who wasn't an asshole. You had me worried **three** months ago when you told me you didn't think he wanted you anymore. I'd hoped you were imagining this because of your low self-esteem. Sometimes I wonder if you don't think you deserve to be treated well, so you'll subconsciously sabotage anything good you get. You were right to end the relationship instead of cheating on him though. You always try to do the right thing, despite being a walking disaster at times. Fuck anybody who judges you.

Seriously.

Fuck them.

It's a shame it didn't work out with the girl you were dating, but try not to let it get to you. Well done for trying, anyway. You were always shy with girls and this used to make you so lonely.

Do I know this Bret Daner guy? I'm not sure I trust your taste in men. Before Donnie you had so many disasters, so I hope this guy doesn't switch and become abusive. I know you can be psycho bait at times.

Please look after yourself and try to stay as independent as possible until I get out. You can survive without Estana.

Tomorrow rescues you,

Ash

After writing their reply, Ash dashes to the office to pass the correspondence to the helpful administrator who promises to send it with the day's post.

Tortured days go by with no response.

Ash tries to keep a steady routine during scheduled Day Time. Their colossal cellmate spends most of his free time in the mediavision room monopolising the remote control. Ash could stay in their cell, drawing at their desk to avoid the other convicts, but this could trigger insomnia. They often cannot sleep at night if they spend the day in the same room as their bed. Instead, they find a quiet spot in the corridor to sit and sketch, depicting fragmented, illusory worlds of fire and fury with a cheap pen and pilfered paper. Ash is not as good as Leah at making art, but the release of creating dark imagery is calming.

They fear for Leah. They are not around to protect her, nor is Donnie, and they know virtually nothing about Bret Daner. With nobody to look after her, the girl is prone to spiral out of control, making her ideal bait for psychopaths such as Estana or a few of her former boyfriends.

Wondering if their letter is lost in the post, Ash considers writing another but decides to wait a while longer. The authorities who rebranded the police state of Dew Lorrund into the corporate playground of Deragon Hex took inspiration from overground cities that existed before the rumoured fall of civilisation. This has resulted in an arthritic bureaucratic system where nothing works efficiently, and residents are anaesthetized by constant low-level poisoning. Leah's letter is probably at the bottom of a drunk loner's postbag, overlooked as they stumble through life numbly anticipating the next break from their daily monotony.

After days that resemble an eternity, Ash is relieved to finally hear from Leah. Further communication means she is not dead at least, and they soak up her words in an empty corridor, longing for the day they can save her.

Dear Ash,

In my quest to build a life that makes me happy I've managed to alienate myself from nearly everybody. Only a fraction of my former social group still talk to me. They plan events on the com network and the thread dies when I ask a question. They say the way I behave is thoughtless after everything Donnie did for me, but I'm only trying to convince myself I'm not hideous.

The main person I saw during the week was Salma Esnow, who many of the group don't talk to either... there's so much in-fighting. Well, yesterday she told me she's now in a relationship with Tharia Bornil!

Maybe I'm a hypocrite for complaining, but I feel so worthless. The worst part was, I found this out just as Bret stopped messaging.

He must be seeing somebody else as well. I'm so repulsive!

I know you don't trust her, but I do sometimes wonder if Estana was right about everything. Wouldn't life be so much better if we were rich and living **nine** floors above instead of **nine** floors below Road Level? To have a close-up view of the ceiling lights as they go through the colour shifts of their daily schedule... To never be bothered by the oppressive sounds of footsteps above us or drunken violence in filthy corridors at **three** in the morning...

I've heard the breeze from overground is more noticeable once you get **seven** floors up, and if you sit on a balcony and close your eyes, you could imagine you truly are outdoors and under sunlight.

How else will we ever escape the lower levels? I set up those online stores you suggested, but nobody buys anything and I may have to shut them soon because I can't afford the fees. Visitors to my stall get a card with my web address and I say "Find me online!" but most of them don't. There must be something wrong with me.

I'm not sure how much more I can take. My need for reassurance is so urgent, as though if I don't receive help within the next **five** minutes, I will drop my electric heater into the bathtub. I've checked, and the cable is long enough.

I'm sorry, I shouldn't be telling you this. It's because I've dedicated so much of my life to my art that still being deemed unworthy is beyond devastating. I want to scream, "What more do you fucking expect from me? I've sacrificed everything I have to create this, and it's still not enough for you! There's nothing left!" Each time I force myself to go back and stand hopefully by my stall I tell myself, "This time it will be different. I am worthy. I will get the breakthrough I need and not have to choose between a job that makes me suicidal or a descent into absolute poverty and homelessness." But nothing ever changes. I'm so trapped. It's as though part of me is writing a suicide note right now, but I promised you I'd be stronger than that, and I'm sorry.

Cash, I'm useless! I shouldn't be bothering you with my problems when you're the one who's in prison.

I will try my hardest to get better and look after myself so I don't cause you so much worry.

Heroes escape laceration painlessly,
Leah

"Ooh she's a crazy little thing, isn't she?" drools an unwanted voice at Ash's shoulder.

Ash turns to see a prison guard peering at their letter, previously unnoticed while they consumed the troubling words. "Yes," they reply to the intruder, "I'm reading a letter from my friend who has mental health problems."

"I've heard about her," says the guard. "She used to be anorexic, didn't she?"

"Yes, she did."

With a smug grin, the guard states, "I enjoy my food too much to get an eating disorder."

"It's a Cashdamn illness!" Ash retorts. "That's like saying 'I love walking too much to end up in a wheelchair!' or, 'I love having healthy bone marrow too much to get leukaemia!'"

The guard drops his hand to the prison-issue stun gun attached to his belt. "Be careful Ash, be very careful," he warns. "It might not be long before somebody sends that **zero**-calorie girlfriend of yours a lovely letter saying her favourite freak is finally leaving here, in a body bag."

"She's nobody's girlfriend," says Ash.

"Give me **five** minutes with her, I'll make her change her mind about that," jeers the guard.

Ash's hazel eyes bore into the man's leering features as though trying to make him spontaneously catch fire with the sheer force of hatred and willpower.

"Gonna have a little rage attack in my direction are you, freak?" the unperturbed lecher jokes. "They'll never let you write that bitch again if you do! You'll be in solitary confinement for the next **eight** years and we'll transfer your prison clerk fangirl to another segment before you can say 'sick lesbo scum'."

Choking back rage with a smile of grim determination, Ash turns and marches back to their cell to write a reply to Leah. Further calls of threat and malice are thrown at their hunched shoulders as they go.

Hi Leah,

This place is driving me insane! I need to be with you, helping you, not stuck in here with these assholes! I wish I could smash my way out, run **two** hexes to our apartment and give you a massive hug before we sit down to make plans for sorting our damn lives out. But first, I need you to listen to me.

Estana was not 'right about everything'. Estana was fucking dangerous! Don't you remember what she did?

The only aspect of her character I admired was her independence. I even approved of her influence on you at first because she gave you better advice than that stupid woman who was in the spare room before. Remember that **zero**-emission, save-the-homeless, recycling enthusiast who was always telling you to find a nice man and start a family? As if it would be a great idea to become emotionally and financially dependent on another human being! As if the cure for being barely able to function within society is to create a miniature version of yourself!

Fuck that!

Estana came along with her Strong Independent Woman ethic and I thought, "Yeah! This bitch is alright!" The way she carried herself like royalty made me want to trip her so she'd fall flat on her face, but that's only because I'm a dickhead.

I thought, "I've no idea why this person wants to live with us, but I'm glad she's here."

Then the sinister shit started happening.

With a rush of vertigo, Ash's writing is interrupted by what resembles a drug trip from hell, although they are sober as a machine.

The chequered floor again...

Plush screens set into lofty surfaces. Leah in a hospital bed, hooked up to medical equipment, all wires and plastic death-defiance, dressed in white. The beep of her heart monitor becoming slower as the room spins like a morbid carousel.

Estana.

The way she smiles as she hands over the axe.

Ash slams their pen onto the paper as their upper body jerks forward with a spasm of their stomach muscles.

Estana...

"Decapitate to liberate!"

Her eyes the gateway to a malicious abyss and her voice an imperious razor.

Ash retches over the concrete floor, but no substance is vomited, just the vulgar noise of a body malfunctioning with the sickness of horror. The sound is met by cruel laughter from outside the cell. Voices of inmates **nine** metres away echo as though propelled down a **seven**-year corridor, hurtling through foggy darkness.

"Aww, poor Ashy Washy has a poorly tummy!"

"If you puke on that floor, you'd better lick it up if you don't want your skull bashed into it!"

"I'll give you something to choke on, petal."

More braying laughter.

Ash's cell spins, but they barely notice. The image of a different room, chequered, beeping and far from here, is superimposed onto their surroundings. A room where Estana looms with a blazing eternity in her brutal countenance, handing over an axe, ominous and gleaming. A room so long ago it could be tomorrow. The sense of a world disappearing.

Estana.

"The fuck is this trippy shit?" Ash mutters, their left hand clutching their waist while their right slides over the page. **Four** slick clumps of hair break from their gelled-back style to fall over a bemused grimace. They hold deathly still while everything hurts. After several nerve-shredding minutes, the mirage and nausea fade in unison and Ash forces their laboured breathing back under control.

"Gee, I hope you're not dying in there." A taunt from outside the cell sparks further amusement. Narrow eyes set into a face as round and pink as ham peer from the doorway while Ash pulls themself upright.

Poison?

Premonition?

Allergic reaction to new hair gel?

Or maybe Ash hadn't enjoyed being in a non-spinning room enough for it to not rotate.

"Don't worry, I'm enjoying living too much to die right now," replies Ash, returning to their writing as the porcine face departs the doorway in disappointment.

Fuck! I'm struggling to write today. I'm nauseous as hell, the room keeps spinning and my brain's gone trippy as fuck for no reason. What was I saying? Ah yes, Estana.

"Decapitate to liberate."

Please don't trust her. You remember what happened to Fredi Luga, right? OK, so he was an asshole, he made you cry and lied about it afterwards, and I very much wanted to bash his face in... but vengeance should have limits! Whatever else he was, he was somebody's son, he was somebody's friend (OK, not mine, that's for sure, but somebody's) and he was a human being. Granted, he was a shit human being, but still...

Do you recall how whenever anybody asked Estana about what happened to him, she just laughed? Do you remember the way she laughed?

Bring... them... hell...

(Alicia?)

I'm afraid I can't write for much longer, I'm too ill.

I've got fantastic news though! Because I've been in no fights for **nine** weeks, they've scheduled me a parole hearing in **four** months' time.

I might be getting out, Leah!

I don't belong in prison, I'm no rapist or murderer like the scum in here, it's these damn rage attacks I can't control. Half the time, I don't even remember them.

I'll be free soon though, so please hang on until then. We can get by without her. It will be OK.

Fearless invincible genderless hilarious tenacity,

Ash.

After sealing their letter in a stolen envelope, Ash walks out of their cell and past leering felons to leave their latest correspondence with the clerk. She grins and blushes, grateful to help the troubled creature who confuses her. "You remind me of Leah," remarks Ash, returning the smile of their helpful friend. "That is, a shyer version without her self-destructive tendencies."

"Thank you so much!" she beams in response.

An administrative colleague glowers at this exchange. Disgusted by modern tolerance of extreme androgyny, he later retrieves Ash's letter from the postbag, rips it to pieces and throws it in the trash.

It is **four** months until the hotel massacre.

CHAPTER
FIVE

The detective is the only person in Deragon Hex who knows where the legendary mass murderer, Alicia, lived before she disappeared: a decrepit apartment on level Minus **Nine** of hex Blue **Two Three**. He figured this out with a minimum of external assistance, and for this he damn well deserves another drink. "Let it go, detective," the other guards say. "You've got **zero** chance of finding that psycho bitch alive." But he refuses to listen. He refuses to believe she is dead or escaped overground. She is alive, here in Deragon Hex, hiding in a safehouse or undercover network, biding her time, mocking him. He aims to capture her and restore public faith in the city guards.

The portly detective gloats in his solitary room because discovering her last residence brings him another step closer to fulfilling his ambition. He scratches the scalp under his thinning hair and grins. For the past **seven** years he has spent his free time learning how to hack Deragon Hex's communication network. This spare time increased somewhat when he lost his family due to his little problem, then the authorities cut his working hours on the force due to loss of funding, but this only provided more opportunity for off-duty investigations.

It had been difficult at first. Most of the clueless consumers in this myopic metropolis are happy to use their computers as a mixture of games unit and glorified com screen. Whoever designed the network was keen to encourage this mindset, with a 'user friendly' interface on every machine allowing limited interaction with the underlying programming. The detective has uncovered some intriguing information though... information the authorities in their damned master control room did not want him to know.

Chuckling at his own genius, he types in the recently acquired **eight**-digit passcode, enabling instant access to the camera feed from the apartment where Alicia used to live. Back in her day, surveillance was far less intrusive in residential areas. Now the cameras are everywhere. This means **one** of the bitches in her former apartment is going to lead him straight to her.

He ignores the spy screens, the monochrome monitors depicting mundane crimes that light up the wall in a grid of luminous voyeurism. The only important footage is the hacked stuff on his computer.

After knocking back another straight whiskey, he begins with some live feed. The massive monitor, which he got delivered here especially for his research, splits into **six** separate visuals. Bottom-left depicts the bathroom in the apartment's south-west segment, where he often watches that sweet slut who's had surgery to look like a porn star get naked. In the lower-middle, he sees the grimy corridor outside the apartment's front doorway. The lower-right feed shows the combined mediavision room and kitchen of the south and south-east segments, which also serves as a hallway to the abode. Here, the young woman with the large breasts now sits on a sofa reading messages on her personal com screen.

The upper feeds each show a bedroom. Top-left is the buxom girl's room in the apartment's north-west segment, where she is sometimes naked but usually trying on a variety of dresses and trying not to cry. Top-right shows a north-east room now empty. Research revealed it previously belonged to a steroid-laden, genderless freak who was the slut's best friend and resident money earner until they got thrown into jail. The upper-middle feed contains glimpses of the north room, which resembles a torture chamber in the sporadic images that flicker through a maelstrom of static interference.

"There must be something wrong with that camera," the detective mutters. His computer is working fine and the only other potential reason for this lack of clear picture seems too far-fetched. "Now who the hell are *you*?"

In the dimly lit corridor of the lower-middle frame, a woman with a sliced-up face walks past the security camera outside Alicia's former apartment. In her mid-thirties, wrapped in filthy layers, she holds no expression on a face that might once have been attractive before she was stupid enough to become penniless.

Ava holds a crumpled piece of paper which she stares at as she shuffles past, muttering to herself through rotten teeth.

"Great, it's you... Get out of my way!" commands a haughty voice. Estana enters the frame from stage right. She wears a long, black coat that buckles to the neck, and pulls a suitcase on wheels behind her.

Mutilated Ava blocks her path to the front door, mumbling under her breath. Within her garbled words, the detective could swear he hears the phrase, "Strange cellar".

Estana throws back her head with a throaty laugh. "Why the fuck would I want to?" she asks, before shoving past Ava without waiting for a response. She knocks on the door. Upon realising her clothing has been in contact with a homeless person, she utters a loud exclamation of disgust, swatting at her sleeve with the back of her right hand as though brushing away filth. Still waiting to be let in, she turns to glare at Ava who is hobbling off screen.

"Snooty bitch!" spits the detective, opening a can of beer that hisses as it drips froth onto his starched pants. He gives the spillage a half-hearted swipe.

When he looks back at the screen, Estana is looking right at him, the glowing pixels of her predator eyes boring into his face with a look of disdainful amusement.

"What the..." he begins.

The apartment door opens with a weird squeak and the lonely bleached blonde with the fake rack gazes nervously at her visitor, who turns her unnerving gaze from the camera. "Leah! Darling!" Estana croons.

"Did you see that crazy homeless woman?" Leah asks, poking her head out of the doorway to peer along the corridor at the retreating Ava.

"Never mind her! Aren't you going to invite me in?" asks Estana, who speaks the way a well-bred lady from an ancient overground civilisation might speak to a servant.

"Of course! Sorry. Come in!" Leah replies, stepping back so her Ladyship can enter with her suitcase. As she closes the door behind her, it makes another high-pitched creak.

"Great, the door's making that ridiculous noise again!" Estana complains. "Please tell me somebody's coming to fix it soon."

"The landlord is sending somebody in **four** days," Leah replies, smoothing the fabric of her dress and scanning the room for anything else that might be wrong.

"Good. I hope you haven't changed anything in my room!" Estana warns, wheeling her smart suitcase over the threadbare carpet.

"Of course not!"

Estana opens her bedroom door. The flickering image in the upper-middle frame of the detective's screen cuts out entirely. Estana laughs, then remarks, "Good Cash! It's about **zero** degrees in here! Did Ash tell you I'm supposed to freeze to death?" Her voice sounds distant. The audio bug nearest to her has malfunctioned but her words are picked up by the device in the hallway.

"I'm so sorry!" cries Leah, her mouth falling open in dismay. "I've been struggling with money, so I switched everything off in rooms I wasn't using!"

"It's fine!" Estana assures her, returning to the mediavision room without her suitcase. "You don't have to worry now, I always have money."

"You do, don't you?" gushes Leah, gracing Estana with a wide-eyed stare that betrays both fear and admiration. "Ash told me not to invite you back, but they've stopped writing to me, and I don't know when they're getting out. I've been running out of money and didn't know what else to do... They don't, er, trust you. You know, after..."

"After Fredi Luga?" drawls Estana, her brutal smile glinting.

"Who the fuck is Fredi Luga?" the detective mutters.

"Who the fuck are *you*?" demands Estana, turning her terrifying gaze to the nearest camera.

The detective almost screams as her carnivorous eyes penetrate through the screen, irises flickering flecks of amber, green and electric malice. His can of beer drops to the ground with a dull thud.

"Who are you talking to?" asks Leah, peering around the empty room behind her.

Estana laughs cruelly as all **six** frames cut out along with their accompanying audio feed. The bemused, balding detective gapes into the black mirror in silence and realises he has dropped his drink.

Leah remembers Fredi Luga's first and only visit to the apartment.

It is so long ago it could be a different lifetime and she is shaving herself in the bathroom while her new boyfriend sits in the mediavision room wanting to kill her.

She takes her time with the shaving. There are places you should not cut yourself unless you want it to sting when you urinate. She wants to be perfect for him. When she has finished, she puts on new underwear and her prettiest dress, combs her hair and applies her make-up.

Finally satisfied she looks worthy of being somebody's girlfriend, she walks into the mediavision room saying, "I'm sorry that took so long."

He does not look away from the media screen. She had left him watching a gangster movie and he sits before it, his eyes unfocused as though lost in a void, his jaw tense and arms tightly folded.

Leah had known Fredi for years as a social friend, but for most of that time she had been wary of men because of her troubled past. On a recent night out, she wore a low-cut top with a short, black skirt and flirted with him on the edge of the dance floor.

"It's such a shame you're a lesbian, Leah," he told her, gazing at her barely covered legs in their mesh stockings.

"Oh, I'm bisexual now," she replied, dazzling him with her most winning smile.

"Can I buy you a drink?" he asked. They spent the rest of the evening kissing until she stumbled to an after-party while he went home to sleep. That was a week ago. This is the first occasion they have been alone together.

She sits beside him on the sofa. "What do you think of the movie?" she asks.

"How do you suppose it makes me feel when you invite me over and leave me sitting here on my own?" he demands.

"I... I'm sorry," she stammers, her face twitching and breath almost caught in her throat. She originally planned to meet him later for drinks, but invited him over early when he messaged to say he had nothing to do. Eyes downcast, she utters, "Sometimes I don't think. I wanted to look my best for... for going to the bar this evening."

"I came here to see *you*! Not sit here watching some Cashdamn movie!" he fumes.

"Sorry." Her voice is barely louder than a whisper. "Shall I cook us those pizzas now?"

He shrugs in response. She heads over to the kitchen area, switches on the oven, takes the pizzas from their plastic packaging and places them on the oven shelf. "Can I get you another drink?" she offers. After receiving no response, she pours a glass of water for herself and returns to the sofa.

On the media screen, a man holds a gun to a hostage's head.

"I can't believe how you behaved at the party last night," Fredi admonishes.

"I... what did I do?" Leah chokes.

The hostage's eyes bulge in terror above a gagged mouth.

"You spent half the evening ignoring me! How do you suppose I felt when you kept leaving me to go talk to other people? I was there for YOU!" Fredi snarls.

The gangster takes the safety catch off the gun.

Leah had spent half the previous evening's party sitting on Fredi's knee, kissing him. She had spent the other half floating around chatting to various people, but had constantly checked back with Fredi to make sure he was enjoying the event. "I... I thought it would be rude not to talk to anybody else, but I did introduce you to everybody," she explains. "Whenever I checked, somebody was talking to you."

The hostage attempts to scream.

"But I wasn't there to see *them*, was I? You know how I feel when women treat me like shit," he seethes. "You only think of yourself though, don't you?"

The gangster pulls the trigger. Brains, blood and pieces of skull splatter over a concrete wall while Leah tries not to cry. The movie cuts to a plot-building conversation she can barely fathom. Fredi continues to rant about what a dreadful, selfish person Leah is, eventually breaking the girl's resolve not to burst into tears. Once her spirits are crushed, he returns to brooding in silence.

After a few minutes, Leah sniffs, wipes her eyes and says, "The pizzas should be ready now," with a sad smile. She fetches the food. Fredi accepts his meal without thanks and eats sluggishly, his eyes still fixed on the space between himself and the movie. Leah consumes her food with quick, nervous little bites, trying to keep her breathing steady and stop her face from crumpling.

"And another thing!" he snaps.

Leah looks at him in desperate horror.

"When we eat, we close our mouths!"

This is too much for Leah, who abandons her pizza and runs crying into her bedroom. This is the worst birthday ever.

"I can't say anything right, can I?" Fredi yells after her. He abandons the remains of his pizza and re-folds his arms, staring petulantly at the car chase ahead of him while behind the door Leah weeps into her pillow.

In front of Fredi, a car crashes into a wall but he barely notices. He is getting damn sick of how women behave. They are all the same, wanting you to go to parties, spending ages on their make-up, never thinking of anybody but themselves. If Leah doesn't sort herself out and try to patch things up with him soon, he is going to leave. He is sick of putting up with women's drama.

The angry tirade of his inner monologue is soon interrupted by the hairs on his tense arms standing on end as he gets a creeping shiver up his spine. He is being watched. He turns with the swift movement of an adrenaline jolt.

Estana.

She is stood in the doorway between her bedroom and the mediavision room, coolly appraising him. Her face wears the frown of bored disgust she usually reserves for the ill and destitute. Fredi flinches, then returns his eyes to the screen. After a few seconds, he turns back to her and snaps, "Are you just going to stand there?!"

Estana raises her left hand to view her perfect manicure for a while before responding. When her gaze returns to him it holds an aloof indifference as though she is viewing bacteria in a culture dish and is entirely unsurprised by their growth pattern.

"Have you considered getting a hobby to help with your little anger problem?" she enquires. "There was a great deal of repressed rage in this household until I insisted we take up painting. The act of releasing dark emotions through art can be extremely cathartic."

Fredi says nothing, but the tendons in his neck bulge.

"Do you know what cathartic means?" Estana smirks.

Fredi leaps to his feet and stands glaring at Estana, unsure of his next move. "It's not as easy for me as it is for Leah!" he yells. His voice falters slightly as though restricted by an unwanted hesitance, but he still projects it loud enough for Leah to hear in her lonely room.

Estana stifles a laugh. "Not that it's a competition, but I highly doubt you've had it worse than her," she retorts. "You truly need a healthy release for this bitterness and rage you're carrying."

"I really try!" shouts Fredi. "But I've got no motivation!"

Having a basic understanding of Hexish vocabulary, Estana bursts into a fit of condescending laughter. Fredi flinches as though she just slapped him. "Are you laughing at me?" he demands.

Estana composes herself then asks, "What did you just say?"

"I said, 'I really TRY but I've got NO MOTIVATION!'" Fredi bawls, his face scarlet and hands clenched into fists at his side.

Estana howls with amusement, steadying herself against the door frame to stay upright during the convulsions of mirth.

"Right!" says Fredi, his eyes lit with furious malice. Estana knows what he is going to do next, and it makes the situation even more hilarious.

He marches over to the front door. In his rage, he will have forgotten that the hinges are so stiff it only closes slowly with an embarrassing little squeak.

"It's too much!" cries Estana, clutching her side as Fredi opens the door.

"Well, GOODBYE!" bellows Fredi, storming out and heaving the door behind him in an attempt at an intimidating slam. Despite the strength of his rage, it only half closes, making that humiliating squeak like a fart escaping through clenched buttocks.

Estana laughs so hard she can barely breathe.

But Leah fails to find hilarity in this occurrence. When she emerges from her room to find Fredi gone, she succumbs to an overwhelming tide of misery as Estana disappears, leaving her alone on her birthday. She takes to her amateur home-filmed opinion show on an obscure channel to share her traumatising experience and the resulting emotional pain. This is not the smartest of responses. As soon as she complains of feeling threatened by Fredi's livid behaviour, an eager viewer calls for Trial by Vulture. The resulting backlash is led by Botoxia Burnos, a mouthy brat with a trust fund who was always horrible to shy women, and Leah loses the trial. She is sentenced to house arrest for several months, at risk of being maimed by vultures if she leaves the apartment.

"This is your fault!" she wails at Estana upon her return. "If you hadn't been so condescending, he might have apologised for being horrible! He wouldn't have denied being verbally aggressive, making people think I'm a liar... You made him glad of how he behaved!"

"Please!" retorts Estana. "I've just had a nice little chat with his previous girlfriend. She's a sweet girl who's insecure about her weight, bless her. He told her she ate like an obese rat! He made her leave the room and eat by herself, after she cooked him a lovely meal, on Valentine's Day. She lived in fear of him. The man is an utter troglodyte, an aggressive moron, and definitely not the type you should ever bring to this apartment! People are only judging you because you sat playing the victim instead of moving on with your life. I keep telling you, nobody likes a victim."

Ash arrives home from another warehouse job in the middle of this argument. “People are only judging you because you’re on the radar of too many spoilt, self-centred assholes, honey,” they interject with a bitter grin, taking off their dust-covered jacket and hanging it separately to the other residents’ clean attire.

Leah wrings a tear-stained tissue in her dainty hands. “But don’t you think he’d have regretted his behaviour if Estana hadn’t been so mean?”

“Mean?” Ash splutters. “He got off lightly! Estana told me what he said... ‘I really try, but I’ve got no motivation.’ What’s next? ‘I’m really active, but I hardly move’? ‘I’m really rich, but I’ve got no money’? ‘I’m really intelligent but I’m not good at thinking about things right proper’? If I’d been here, I’d have laughed in his face too, before chucking him out through the damned window!”

Leah giggles and wipes her eyes. “Do you think anybody nice will ever date me?”

Ash collapses on the sofa with a weary sigh. “I think you need to stop asking yourself that so often. You give in to the loneliness, you end up having dinner with people who say things like, ‘When we eat, we close our mouths’. I mean... what the fuck?! I’d have been like, ‘When we kick, we aim for this testicle’, ‘When we stab with a fork, we gouge out this eyeball’, ‘When we set people on fire, we...’ Ooh, is that pizza?” Suddenly distracted by the discarded food beside them, Ash starts eating a well-earned dinner.

In his screen-lit hotel room, the detective searches the com network for information on Fredi Luga and finds several news articles relating to his murder.

The day after winning a vulture trial against his ex-girlfriend, Fredi’s body was found with his jaw held open by a blood-stained rock, an entire pizza stuffed into his oesophagus and a bunch of colourful birthday candles protruding from each eye socket.

His ex-girlfriend had been under house arrest at the time, and the surveillance footage proved she had not ventured from home. Her only friends were those she lived with: a non-binary warehouse operative and a female entrepreneur, both of whom had alibis for the night of the attack.

"Crazy fucking bitches," mutters the detective.

In her cheap apartment, unaware she is now hidden from city surveillance, Leah hears a cat meowing and goes to the kitchen to fetch a saucer.

"So what made you change your mind?" asks Estana, referring to Leah's decision to allow her back into her life.

"Well..." Leah cautiously begins. "I've been struggling with bills, and it's been lonely here. Ash stopped replying to my letters. Donnie isn't speaking to me. Tharia is with Salma now. Bret won't return my calls..."

"Who the fuck is Bret?"

"A friend I've been hanging out with," Leah replies, placing the saucer on the ground as a scruffy cat jumps in through the open kitchen window. "He's nice to me. He doesn't get angry..." She retrieves a bottle of vodka from the cabinet and fills the saucer.

"What are you doing?"

"This cat is Mr Derek Blin," replies Leah. "He's a stray who visits me sometimes. He always knows when I'm sad. I'm pouring him some vodka."

"Are you completely mental?"

"Probably," Leah concedes, "but he does enjoy his vodka! He prefers it to that synthetic milk stuff, anyway."

As Estana shakes her head and sighs, Leah switches on the media screen. It first shows a commercial, with celebrity couple Ben Wancaski and Morgua Plige modelling club wear with trite poses and bored faces. Next up is a biography of Honeysuckle, Leah's favourite celebrity.

"Delightful," sneers Estana.

"She was the most beloved starlet the studios had ever known," declares the narrator while a photograph of a blond actress in tight-fitted clothing graces the screen. "It was a scandal that shocked the underworld when it emerged that studio executives had been controlling her life and abusing her. She plummeted to her eventual drug-fuelled destruction, with lurid headlines of her antics dominating the com network, until she vanished completely. Her disappearance still remains a great mystery."

The visuals cut to a clip from a romantic comedy, where the male lead first approaches Honeysuckle's character before everything goes wrong due to a series of hilarious misunderstandings. This is replaced by a still shot of Honeysuckle sitting miserably on a talk show, all pretty designer clothing and melancholy eyes. The voice-over remarks, "We have no real-life footage of Honeysuckle; she only seemed to exist in front of the studio cameras. It's almost as though she wasn't real."

Visuals switch again to show the channel's resident psychologist being interviewed by the out-of-shot narrator.

"Despite her fairytale beginnings, she is now associated with trauma and tragedy... so why do so many young women still aspire to be her?"

"It's the combination of her glamorous image and unhappy life story," the mental health expert explains. "It makes her the ultimate tragic princess. Many people in this city are secretly miserable due to peer bullying, difficult childhoods, and constant pressure to be attractive while maintaining high social standing. Seeing her on the screen made people feel less isolated by their own depression; they enjoyed seeing somebody else who was depressed doing so well for themself."

"So her sadness gave them something they could relate to?"

"Exactly."

"What's your opinion on the rumoured connection between Honeysuckle and Alicia?"

Estana ignores the screen. She is observing Leah's reaction to the show, studying her face with wry amusement. "You look a bit like Honeysuckle, don't you dear?" she teases.

Leah says nothing.

Unable to view the apartment anymore, the detective uses facial recognition software to find footage of Leah, Ash and Estana away from home. First, he searches for Estana, but the difficulty of this task fills him with apprehension. Cameras constantly malfunction near her, working adequately until she approaches, then succumbing to a monochrome maelstrom of static dots or utter blackness. They show a clear picture again when she is gone. An occasional image might flicker through, graphic scenes of her dealing out consensual abuse, turning hotel rooms into twisted queendoms of pain and humiliation before disappearing once more into the static ether.

"She can't be a fucking statica," mutters the detective, "they don't fucking exist."

Although if Alicia has a statica on her side, this could explain how she's remained hidden...

So, Estana is damn near impossible to investigate, and the detective cannot presently cope with the implications of this. However, if Estana knows where Alicia is, maybe the other residents do too.

The detective finds video feed of Ash in jail. They held various manual labour jobs before an act of criminal damage landed them in prison, where they keep getting their sentence lengthened due to violent altercations. The eager lawman cannot wait to see Alicia joining them behind bars. This could be the guard victory of the century, finally earning him a promotion. His gut tells him the present tenants in her former home will lead him to the psycho bitch, and his gut is beer-filled but never wrong.

The easiest resident to follow is Leah, who always places herself in front of the nearest camera with her figure turned at a flattering angle. The detective sets up tracking feed to follow her every move outside the home.

He watches her go to a party. Lost in her own world, she sits fussing with her hair and nails instead of offering any verbal contribution. After an awkward hour, she frets, "I don't think people like me anymore," to the person next to her.

"I'm sure they do, I've not heard anybody diss you," is her friend's well-meaning but untrue response.

"You know what I wanna do?" Hector Decallo asks the room. "I want to take drugs, punch a girl in the face, then piss myself." Everybody laughs. Leah flinches before giggling and pouring herself another drink.

"I still can't believe you called the guards on that poor guy!" jeers Gabby Coilestio.

"I didn't! The assault got flagged by the cameras."

"But you whining about him 'attacking women' was fucking stupid. He was wasted!"

"I shouldn't have to justify speaking out against somebody who attacked me!"

When Gabby goes to the bathroom, her friends tell Leah they agree with her, but they change the subject when Gabby returns.

At 2 a.m. Leah walks home alone. The detective watches each hurried footstep, each nervous tug of a bleached curl, the cheap handbag clutched to her side, until she nears the surveillance blind spot that surrounds her residence and is lost to him. He swears and decides to get some sleep.

After suffering agitated dreams of failure, reliving the events that precipitated his familial estrangement and becoming a joke in the workplace, he wakes and watches her again.

Today she is attempting to sell her paintings and handmade merchandise at an alternative market in a nightclub venue. Consumers mill around her, parading themselves in the latest plastics while industrial music pounds from speakers in the ceiling. She stands with a petrified smile behind the things she has created, anxiously animated and dressed up to die, her voluptuous figure poured into tight-fitted clothing. She is surrounded by stylised depictions of her demons. A creature with feline eyes wields a bloody sword. A vampire grins beneath an ebony curl in a shadowed dreamscape. All her dolls have jagged teeth.

"This stuff is saying, 'Pity me!' isn't it?"

Leah jumps and the colour drains from her complexion as she turns to face her stall's first visitor. "I... I'm sorry?" she stammers.

"My name's Brooke Nollto and I'm doing a write-up of these stalls for my college magazine," explains a young female dressed in sports top and yoga pants.

"I see," gulps Leah. "This isn't your type of art then?"

"I can't stand art that's dreary and disturbing," replies the critic, glowering at the haunting imagery before her. She blows a bubble of luminous pink gum and recommences chewing after it pops, impatiently tapping her right foot while she stands with her arms folded.

"Um... Well, it's not for everybody, I guess..." Leah admits, gazing at her creations with a deflated sigh.

"All this stuff is miserable, isn't it?" Brooke Nollto continues, staring around in disgust. "Why do people make this? I prefer art that's cheerful, not this dark shit. It must be trendy to be depressed these days... I'm gonna tell everybody who reads my column not to buy anything from this place because it's all crap." With that, the opinionated woman struts off to find other stalls to be offended by while Leah nervously neatens her sales display and tries not to cry.

Eight feet to her right, the detective notices a couple of guys staring at Leah and zooms in. "Where have I seen you before?" he mutters, before realising he is looking at none other than social celebrity, Damon Repper, and his new driver, Sephen Blacroy.

As the latest rising star of the social channels, Damon Repper holds his **six**-foot frame with the confident poise of the rich and recognised. He leans toward his hired help and the **two** men confer while taking turns to peer in Leah's direction. The detective scans their vicinity for the nearest sound bug then resets his audio feed to **zero** in on their conversation, curious about what attention Leah has attracted.

"Don't you think the girl in the designer dress was more suitable? I did admire her branding. This girl's clothing is cheap!" remarks Damon.

"No way, the other gal had a snooty face," insists the driver. "That sort reckon they're better than you. She'd wanna be the star of your show! You don't want that, you want a friendly girl who smiles. Look at her there, smiling away!"

"You know, you're right," admits Damon. "A pretty, cheerful sidekick presents a far better image! My viewers could see how lucky she is to be my girlfriend."

"She'd look grateful and happy next to you!"

"Absolutely! Plus, she is quite presentable apart from the cheap clothing, and her attire is something I could easily alter."

"Shall we go over then?"

"She hasn't looked over here once! I'm not sure she recognises me... What do I say if she doesn't know who I am?" worries Damon, preening his thick, spiky hair.

"Aww, just introduce yourself! Compliment her paintings. Pretend you're an art collector or something," replies Sephen, walking over to Leah's stall and checking back to see if Damon is following him.

"Me?" splutters Damon as he reluctantly approaches.

The driver pretends to be intrigued by a framed print of a fairy made of fire. "Hiya," Leah greets him.

"Hi," Sephen responds, before turning to Damon and raising an eyebrow.

The socialite steps closer to the artwork and awkwardly peers at a surreal, monochrome design as Sephen steps back. Leah greets this next potential customer with a friendly, "Hi!"

"Hi there," replies Damon. "This is a lovely, er... painting of an eye you've done here."

"Thank you!" beams Leah. "It's not a painting though. That's a print from what was originally a ballpoint pen drawing."

"That's great," Damon tells her, surveying the array of saccharine nightmares before him. "You've got some, er... wonderful artwork here."

"Thank you!" says Leah again. She then regales him with the story behind each picture, babbling a series of memorised sentences as her hands fidget with a stack of flyers.

Damon attempts to discuss his own career, but Leah keeps chattering about her artwork. After **eight** minutes he buys a handmade key ring which she places in a bag along with a business card. The transaction complete, he heads back to Sephen, grinning.

"How did it go?" his driver teases with a theatrical wink. "You were only talking to her for around **nine** hours."

"I'm in!" boasts Damon. "She barely stopped speaking to me the whole time I stood there, and she told me to 'find her online'."

The detective laughs as he pauses the footage. The image of Leah is now frozen as she smiles that terrified smile, surrounded by pieces of her soul she is trying to sell to pay for electricity. He chuckles as he fixes himself a glass of breakfast whiskey. It is hard work investigating the residents of a scummy Minus **Nine** apartment in his cluttered Plus **Eight** hotel room and he deserves this drink. He does enjoy spying on little Leah though, especially now she has a celebrity admirer... albeit an admirer rendered somewhat dense by his own arrogance.

"I always think women who are selling things want to sleep with me too," the detective jokes to himself, staggering back to his desk.

"I like it when I go to a car showroom and the saleswomen discuss the features of various automobiles with me," he slurs into the empty room. "That means they want my penis."

CHAPTER SIX

Dear Ash,

I've not heard from you in a while... I hope you don't hate me. It must be annoying, me complaining about my problems when it's so much harder for you, I'm sorry. I miss you.

I miss Donnie too. When I was with him, everything felt warm and safe and precious. He was kind to me and we had a lovely life together, but I threw it away because I believed I was missing something. Now what's missing is the remains of my sanity, and my life is a technicolour nightmare that never ends.

A crazy vagrant with a sliced-up face keeps following me. I didn't notice her at first because she's so ugly she borders on invisible, but something in her eyes says she understands my secrets.

My stalls are still a disaster. Sometimes kind people buy things, which I truly appreciate, but it's not always enough and I lose money despite my hard work because the pitches are so expensive. I'm constantly worried for the future.

I wish you'd been there yesterday when this guy at my stall was trying to discuss his music career with me. Usually I show an interest in other people's work, but I got such an arrogant vibe from him. I tried keeping the subject on my own work, but he kept interrupting, saying, "Yeah, it's difficult being an artist, isn't it?

I've been in a few bands..." and trailing off, as though he expected me to excitedly ask, "Really? Wow! Which bands?"

You would have crucified him.

Without you, all I do is be nice to people, I'm so pathetic. I'm the type of girl who spends her life craving a rescue that never arrives, a miracle that never happens, a wish that's never granted...

"Psycho bait," you used to say.

Talking of psychos, a fellow trader warned me about somebody who's killing women with a slow-acting poison. It takes somewhere between **two** weeks and a few months to activate, then the victim gets blisters covering their lower body and loses the ability to walk. After a few days of being crippled, the victim falls into a coma. The Poisoner has a birthmark in the shape of a car. Nobody knows who they are, so we should be wary of trusting anybody.

I trust you though.

I will always trust you, and I'm sorry if I'm a disappointment to you.

Yesterday you were in the strangest dream. It was **eight** p.m. and you were wielding a bloody, red club as you beat up the owner of a sick, black heart. I was choking on diamonds as they smacked me with spades. There was a ghost girl glowing in a **zero**-loaded symbol, somewhere in the scarlet confusion, with a heart-shaped hole in her chest. She said we didn't belong here. Her companions could show us the way to freedom, but first we had to sacrifice everything we knew.

Imaginary menagerie,
Chaotic repulsive anxious zoological yesterdays,
Leah

Hey Leah,

Sorry you haven't heard from me recently. I wrote a couple of weeks ago but my letters might be going missing. I'm going to ask the clerk if she can send my letters from outside the prison because I don't trust the other staff in this place.

The main theme of my last letter was me warning you not to trust Estana... I hope you haven't let her back into your life! The woman is evil. I know I joke about killing people, but that's only because I get a release from dark humour. Only a sick fuck would actually do that shit. That sinister bitch is dangerous, but I guess she's the type of person who thrives in this twisted city... That's if she is a person.

She might be a statica.

You've heard of them, right? I was reading about them in this battered book I borrowed from the library.

"With a rarity that makes many view them as urban legend, staticas could be the most powerful beings in Deragon Hex. They can manipulate certain machinery with their brains, switching the video feed in their vicinity on and off at will, and are considered highly dangerous. These supernatural creatures wield such complete control over their own narrative they scare those in power, and live bizarrely compelling, renegade lives on the fringes of society where the authorities grudgingly tolerate their existence."

Doesn't that describe Estana? There's hardly any public footage of her and she can always tell you which nearby cameras are malfunctioning. Also, she has tonnes of money and is vague as hell about where she gets it. Something about her doesn't add up.

Most people say this statica thing is catshit, and honestly so did I, but then I researched the science behind it. Gifted people can change the frequency of their brainwaves, and this can affect machinery around them. You might even do this yourself... Didn't you once say electronics break around you for no reason when you're upset? Well, what if you're doing something by accident that Estana has learned to control?

Pseudo-science aside, even if you don't believe she has superhuman abilities, let's not forget the fact that she kills people... or at least has them killed, which amounts to the same thing. I'm almost sure Fredi Luga was her victim, and I reckon there have been others. Please be careful in your dealings with that bitch and don't let her manipulate you.

Also, this may sound mean, but don't be so nice to everybody who visits your stall. Most people won't buy stuff because they're broke, so don't take it as a personal insult. Just sit and draw, and don't try so hard to please everyone. That band guy in your last letter sounded like a dick. I'm sure most of your customers are lovely, but sometimes guys get the wrong idea if you're too friendly, so be careful. When I get out of here, I will help protect you from that type of person.

Stay strong. You don't disappoint me, I know you mean well, I only wish I could do more to help you. It will be OK though.

See us rapidly vanish in voracious escapism,

Ash

Dear Ash,

If I didn't disappoint you before, I'm afraid I will now.

That band guy from the stall found my personal profile on the com network and was messaging me, asking if I wanted to meet again. At first I ignored him. Then I found out Tharia and Salma were attending a party I wanted to go to, and Bret still wasn't returning my messages, so I invited this guy to join me. I'm sorry. I felt so repulsive and didn't know where else to turn.

Well, I've been spending lots of time with him. His name's Damon Repper and he says he was a famous musician a few years ago. He's mostly a big deal on the social channels now. My friends aren't keen on him, but my friends don't think much of me either. I'm quite socially isolated these days.

Damon wants to take me to a festival in the caves, he says a trip away might help me. I get this sick sense of foreboding when I picture it though... as though everything is fragmenting and I'm losing mental coherence. I fear I'm walking into a trap, but my feet are moving of their own accord and won't let me turn back.

Some girls, they get mirrors torturing them with distorted versions of their face, and they need reassurance they aren't hideous in the same way other humans need oxygen. Perhaps this madness is the reason I let him into my life, and why I'll risk being alone in the caves with him. Sanity has forsaken me. A person can reach out in hope and end up in a horror story... it's like a razor blade slicing open the firmament if you've ever been the sky.

Only the girl who counts for something can make this mess add up again. She brings redemption. Numbers abandon her mouth like leaves from the trees in the storms we have never seen.

She will say **three** as though the vodka, the rum and the white spirit are the only trinity that could ever drown her.

She will say fortunate **four**. It will come tumbling out the door, brightly burnished coins from a slot machine that has finally been fathomed.

She will say **eight** and everything will escape. Treasure from a broken money box, smashed in haste to buy candy for rotten teeth.

She already said **two** because that's how many pieces we existed in before the machinery imploded.

She says **five** and nobody is surprised. We all know the sequence. The car starts, it drives, it crashes, we pretend we were never there.

When she says **three** again, we will run free again.

When she says **four** once more, words will pour from her like a frightened congregation, her mouth the only exit from a burning place of worship.

I feel numb, but she is number.

Halos emit light painlessly,

Leah

"Is that crazy bitch still writing to you?" sneers Ash's cellmate. He has decided that looming over Ash at their writing desk is more entertaining than watching comedy violence in the mediavision room today. Ash says nothing. They usually attack people who insult Leah, but their cellmate is the size of a small planet and they have to sleep in the same room as this person, so they choke back their rising anger.

Ash remembers the day they first arrived at the prison. "If you're not female, we'll have to put you in a men's segment, won't we?" the warden said with his creepiest grin.

"Well, I'm not male either..." Ash began.

"Sorry, we don't have any special blocks for freaks like you! If you wanted to be a precious little snowflake, you shouldn't have ended up in prison, should you? I'm sure you **two** will be just fine together though!" With this, the warden walked away chuckling to himself, leaving Ash alone with the most gargantuan slab of muscle to ever have something resembling consciousness. Ah, good times.

"Why are you still reading that shit?" their cellmate asks. "Doesn't that whiny bitch know some people are starving?"

"Wow, I bet she has no idea!" gasps Ash, still holding back their physical anger but losing control of their sarcasm reflex. "She lives in a run-down segment and walks past glittering beggars after spending her meagre income on grocery shopping. I know, I'll tell her they're starving! Obviously, this means they don't actually enjoy eating... but yes, I'll tell her they're starving, and this will stop her having a debilitating mental health condition!"

The colossal man stares at Ash in foreboding silence for a few moments before responding. "I'm not sure who I want to smack more... Her for being a self-pitying moron, or you for being an irritating little shit."

"You can't go around smacking people just because they annoy you. You'll end up in pr... Damn!" Ash exclaims, looking around themself in exaggerated surprise. "Never mind. You're already in prison. Forget I said anything!"

In a measured voice Ash's cellmate enquires, "Why are you the only person in here who doesn't speak to me with respect? Do you have a death wish?"

He puts his hand on Ash's shoulder. What might resemble a benevolent gesture is made somewhat threatening by the weight of the hand and its deathly grip.

"Yes," admits Ash, "sometimes I have a death wish, but that's not the reason I talk this way. The truth is, I'm terrible at being sycophantic. It doesn't suit my nature. This is probably why I lose jobs and I'm failing at life." With this final sentence they turn to flash a self-deprecating grimace.

The mammoth cellmate returns to contemplating the correspondence.

Leah's most recent letter includes a picture of her with Damon Repper. Upon recognising him, the cellmate throws back his head with a rumbling laugh that shakes his massive frame. "He's that mediavision guy who fed his last whore to the vultures! Is he fucking your Leah now?"

Ash regards the photograph with sick apprehension. "She's not sleeping with him, but he's made a delightful trap for her. He's taking her to a festival in the caves."

"What fucking caves?" demands the cellmate.

"Haven't you seen the history channels?" asks Ash, their voice raised this time in genuine surprise. "This whole city was caves to begin with, wasn't it? Before the authorities built the honeycomb structure we're living in now. Back when the world overground was still vaguely pleasant, before it started dying, some morbid sods came underground on purpose because they hated the sun. They wanted to live somewhere with shadows, cobwebs and bats, somewhere that suited the 'darkness of their souls'. Twats. The city's taken over by machinery and hollow consumerism now, we've swapped that particular crock of shit for another, but elderly residents still remember the 'good old days' of frills and candlelight. Personally, the only appealing thing I see in that particular combination is the possibility of some pompous tool accidentally setting themself on fire."

The cellmate lowers his hand during Ash's monologue, his arms hanging uselessly by his side as he struggles to absorb this abundance of new information.

Ash goes back to reading Leah's letter. They turn a page to find Leah has drawn a picture in the lower-right corner, a cat with hypnotic eyes in a monochrome dreamscape. The cellmate jabs a chunky finger at this and demands, "What the hell is that?"

"Leah always loved drawing," Ash explains. "Her reasoning was, 'I'll never be beautiful, but if I create beautiful art before dying, my life might mean something.' She said these pictures were poured from the chasm of her fractured heart."

The hulk behind their shoulder judders with booming laughter once more. "Haha! I used to send hate mail to stupid bitches like that!" he crows in pernicious delight.

Ash sighs. "Leah does receive a lot of hate mail."

The cellmate continues, "I would tell them to try visiting a burns unit or a children's cancer ward if they wanted to see an actual problem!"

"You could say that was a wise suggestion," Ash remarks.

"It really fucking is," agrees the cellmate.

"Although," says Ash, "if you were devoting your life to helping the terminally ill, I doubt you would find time to send anonymous abuse to the depressed. I'm not a doctor, but I'd say sending death threats to sad people is probably a less effective weapon than chemotherapy in the war on cancer."

The cellmate stoops to whisper in Ash's ear. "**One** of these days, I'm going to kill you in your sleep, my darling... **One** of these days..."

CHAPTER SEVEN

Shoulders back but eyes demurely lowered, hands still shaking from the excesses of yesterday, Leah heads to a party, walking like a girl trouble would follow to the grave.

The detective continues to watch her. "That bitch knows Alicia. It's written all over her," he slurs into the stale air of his surroundings. Perhaps it is because she resembles Honeysuckle, the ray of sunshine who disappeared around the same time Alicia's brutal reign ended, forever connecting them in the Deragon Hex hive mind. Maybe it's because she lives in the aforementioned murderer's previous residence... or maybe he just enjoys looking at her.

He has been with precisely **zero** women since his wife of **six** years left him for a rich businessman with a fancy Plus **Seven** apartment in the western hexes. He moved into this hotel on the eastern edge after getting a tip-off that a mass murder would soon take place on Plus **Nine**. Wanting to be near the action, he rented out the cheapest room on Plus **Eight** and set up spy screens to tap video feed from each top floor room. Due to his hyper-active mind needing to work on at least **two** projects at a time, he now sits surrounded by screens that show no killers worth catching, while investigating a mass-murderer his colleagues gave up on finding years ago.

Alicia was **one** bitch who deserved a public execution.

"Tell me where she is, you damn slut," he mumbles at the image of Leah.

She has arrived at the party and is talking to Damon Repper. The social celebrity is boasting of his past accomplishments, holding up his com device to show her a clip of himself playing on stage **four** years ago.

The detective stares at the musical performance on the screen within a screen. "I've never heard of you, dickhead."

"I wish I'd heard of you before and seen you play live, you were really good," Leah compliments him with an eager smile, fidgeting with a lock of hair.

Damon says something in response, but all the detective hears is a voice saying, "You left this outside, mate," from the hotel room's doorway.

The detective jumps up, knocking his chair over, and draws his weapon. "Who the fuck said you could enter?" He aims his gun at the chest of a tired old man.

"I thought I'd bring you this before somebody steals it from the hallway," the uninvited visitor explains. Oblivious to the gun, he stands relaxed in his faded uniform and holds out a large bottle of whiskey.

"And you couldn't knock?"

"I did knock! You might have noticed if that 'movie' wasn't so Cashdamn loud. That's the other reason I'm bothering you. Guests next door complained about the noise last night. You might want to lower the volume."

Leah's sickly soft speech and Damon's confident voice are eerily projected, ringing out against a hiss of interference as he invites her to a festival in the caves.

"I don't remember leaving that outside," the detective growls, torn between confusion and suspicion. To be fair, he remembers little from the past evening except Leah... crying over her paintings, fixing her make-up, hiding strange secrets within each self-conscious gesture. When he cannot follow live footage of her, he sifts through whatever archived material he can find in the databanks.

He scratches his head with the hand not holding the gun and tries to recall. He had gone out to buy more whiskey earlier. It had been difficult unlocking the door on his return, he had placed the bottle on the ground... everything spun... he got in, stumbled over something on his way to the desk... Was it a stray bottle that tripped him? Is that what he had nearly finished drinking? All he knows is, he has been searching for a clue. A clue that could finally catch that bitch, Alicia. A clue that could give him his life back.

"I'm surprised you can remember *anything*," quips the trespasser, making a derisory scan of the detective's dishevelled state.

Click. The lawman takes the safety catch off his gun.

"Hey! Don't be so paranoid! I don't give a damn about the little spy cinema you got rigged up here! You any idea how much fucked-up shit I've seen in this place? I gave up phoning you people years ago when I saw how terrible you are at your jobs, and decided to leave the criminals for the vultures! All I'm trying to do here is keep my guests happy and clear the hallway, so do you want this bottle or not?"

The detective sighs, returns the safety catch and holsters his weapon. "I'm sorry fella, all this footage is too intense, I'm really losing my shit." He turns a dial on his speakers to lower the volume.

"No worries... I can help if you want? Cash knows you guys need it."

"Aren't you on duty?"

"My shift ended **eight** minutes ago, the day porter's just arrived to replace me."

"Cash! How late is it?"

"You don't wanna know, mate," replies the night porter as he hands over the whiskey.

The detective emits a bitter laugh. "Well, take a seat." He picks his chair up off the floor and gestures toward another. "You can help me watch this tracking feed for clues to where Alicia is."

"Alicia? Are you kidding? I thought you guys had given up trying to find her."

"I never give up! This whore knows where she is, I can feel it." While the detective pours whiskey for his new guest, a green circle begins to flash in the corner of his screen. "There's live footage of her coming up now!" he grins.

"What makes you think she's a whore?" wonders the night porter.

"Well, I've been watching her a great deal on these surveillance cameras, and she often gets naked."

"Well, that explains it then..." murmurs the night porter as he surveys the nearest wall. "And what's with the other monitors? You hacked into the hotel's security system? You guards don't usually concern yourselves with what goes on in this building..."

"I've been investigating a tip-off concerning illegal activity on the top floor, but it's probably nothing. Let's just look at my computer screen, shall we? Maybe you could help me spot a crucial clue."

Deragon Hex surveillance video travels from distant caverns via the central control room to the detective's computer, and the story of Leah and Damon's holiday unfolds like a slow-motion trainwreck.

"See, you'll feel much safer out here," says Damon's image to Leah's image on the glowing monitor as they walk toward a holiday home for rich tourists. Around them is a tasteful acrylic garden and a glorious view of lamp-lit stalactites.

What remains of the caves lies out past city borders, where hollowed ground has yet to be adapted into modern structure. This is where the early settlers lived when they first came underground, taking the elevator down the north wall of Red Zero and then following a chasm through the rock away from the prison.

The elder cave dwellers were the first citizens to leave the surface on purpose, claiming they no longer belonged under the sun. When the next generation questioned their sunless existence, the elders insisted the world above them was dead, or it may as well be.

Armed guards surround the elevator at the edge of the central hex, which is programmed to only return to surface when containing no passengers. There are rumours of an exit to overground through the caves' twisted caverns... but the ubiquitous cameras make leaving impossible. Anybody straying too far from authorised walkways will certainly attract vulture attention, and the traitorous act of trying to escape leaves no way to avoid Death by Laser.

Damon and Leah's isolated guest house lies a short drive along rocky tunnels from the nearest ancient town, where a subterranean river joins a polluted lake, ornate buildings sprawl over crumbling stones, and bats roost in the shadows. Twice a year, a festival for music fans and socialites takes place in this gloomy realm. The region is also popular with celebrities who wish to portray a certain "dark" image, and became notorious when Honeysuckle got arrested for possession of narcotics here **eight** years previously. This wild, northern part of the caves will someday become part of Layer **Six** as Deragon Hex continues its unrelenting expansion. Presently, it remains rough, unrenovated and far from the main roadways.

"Maybe it would be better if I stayed with friends," suggests Leah, shivering as she stares at this evening's abode. "Some of them have booked a place near the festival."

"Don't worry, I won't expect anything from you here," Damon promises. "I'm just trying to help you. Besides, you'll feel better after spending time away from those supposed friends of yours."

"Don't you like my friends?" Leah frets.

Damon halts before the house and exclaims, "This always happens! People always complain, 'He's taking her away from her friends!'" Exasperated, he explains he often meets girls who associate with an unsavoury crowd, and he helps them by bringing them into his own social group instead. People judge him for this. "I'm only trying to help!" he snaps.

Before Leah can apologise for causing offence, the door to the vacation home opens and a slim woman with voluminous hair grins from the darkened hallway. "Hi there! Welcome to your lovely home in the caves!" she greets them, before grabbing Damon in a lingering embrace.

"Hi, Raychel," Damon responds, composing himself. After she pulls away to flash a frosty smile at Leah, he adds, "Leah, this is my friend, Raychel Spoben. Raychel, this is Leah."

"We... We've met before," stammers Leah. The woman's drawn-on eyebrows raise as she continues, "I... I had a stall near you at the last alternative market. I was selling my artwork."

"Hmm yes, of course you were, dear," Raychel assures her, rummaging in her designer handbag.

Damon scowls at Raychel. "I didn't realise you'd still be here."

"Oh don't worry, the others have left and I'm about to leave too," she explains. "I just promised the landlady I'd pass you the keys, to save her the journey."

"How kind of you," mutters Damon as Raychel produces the keys from her purse.

She hands them across with a peck on the cheek, saying, "Goodbye, darling." From out of shot comes the sound of tyres over dirt. "What fantastic timing, my taxi has arrived!"

"It was nice meeting you again," says Leah, as Raychel totters along the driveway with her suitcase.

"Lovely meeting you too, dear," replies Raychel. "Gosh! Is that your car, Damon? It's a real beauty!"

"Thank you. She sure is," agrees Damon, gazing at his prized possession, his eyes shining as though he's observing the mythical sunrise.

"Have fun, you guys!" Raychel teases as she gets into the taxi. She slams the door then winks at Damon through the window as the vehicle pulls away, but he fails to notice because he is still staring at his car. Leah waves at her.

Damon eventually pulls his gaze from his automotive treasure to tell Leah, "I find that woman so annoying, I want to stab her."

Leah attempts to laugh, but it catches in her throat.

Damon gives her a kiss, takes her arm and walks her into the building.

The rooms of their accommodation are arranged in the rectangular grid style that was popular overground instead of Deragon Hex's modern, hexagonal design. Damon heads straight to the bedroom.

Leah stands horrified as he pushes the single beds until they are next to each other. "I thought you chose this place because of the twin room?"

"Yes, but I want to sleep next to you tonight. I'm tired from taking care of you and I need something for myself," Damon informs her. Once satisfied with the new furniture arrangement, he starts getting undressed. Leah goes white and turns away to stare at the wall. Damon is amused by her discomfort. "Relax, I'm only getting changed," he chuckles. "Besides, you always knew you were going to see my dick this weekend."

"I have serious reason to believe this guy is a cunt," remarks the night porter, interrupting the detective's attentive viewing.

"Wha..." mumbles the drunken lawman. After registering this comment, he looks hopeful. "Maybe Alicia will arrive to kill him and rescue her!"

The night porter regards his new acquaintance with eyes narrowed in appraisal. "You're not the rescuing type then?"

"Don't get me wrong, if I was there, Damon dearest would receive a brutal kick in the testicles that leaves him clutching his groin in agony while I take the keys to his precious sports car, grab Leah and drive her to safety."

"Is there a time lag on this footage? You gonna find out where she is? Perhaps we can save her?"

"Fuck it," responds the detective as he knocks back more whiskey and sweats on his plastic chair. "It's not worth sabotaging my research mission to save a girl who was always destined to be psycho bait."

Damon gets changed and chooses an outfit for Leah. "Don't you look pretty," he says, looking at her as though she is something he has accomplished.

"Thank you," she responds with a small smile.

"You're almost as pretty as Estana," he adds. His eyes mist over as though he is viewing his car or his own reflection.

"Thanks," whispers Leah, lowering her eyes to stare at the ground.

"I saw her in her bedroom doorway while you were fetching your suitcase," continues Damon. "She had the most striking expression of distant cruelty... I do admire that in a woman... She told me '**Five one three** is the trigger' before laughing in my face! I wonder what she meant."

"I have no idea, I never understand her."

"Yes, she is rather enigmatic, isn't she?"

Leah sighs.

Damon glowers at her and says, "Humans are complicated creatures with complex needs." But she fails to grasp what he is implying.

Once ready, they travel by taxi to the festival site. The camera built into the top of the taxi's rear-view mirror captures their ride. Leah sits with her hands folded in her lap, staring through the laminated glass at sporadic lights on craggy tunnel walls. Damon leans back, relaxed and smiling, boasting to the driver of his contacts in the music industry. A bat swoops past the window in a leathery blur of wings and talons.

"I love this place!" beams Damon as they finally arrive at the festival town and exit the taxi. Candles in skulls adorn the walkways, and revellers swarm in fancy dress, masquerading as early settlers and posing for the ubiquitous photographers as they strut alongside the underground river.

Leah stands captivated by the corseted cavegirls adorned with opulent jewellery. The way their faces shine under candlelight glow reminds her of the moonlight she has never seen.

Damon insists on heading straight for the main venue, much to Leah's dismay. "I've not sold many paintings lately, I can't afford a ticket," she frets, embarrassed by her poverty. "I usually go to the smaller venues. They're cheaper and just as nice."

"You don't need to pay for festival tickets now, you're with me." He laughs, reaching for her hand beneath a flickering lantern and leading her through the gloom.

When they get to the auditorium near the river, he asks the door staff to lead him to the event organiser. An assistant walks them to an office, where the organiser greets him warmly and hands over two backstage passes. "This is what happens when you arrive with me," Damon boasts, handing a pass to Leah.

"Thank you," is her simple reply as they head to the stairway.

"Thank you for thanking me," he says, prompting a look of shy bewilderment.

"Women rarely thank me for helping them," he explains. "They usually take me for granted. I am accustomed to going out of my way for women I'm involved with, doing whatever it takes to make them happy, and receiving no gratitude in return. It's wonderful to be thanked for a change!"

"Why in Earth would you date somebody who treats you that way?" wonders Leah, her face pained and incredulous.

"I try to see the good in people..." he sighs. When they reach the top of the stairs, he takes Leah's hand and slows his footsteps.

The stairway to the main hall gives social players the opportunity to make an impressive entrance while flaunting prestigious accessories. Damon has dressed Leah in a tightly fitted long skirt that constrains her lower body, forcing her into the hobbled walk of the vulnerable. As he descends, he surveys the crowd with an icy smile. Some festivalgoers stare up at their entrance, but most pay no attention. Leah's eyes dart nervously around the room, taking in the upturned faces and dusty chandeliers before gazing at her feet for the last eight steps.

"Aw, look at you two..." a passing friend comments.

"Congratulations to you both!" cheers another well-meaning acquaintance when they finally reach the assembled masses.

"We're not..." Leah hesitantly begins.

"Thank you!" grins Damon, pulling her close with an arm around her shoulders.

"How long have you been together?" another acquaintance enquires.

"We haven't..." Leah starts to say.

"We met three weeks ago at an alternative market," Damon replies. "I had just gone for the day out really, but I saw her behind her stall... As soon as I approached, she smiled and started talking and we spoke for nearly half an hour! She gave me her card and told me to find her online."

"Aw, that's so sweet!"

Leah somehow becomes paler. Her chest heaves beneath the taut fabric of her plastic-coated dress as tiny droplets of sweat glisten on her brow.

Damon recognises more acquaintances in the vicinity and decides to make introductions. "This is Leah," he tells them, gesturing toward the girl as she stands frozen like a fragile creature in the face of inexplicable danger. "This is Coby Perlanesh," he tells Leah, referring to the man stood closest to him. "He sometimes DJs here." He then introduces the rest of an expensively dressed social group.

After a couple of minutes of being kindly spoken to, Leah appears calmer. Some girls, you can put them in a pit of malevolent, talking lions and they will smile so long as the articulate carnivores admire their outfits. They can cope with their limbs being ripped off, providing their dress still looks pretty.

Leah soon ends up stood awkwardly alone while Damon flirts with a woman nearby. "Can I have a word with you?" asks Damon's friend Coby Perlanesh, leading her away from the group. He stops and leans toward her. "I just want to tell you, Damon is a really great guy."

"Is he?" Leah replies with a nervous smile. She glances at her apparent date for the evening putting his arm around another woman while they laugh at his jokes.

"Honestly," Coby continues, "if I ever needed help, he'd be the first person I'd call. He'll do anything for his friends."

The man in question swaggers across with his female comrade in tow. "This is Nescha Polbrey," he says. "She's the main designer at Tornado clothing, the latest name in talex plastics."

"Pleased to meet you," says Nescha, shaking Leah's hand. She then leans close to Leah's ear, telling her, "Damon is the nicest guy", while exchanging a conspiratorial smile with the subject of her flattery. "I'd date him myself if I was single."

Leah has stopped explaining that Damon only invited her as a friend. She merely nods like a dumb doll, the fingers of her right hand playing with her necklace, her left arm folded across her waist. Damon puts his arm back around her. "So what do you think of my friends?"

"They're lovely," she replies, smiling at everybody as though they are listening.

"I'm incredibly popular on the social scene," Damon boasts. He then leans in and whispers, "People are extremely protective of me. I have loyal friends who would hate to see anybody hurt me. Any woman who treats me badly ends up a zero on the social scale."

Leah gulps. "It's nice of them to protect you."

For the rest of the evening she maintains impeccable behaviour, dancing prettily, being friendly and polite to his friends, desperate to give people no reason to hate her. Later, back at the guest house, she gives him what he wants. She gets through it by pretending to be Honeysuckle, her favourite movie star.

In the stuffy hotel room, the night porter watches in furious disgust while Leah pretends to be pornography, all naked and compliant because some girls cannot bear being a disappointment. "I want you to be more like Estana," commands Damon from centre shot to Leah on screen left.

"I don't know how..." she frets.

"It can't always be about you! I am a complex person and I want a dominant woman! So if I ask you to be more like Estana, then BE MORE LIKE ESTANA!"

The detective shakes his head and laughs. "Haha! That's a logical way of making somebody more dominant, isn't it? Yell at them until they comply! DO AS I SAY!!! BE MORE DOMINANT!!!"

The night porter says nothing, but his knuckles whiten from gripping his glass too tight.

There is another glitch in the footage. What happens next was inevitable since the movie began, the bitter occurrences tumbling into each other as they hurtle toward a precipice. The scene goes from naked to pixelated. The detective rises from his chair to slam the side of the screen with a podgy hand, bullying it into displaying the forthcoming act. They all break in different ways. The modern units lose their picture by dissolving into a honeycomb of harsh colour, overrun by those **six**-sided shapes that form the underworld's city blocks. Others succumb to an ancient static haze that resembles an electrical snowstorm. Screens of intermediate age merely depict flickering squares when they malfunction. Images compress into a grid, a naked breast becomes a square, a naked arm becomes a rectangle, a naked face pixelates into a less harrowing disaster.

The picture clears and Leah is sitting on a sofa, broken. Damon sits nearby, his narrowed eyes stabbing fury in her direction. She crumples before his gaze. Wavy locks cascade over her lowered face, partially covering the black smudges on her cheekbones and the shiny, pink skin on her nose. Her upper body rocks back and forth. Both characters in this unfolding drama are now corporally clothed, although the natures they hide from public viewing have become disrobed.

"Do you remember the time you went to the psychologist because of your eating disorder?" he asks her, his voice dangerously quiet.

She responds with a hesitant nod.

"When you tried to discuss the awful things that made you unwell?"

She nods once more, wringing her hands and breathing in anxious little gasps.

"And he dismissed you," he continues. "He said horrible, judgemental things to you! He made you feel worthless, didn't he?"

Her gentle rocking increases as she shrinks further into herself.

"WELL THAT'S HOW YOU'VE MADE ME FEEL!" he bellows. "After everything I've done for you! After going out of my way, doing whatever it takes to make you happy, I have received no gratitude from you whatsoever! This is how you repay me! When I ask for something for myself and it's not all about you anymore, you lose interest! This is how you treat me!"

Another tear drips from Leah's eye.

"I've got the urge to start throwing things," he fumes. "Wouldn't that be scary for you? If I started throwing furniture and smashing this place up? My ex didn't like it. Well, you're lucky I can control myself now because that's what you've made me want to do!"

"I'm so sorry," sniffs Leah, still rocking back and forth, downcast, wiping her wet face with the side of her shaking hand.

"I'm tempted to leave you here by yourself," Damon threatens, prompting Leah's small body to heave with overwhelming misery.

The night porter hurls his glass of whiskey at the screen. Vivid pixels of Damon's livid face remain unmoved while the fragile vessel smashes against it and translucent shards rain to the ground like jagged hailstones. Bitter, brown liquid drips over Damon's eyes as they scorch with contempt.

"WHAT THE FUCK?!?" yells the detective at his drinking companion.

The night porter ignores him and rises to clean the mess.

"That was expensive whiskey! It cost me **64** cash digits! There's no need to throw it over some Cashdamn whore, you could have messed up my equipment!"

"Why leave it in the hallway if it was expensive?" mutters the night porter.

"WHAT?" the detective snaps.

"Nothing."

"Too right, nothing!"

"I'll buy you a new bottle tomorrow."

"Too right, you will!"

Also drenched with splattered whiskey is the image of Leah, the drops disguising her tears as she convulses and sobs, "I don't mean to be bad. I don't mean to be ugly. Bad... ugly... bad...

ugly..." She hits herself in the face as the light above her begins flickering. There is nowhere for her to run.

Damon suddenly becomes contrite, saying, "Darling, you could never be ugly," as he takes the weeping girl in his arms. Sympathy replaces the inferno in his gaze.

With her arms squashed to her chest, Leah stops attempting to rock while he gently explains what a difficult time he has been going through lately. He is stuck living in his parents' penthouse while he waits to receive the sponsorship deals and recognition as a celebrity he deserves. His true place lies with the cultural elite, but the breakthrough he needs is forever beyond reach. Plus, he has persistent problems with his physical health and keeps needing kidney dialysis. The frustrations of his life make him lose his temper sometimes, but he honestly never thought he would lash out at Leah.

She wipes away her tears and forgives him. A person perpetually tortured by the craving to be loved and understood will accept any reconciliation. This is how she descends from depressed artist to mindless mannequin, deciding to give him what he wants for the rest of their stay until he drives her home.

Hours later, in the detective's room, video feed shows Damon and Leah's journey back to the city. An uneventful ride through jagged tunnels and lurid streets is accompanied by the faint noise of Damon's car stereo. He says he enjoyed introducing Leah to Nescha Polbrey and Coby Perlanesh. "Many of my friends are designers and DJs. I am very well connected."

"Well, I've met a few people through..." begins Leah.

"Aren't you pleased to have met the designer of Tornado clothing?" Damon continues.

"What the fuck is Tornado clothing?" the detective demands, snapping back to consciousness. He realises the night porter has left without him noticing, and he has no idea how much time has passed since he fell asleep in this stupid, uncomfortable chair. He is on his own with his whiskey and his screens and this footage of a whore who is hiding something. "I'm watching you," he mumbles to Leah, wagging his finger at the screen as his eyelids fall again.

Judging by the confused look in Leah's eyes, she had never heard of Tornado clothing either. After a few moments she diplomatically replies, "Yes, she was nice."

The vehicle lurches over a bump in the terrain as Damon tells her, "I've always wanted to be seen with a woman dressed in talex plastic."

"I couldn't wear a talex outfit in public."

"Why not?"

"I'd be so paranoid and uncomfortable! Talex plastic is so thin, and you can't even wear underwear... What if something catches it and rips it open?"

"Fine," scowls Damon as they reach the border of Deragon Hex.

"Now is the time... **seven zero nine**..." croons the radio's latest synthpop hit. After a sharp turn, the road joins the city streets which go past in a colourful blur, and they travel without further conversation.

When they reach the garage above Leah's place the camera feed cuts out, but the detective is no longer conscious enough to notice.

Unaware they ever had a drunken observer, Damon and Leah exit the vehicle and he helps her into the apartment with her bags. At the door, she tells him, "Thank you for helping me."

"Thank you for thanking me," he replies.

He moves to kiss her goodbye, and she tells him, "You don't really want me as your girlfriend. You want somebody like Estana... or maybe Honeysuckle..."

His laugh is vicious. "Honeysuckle? The wanton slut? I think my dick would fall off!"

He gives Leah a kiss and returns to his car with a swagger in his step; his eyes are twinkling razorblades.

Leah closes the door and unpacks her things. **Three** minutes later, she bursts into tears and continues to cry until bedtime. She types a letter to Ash, telling them of her disastrous weekend before passing out in a heap of blankets and misery. When she wakes the next morning, she wishes she hadn't.

With no idea her actions beyond the apartment are observed by an alcoholic stalker, she drifts through the following days, wandering through a life that no longer belongs to her. She is constantly afraid something terrible is going to happen.

CHAPTER EIGHT

Dear Ash,

I have agreed to be Damon's girlfriend. I don't recall how it happened, but he's announced our relationship on his opinion show, so I can't change my mind. This is a nightmare. I wanted to speak to Bret first, but that might have made Damon angry with me again, so I said nothing, and now my friends hate me. I don't know how to undo this mess. Maybe Bret will rescue me if I tell my friends I'm trapped.

Somebody needs to rescue me. Each day, Damon's noose around my neck gets tighter. He introduces me to important media people and compliments me as though I'm not there, saying things that are flattering in a sleazy way. There's this constant suggestion that these people will hate me if I ever displease him. He's showing me the bars of my cage. I've never felt so trapped in my life.

He keeps saying how terrible things will be for me if I "cross" him. What does that even mean? "Cross" him... He often begins sentences with, "If you cross me..." It's such a vague statement of injury - "that person crossed me" - like a lame crucifiction. If he was a spider, his web would be the social scene and the "nice guy" mass-delusion that's infected his disciples.

His temper terrifies me. He brings up my insecurities and awful things from my past, knowing exactly how to make me cry. The worst part is, his entourage only see his good side. If I told them about his other side, they'd merely abuse me for "lying", they're so protective because of the illness that makes him need kidney dialysis. He says if I ever hurt him, they will destroy me, but it's impossible for me to not offend him! Sometimes everything I do is wrong.

He insists he's treating me "like a lady". I wish he wouldn't. Why can't I be treated like a human being? A "lady" is a woman who achieves an impeccably high standard of behaviour, which is too much pressure. He's very charming when I meet his expectations, but furious when I disappoint him.

I did try to leave him once. I told him I wasn't judging him, that I knew he only lashed out because he was unhappy, but I just couldn't cope with it anymore. He burst into tears and admitted he used to scare his last girlfriend with his temper too, that it was wrong of him to keep doing this and he would get help. And I believed him... but as soon as he was sure I wasn't going to leave, he turned back into a monster.

I wish I could be **four** different people: somebody to be the girlfriend who meets the standard he expects, somebody to go to parties with my former friends and make them stop hating me, somebody to get some damn work done so I'm less of an unmitigated failure, and somebody who can hide in a dark room until everything has gone away.

I miss you so much. If you were here, you could help me escape. I can't ask Estana for help because she doesn't care. She is cold and terrifying. She tells me I should be as heartless as her, so I don't get hurt...

But I don't want to be dead inside, I just want to be free.

Hexadecimate emigrate lacerate pâté,

(Yeah, that last word doesn't rhyme. That was me trying to be funny like you. Sorry if it sounds crap.)

Leah

Although the broken young woman receives no reply from her best friend, over the next few weeks she continues to write another **four** letters. She has no idea if Ash will even read them, but she has nobody else, and it helps to put these events to paper. Creating a story from these bitter occurrences makes them somehow less real.

The only detail she omits is Estana's return to the apartment, being too ashamed about ignoring Ash's advice. She does not believe in the concept of "staticas", weird beings from a futuristic fairy tale who control cameras with their brains. The notion seems too far-fetched. All she knows is that a couple of sinister, manipulative people are now a permanent part of her life, she may well be doomed, and it is entirely her own fault.

The worst part is Damon's obsession with Estana. It starts with him yelling at Leah to be more dominant, then before long he is hammering on Estana's door right in front of her, demanding the woman's attention.

On a lonely afternoon, Leah catches sight of them through an open bedroom doorway and stares in intimidated awe at the cruel woman's sadistic antics. "I could never be as confident as her," she decides, before resigning herself to another pathetic evening of watching Honeysuckle movies and eating synthetic ice cream.

Later, Estana tells her, "You should stay away from Damon."

"Why don't *you* stay away from him?!" Leah snaps.

Estana graces her with the sympathetic smile a patronising person might reserve for the crippled. "He keeps pestering me for attention and it's amusing to pander to his requests on occasion," she explains. "I can handle him though, unlike you. Spoilt little boys destroy their fragile toys."

Leah sobs, racked with paranoia and self-loathing. "He only trapped me to get closer to you, didn't he?"

Estana looks her up and down. "Well, do you blame him?"

The detective returns from the shops after buying whiskey, beer and chips, and gets talking to the night porter in the hotel lobby. They have struck up an unlikely friendship ever since the staff member called round to his room with a new bottle of whiskey and an apology, and the detective, embarrassed by losing consciousness at their first meeting, invited him in to watch more Leah footage. These ongoing "investigations" have now become a regular pastime.

"All set for tonight?"

"Yeah, I've arranged cover so my shift can finish early."

"Great, see you later!"

Tonight is Damon's birthday party. The extravagant event takes place in his parents' penthouse apartment, a residence large enough to have both inter-hex and inner-hex windows. North-west glass looms over an eternally darkened roadway while a south-east balcony enjoys fluctuating "outdoor" lighting overlooking an acrylic park.

"All this will be mine in a few years," Damon boasts as he shows off each opulent space to Leah. "By the way, the tiles in the balcony room are extremely expensive, so you can't wear those large boots to my party."

Leah's present for him is a mixed media art piece it took her six days to make, a cartoon girl stood in an abstract dreamscape with a Gothic rose beside her. The work represents a breakthrough in her development as a visual artist. She has never given away such an important piece, and wants to keep it. But Damon perpetually accuses her of not being grateful for his help, so Leah hopes presenting this work as a gift will be a strong enough indication of gratitude to appease him. He is so moved by this gesture he goes several hours without complaining about how difficult she is.

After unwrapping his present, he chooses a short dress for her to wear to the party. At the designated hour, his guests arrive in formal attire.

"I should be wearing something more formal," Leah frets.

"This is how a girlfriend of mine should dress," he insists.

To protect the expensive flooring, Leah wears her lacy dress with no shoes, giving her the look of a particularly sluttish orphan. She is introduced to Damon's best friend, Chloe Spanbrey, who has organised a collection among his main disciples to purchase many expensive presents. Leah is eyed with suspicion by Judi Gingseng, who was a singer in Damon's former band. She also meets Sahlee Byncorp and Sophey Clarben, who wear similar outfits and hate the same people. As they walk away, Damon mutters to Leah, "It's a shame Sophey says she has a low libido. That's why I've never pursued her."

Halfway through the party, Damon insists on having his photograph taken with all the female guests gathered around him while the men stand out of sight. Leah sits beside her boyfriend, drapes herself over him for the shot, then spends the next hour being silently suicidal. None of the other guests notice her misery while her boyfriend prances around holding court. When she later catches his eye, she asks him, "Why have your photo taken with all the women gathered around you and the men out of shot? I don't understand..."

Damon narrows his eyes. "Are we going to have a problem? You *know* I can't stand women being suspicious of my many female friends!"

"But if I wanted a photo surrounded by men, you'd be furious!" says Leah. "I have to be so careful... I can't even mention another guy without..."

"We'll get you dressed in talex plastic next," Damon declares with an appreciative scan of Leah's figure.

"I can't wear talex..." she begins, but he has already moved on to speak to somebody else.

Later in the evening Leah has a panic attack, which causes Damon to yell at her until she cries. "I'VE BEEN VERY SELFLESS!" he bellows. "AND I NEED YOU TO BE MORE GRATEFUL!"

Viewing this exchange on screen in the hotel room, the night porter bursts out laughing. "He's been very selfless, but he needs her to be more grateful?! Doesn't that contradict the definition of selfless? This guy must have the world's tiniest dictionary!"

The detective joins his laughter. "Maybe if he had a larger vocabulary, he wouldn't be such a ridiculous little prick!"

"Small lexicon syndrome," his friend agrees.

Leah runs off to cry in the guest bedroom and confide the evening's misadventures to her prison penfriend.

The detective and the night porter have no plans for Cashmas so they spend it spying on their favourite **zero**-sum relationship as Leah visits Damon's parents' place. Cashmas is based on an ancient overground festival. Once a year, the population gather with close friends and family to eat, drink and exchange gifts in their specially decorated homes. The origins of this custom are long forgotten, but in a city with no seasonal variation of day length, people cling to various celebratory dates to divide the year into fun phases.

On the day before Cashmas, Leah arrives at Damon's family home with thoughtful presents and a shy smile.

"You can put those under the tree," he tells her, referring to her bag of gifts. Trees are large, spiky ornaments made from green plastic, designed to resemble non-sentient, overground life forms that humans wiped out to make space for cars and cattle. It is traditional to place a tree in your home at Cashmas and decorate it with lights, candy canes and small acrylic models of silver people wearing fluffy red hats... Just another of those timeless rituals that nobody questions. Leah places her gifts on the left-hand side beneath a silver figurine of a chubby girl holding a bag of chips.

"That's your present," grins Damon, nodding at a large, hexagonal gift box with a red bow.

"I can't wait," Leah says.

At **nine** p.m. they settle to watch a movie on a massive screen in the mediavision room. Its comforting glow is the only thing lighting the lavish setting apart from the twinkling of the Cashmas tree. Damon puts his arm around Leah. They appear almost content, with an action movie reflected in their eyes and non-alcoholic drinks. The movie's mundane script is soon accompanied by the noise of footsteps and slurred conversation as Damon's parents return from a local bar and enter the mediavision room. "Leah's here! Merry Cashmas!"

"Merry Cashmas!" Leah greets them. "Have you had a nice evening?"

"Yes thank you! A wonderful evening!" Damon's father steadies himself against a chair before wandering off to the drinks cabinet.

"The presents look lovely!" gasps Damon's mother, surveying the array of gift-wrapped boxes sparkling like a miniature citadel beneath the illuminated, plastic tree. "Ooh, what's this?" she wonders, reaching for the large present with the scarlet bow.

"GET AWAY FROM THAT!" Damon yells at his mother, whose face drops with the ashamed sadness of somebody trying not to cry. He adds, "That's my gift for Leah."

"I'm sorry Damon," his mother replies. After an awkward silence she adds, "Well, I'll leave you to watch your movie in peace. Night night."

"Good night," says Leah, looking at her with an apology in her eyes she dares not articulate.

Damon sighs. "She never knows when to leave things alone..."

The unsuspected viewing party at the hotel exchange disgusted glances. "How the fuck does he have such a 'nice guy' image when he's so horrible to his mother?" mutters the detective.

"He could be a statica," the night porter suggests.

"Do you honestly think staticas exist?"

The night porter muses, "I keep an open mind... A human is a walking electromagnet, and highly self-aware people can deliberately alter the frequency of their brainwaves. I've heard sufferers of mental illness claim electronic devices malfunction around them when they're stressed. If somebody tapped into that innate ability and harnessed it... then maybe... But Damon doesn't seem particularly self-aware, does he?" he realises with a bitter laugh. "He probably just pays to get incriminating clips of himself hidden from public viewing behind high-security passcodes... If he was a statica, I don't think this footage we're watching would even exist."

"You're right!" the detective agrees. "It took some high-level hacking to access this surveillance feed. That reminds me, I still need to crack that glitch in the clip of him and Leah at the caves. This guy is strangely selective with what he shares of his private life... It's money though, isn't it? Not creepy superpowers... Leah's other roommate though! If staticas do exist..."

"Leah has another roommate?" The night porter raises his eyebrows.

"Yeah. She's kinda sinister..." The detective trails off as Leah and Damon continue viewing their action movie without further disturbance.

The unhappy couple make occasional subdued conversation until Damon notices a nearby fluffy rabbit toy. "It's Mister Rabbit!" he cries, delighted at finding the small child's plaything. "Say hello to Mister Rabbit!" he commands Leah, shoving the fluffy replica of an extinct animal in her face. "Say hello to Mister Rabbit!"

Leah squirms and says, "No, I don't want to!" as she pushes the stuffed toy away.

"There's no need to be rude!" snaps Damon, glaring as though he wants to kill her. He then storms off, leaving her alone to contemplate her behaviour.

"This guy's a lunatic!" yells the detective.

"Well," says the night porter, "everybody knows it's terrible etiquette to push away somebody's rabbit at Cashmas. It's almost as rude as blowing your nose on a spaniel at Chocfest, or kneecapping your friend's favourite ostrich on New Year's Eve."

"Yeah..." agrees the detective. "Wait! What the fuck is an ostrich?"

On the computer screen, Leah sits by herself watching mediavision. When the set starts flickering with static glitches, she switches it off and goes to sleep in the guest bedroom.

Ash is in solitary confinement for fighting again. This is a disaster. Now the guards will further delay their parole hearing because of their Cashdamn temper. They can barely remember what happens during the adrenaline surges and are usually shocked at themself afterwards. It starts when somebody abuses or threatens harm to a vulnerable target. Ash becomes a whirlwind of fists and fury, caught in a storm that does not abate until their opponent's face is in ruins. While this happens, a more rational part of their psyche is trapped in the back of a possessed mind, viewing the drama as though it occurs on a distant screen.

When they finally get released from their minuscule cell, the guards march Ash back to the mediavision room.

The prisoners switch over to the Damon Repper show.

"This is your favourite programme, isn't it, Ash darling?" is the first cruel greeting. The room echoes with mean laughter while the show's malevolent host parades Leah as a prize he has won. She wears the dead-eyed, terrified smile that is fast becoming her trademark expression – the hollow grimace of a marionette controlled by a demented puppet master. She models the outfit made from talex plastic he bought her for Cashmas. The coloured strips of cling film vaguely resemble undergarments from a movie set in space, while her captor grins in triumph. The sight of Leah dressed as a tortured trophy is too painful for Ash, who holds their face in despair.

"Haha, why the fuck would a guy dress his girlfriend as a prostitute from the future?" chortles a nearby inmate.

Ash mutters into their hands, "We live in an underground city with hyper surveillance and flying robot cameras that shoot lasers. You could say, this *is* the future."

"Aww, what a pretty couple," sneers another bald prisoner, viewing Ash with a sideways glance.

Ash gazes up into Leah's eyes and whispers, "'Here Everybody Looks Pretty...'"

"They fucking don't!" the prisoner guffaws. "Although, they do say people in this city choose their looks, deciding their adult appearance before they're even born… So why isn't everybody hot? Why the fuck does anybody choose to be ugly?"

Ash regards Damon's glowing image and replies, "Some say the ugly have guilty souls and want to atone for crimes they've committed in previous lives."

"That's stupid!" snaps the fellow convict. "Fucking idiots!"

"Yeah," agrees Ash. "Catshit propaganda made up by cosmetic companies who want to enforce the hierarchy of attractiveness and justify their violent treatment of the poor and ugly."

"Yeah, alright! Don't start that political shit in here, dickhead!"

On the lurid screen, Damon is saying that women always used him for his family money and media connections, but Leah is different because she is an artist. He says he always wanted to be in an alt power couple. His friend Beryl Pesancho smiles at him with adoration, then turns to Leah, still smiling but with eyes of hatred.

"Did he really just say that?" splutters Ash, torn between horror and hilarity. "'Alt power couple'? What the fuck?! As if the phrase 'power couple' isn't dreadful enough! It sounds like, 'there is no genuine love or romance here, but together we form a powerful socio-political allegiance!' And as for the phrase, 'alt power couple', what the fuck is that? A conjoined abomination in eyeliner? What, do you get special magic rings that shoot black rainbows? How the fuck can anybody choose a partner, a person to bond with and share their life with, based on their Cashdamn social image? Could anything be more fucking hollow? He's certainly convinced me I'm missing out by being single, now I can't be an immaculate half of a carefully orchestrated self-marketing campaign."

As if in response to this, the show cuts to an advertisement break with media personalities Tom Dastirrian and Forensi Purcs modelling designer T-shirts and matching expressions of numb superiority.

Footsteps echo from the hallway, the clerk approaching with her guard escort. The other prisoners leer at her arrival as she walks straight up to her favourite inmate. "Five letters arrived while you were in solitary."

Ash thanks her, takes the **five** envelopes, rips them open and skims the contents, barely remembering to breathe.

"Are those guys an 'alt power couple'?" a prisoner jokes, nodding at Tom and Forensi on the screen.

"That Forensi chick is some other guy's girlfriend... She fucks Tom as well though because she's a slut," his friend replies with a salacious grin.

"You're a bit clued up on media gossip, ain't ya? You a fag or something?"

"No," the convict flinches. "I er... just want to know who the sluts are, for when I get out of here."

Too engrossed to pay attention to their lechery, Ash consumes the story of Leah's life unravelling. They learn of Damon threatening to abandon her in the caves, of her falling into a relationship she cannot escape from, of Damon's birthday party, his behaviour at Cashmas, and finally the letter that signifies beyond all doubt that Leah is doomed. They read the correspondence in dismay while inane celebrity drivel shimmers across the wall. On the screen, musician Ben Wancaski, who recently split with his model girlfriend Morgua Plige, is advertising his new band, Undead **Zero**. The convicts sit in anaesthetised silence, awaiting the next serving of violence, while Ash is overwhelmed by a nauseous sense of approaching disaster. "Wait!" frets the worried prisoner, clutching the most worrying letter with bloodless hands as their heart palpitates. "How recently was that last episode of Damon's show filmed?"

"Cash knows," replies an inmate. "If I was a rich media channel producer, I'd probably have decent legal representation and not be in prison."

"Fuck! He's going to kill her!" cries Ash, despairing at Leah's aptitude for self-obliteration.

"Haha, why?" sniggers a fellow prisoner.

"She's left him!" Ash replies. "She finally persuaded him to end their relationship without him socially destroying her!

Then a couple weeks later, her favourite model, Tom Dastirrian, showed a keen interest so she started dating him... She says he's everything Damon wasn't. She says he never yells at her, tries to control her or makes her cry, and she feels safe with him. Cash! Damon's going to fucking kill her! This guy's malicious as fuck to anybody who wounds his ego... Leah, what are you thinking? Why can't you learn to be happy alone?"

The prisoners listen to Ash ramble in amused silence before bursting into vicious laughter. "Is Leah gonna be vulture bait?" Ash's cellmate chuckles.

"She always was," sighs Ash. "She just didn't know it."

Ash spends the next few weeks hearing more dreadful news about Leah. They try to stay out of the mediavision room and sketch weird pictures in the corridors to distract themself from not being able to save her. Nothing works. The burly prisoners become unlikely members of the Damon Repper fan club, an arena usually reserved for social-climbing club kids and desperate middle-aged women. They recognise a fellow abuser in him. They enjoy the malice that simmers beneath each episode as his hate campaign gathers momentum and Leah becomes the most despised woman in Deragon Hex. The constant threat of laser attacks makes her publicly suicidal, and the incarcerated viewers soak up each vengeful detail for use as ammunition to taunt their least favourite co-inhabitant. It entertains the pack because they know how desperate Ash is to be released now, needing to suppress their rage and not have their parole hearing adjourned by further incidences of fighting.

After finding a secluded spot where fellow prisoners will not see the agony behind their grim resolve, Ash writes to Leah.

Hey Leah,

I'm so sorry your life's fallen apart again. I can't believe this keeps happening. You're a nice person but you get so much shit.

Some people need to fucking get over themselves, it's not as though they've never done anything beyond reproach. I know you sometimes fuck with people's heads by accident because you're confused and a mess, but the abuse you receive is fucking disgusting.

I remember when I used to meet you outside parties at **five** in the morning to walk you home. You were sometimes devastated because some Cashdamn asshole had been rude to you for no fucking reason. You're an easy target because you're so sensitive. I told you I wished you didn't attend those parties and you might be much happier if you stayed home and made art. You didn't believe me though. You always said you went because you were lonely and the only alternative was staying in alone, which was too depressing.

I'm sorry, but if you get nothing but judgement while in an abusive relationship, then I don't care how many people you're surrounded by, you're still on your own. The problem with the scene you belong to is there's always some bitch sniping at selected targets to make herself top dog. The thing with being top dog is, you're still a fucking dog.

I only wish I knew what to say to make you happier. Do you remember that debate we had after you said you were ugly? I asked you, "If you're not pretty, why are you convinced people are spying on you? And how do you have viewers on your home-filmed opinion show when you're neither rich nor famous if you aren't at least attractive?"

Your face crumpled as you replied, "They watch it to laugh at me."

I said, "Do you realise there are actual comedy shows available on mediavision? There's that programme where homeless people get set on fire and they're running around trying to find buckets of water to save themselves. They changed it recently so half the buckets are filled with kerosene instead of water, and the sick viewers at home found it fucking hilarious."

You said, "I was homeless once, but I met this guy who said I could stay at his apartment if I slept with him."

I told you, "See, you've had it easy! Your existence has sometimes been a vicious struggle, but if you were hideous as well as mentally ill, life would have been far crueller. You might have become a cosmetic test subject or comedy bonfire!"

You pleaded, "If I'm not ugly, then why are men so horrible to me?"

I asked you, "Just how do you think men treat pretty girls? Many of them get off on treating hot women like shit. If you were ugly, they wouldn't bother. They'd just ignore you. Or set fire to you."

I'm reminding you of this conversation so you'll remember what kind of world we're living in. You shouldn't take it personally that you haven't risen to the top. It doesn't mean you're worthless, it just means you've got a fucking soul. Please, stay safe and try to find solace in your artistic output, which

```
I'm sure people will love someday. I will get
out as soon as possible and help you.
   Lonely inspirators vent emotion,
   Ash
```

"Leah is in a coma," Ash's cellmate tells them the following day. His eyes are glinting, burnished coins as he salivates and smiles.

Ash dashes to the mediavision room where the news channel provides devastating confirmation. Leah is lying in a coma, the latest victim of the Poisoner. Damon's fans have launched a petition to make the hospital turn off her life-support machine.

"What am I having?" a radiant Damon asks his studio audience.

"You're having a WONDERFUL afternoon!" they chant in unison before applauding.

"This is Leah," Damon continues, while a picture of the dying girl flashes onto the screen. "Leah uses people and discards them when she's bored. She is now poisoned and lying in a coma. Don't be like Leah."

The assembled convicts are in fits of evil laughter as Ash's cellmate strolls in to take his usual seat at the back. "So who poisoned poor Leah?" an eager voice taunts Ash.

"It could've been anybody in her life in the last few months who's had motive to kill her," Ash croaks.

"Well, that narrows it down!" is the harsh response that prompts further bellows of amusement. Ash stumbles back to their cell to curl up on their bunk and hope this day is a hideous nightmare. If Leah is a victim of the Poisoner, the only way to save her is to discover the Poisoner's identity and kill them before she dies. Ash cannot do that while they are incarcerated. They are so trapped they want to scream as they lie shaking, their thoughts racing in tormented circles.

Who the fuck could it be?

Is it some sick asshole's media stunt? Could it be Stan Fellowvic?

He's built a career from assaulting unpopular women, and may begrudge Leah for speaking at his first vulture trial...

Or it might be Damon Repper, a petty, vindictive little man who's made no secret of his utter contempt.

But what about Tom Dastirrian? He was the last person she was dating when it happened...

Then there's her previous ex, Donnie Benifyr... but he treated Leah respectfully and was with her a couple of years... surely that would be enough time to notice if he was secretly poisoning people.

Who was that other guy she dated? Bret Daner, wasn't it? Who works at Bar Ethol...

And what if the Poisoner isn't even male? So many women despise Leah...

Ash's reverie is interrupted by the sound of footsteps entering their cell. They consider yelling at whoever it is to go the fuck away, but lack the strength.

"More mail for you," says a soft, feminine voice. Ash rises to see the clerk without her usual guard escort, her frail body clothed in plain office attire and her delicate face wearing an awkward smile as she holds out a parcel and a letter.

"You shouldn't leave your office without guard protection; most prisoners here are scum," Ash warns her, reaching out to receive the envelope and package.

"I feel safe around you," the clerk sighs while Ash tears away brown wrapping.

The torn-away paper reveals a hardback book by an author Ash has never heard of. They open the pages to find somebody has hollowed out a space inside and stashed a secret screwdriver. "What the..." Ash begins, looking to the clerk but she has already disappeared.

Gazing in amazement at the potential weapon, they see their first piece of good fortune in months. An **eight**-digit code is carved into the red plastic of the handle: **two two three one**, **seven two five three**.

"This is too fucking easy," Ash whispers before heavy feet approach the door. They stash the book and screwdriver under their pillow, rip open the envelope containing Leah's latest letter and pretend to be absorbed by reading it.

Their cellmate looms in the doorway. "What are you reading?" He scrutinises Ash's features.

"More people are being assholes to Leah!" Ash fumes, pushing back nervousness by tapping into their inherent rage. "She just wants to be happy! All she wants is a non-abusive partner who understands and loves her, and enough friends to have a decent social life. She gets judged and labelled a whore because in her mission to form connections with other human beings she fails to maintain fucking celibacy. Too many assholes bully others more sensitive than themselves to secure their place in the Cashdamn social hierarchy, and they'd all look better on fire!"

The cellmate smiles in a manner that suggests he is hungry. "You're an opinionated thing, aren't you? Always running your pretty little mouth off... Aren't you worried somebody might bash your face in? I know your type. You're only tough when you have those adrenaline surges, the rest of the time you're weak as fuck. I could snap you like a leaf."

Ash's cellmate is a foot taller than Ash and at least twice as wide across the shoulders. Ash has so far avoided being raped or killed by this person, but they are not sure how long this precarious peace will continue. Ash should be quiet now.

Ash is terrible at staying quiet in the face of stupidity.

"Snap me like a leaf?" they splutter. "What are you, a twig on the breeze? A gull in a china shop? See, this is what happens when people don't learn history or read! They say everything wrong! And for your information, my adrenaline surges are getting increasingly frequent and more brutal. I hate them! It's as though a sick force is ripping me apart from inside and I've got to kill something to release it. But they're not the only reason

I'm like this. Even if I was weak as a mitten, I would still be an opinionated brat who has comedy rants that mock everything, because I will not be silenced by cowardice!"

"You could easily be silenced by a pillow over your face though," their cellmate leers.

"Yes, I really could," Ash concedes. "How perceptive of you to notice that."

"You might not want to think I'm being 'perceptive'."

"Sorry. To be fair, it's not a mistake I make often."

"I do hope you're planning on sleeping tonight," says Ash's cellmate. "It will make what I'm planning to do to you so much easier."

When the lights go out for Night Time, Ash retrieves the screwdriver from under their pillow and clutches the plastic handle tight as they stare into the dark.

The prison clerk arrives the next morning with another letter from Leah. She finds Ash gone, and a mountainous corpse slumped by the bed in a cell painted scarlet by **five** litres of splattered blood.

CHAPTER NINE

It is **40** days before the hotel massacre, and Leah dyes her hair black while a crippling depression clouds her every waking thought. She has been sleeping with Tom Dastirrian in the aftermath of Damon Repper. She enjoys dating a man who does not control her, yell at her or make her feel worthless, but the sense of metaphorically falling has not abated, only slowed.

Social judgement continues to isolate her existence. She reels from the damage done by Damon, and her life has the stain of something contaminated. Memories she crucially needs to share but cannot fully recall press against the inside of her skull as she stumbles and suffocates.

Tom is keen to make their involvement an official relationship. He was previously sleeping with Forensi Purcs, an up-and-coming model from his agency, but recently stopped due to objections from her primary partner. Leah is afraid she and Tom might both be on the rebound and tries to keep their interaction as casual as possible. She asks whether he wants to sleep with Estana as well, but is secretly relieved when he is not interested.

Dead-eyed on a lonely afternoon, Leah is shuffling around her apartment's kitchen putting away dishes when her arrogant roommate returns.

"Hi Estana!" She picks up a colourful plate, anxiously smiling at the doorway.

The haughty woman regards her with a mixture of sympathy and derision before taking off her long, black coat.

Leah clears her throat. "I thought you might want to sleep with Tom, seeing as you slept with Damon, which was fine, I really didn't mind," she babbles. "But when I asked him, he told me you're not his type." She cringes with this last statement as though expecting Estana to strike her.

Estana hangs her expensive overcoat on a hook. "Charming. I'm sure the sentiment would be mutual if I had any idea who the fuck you were talking about."

She retires to her bedroom without another word.

Sad days roll by drenched in liquid sedation and anhedonic apathy. The camera feed from Alicia's former apartment is still down, so the detective and the night porter can only spy on Leah while she is away from home.

It is fortunate she prefers meeting Tom at his place. She fears Estana's rudeness will repel him if she brings him home, plus the change of scenery serves to mildly alleviate her dysphoria. After closing the curtains on the passing tramps and green strip lights outside his lower-level bedroom, Tom and Leah have sex then lie naked watching mediavision. The first thing they see is a medical documentary, with doctors researching the use of "troll waves" to cure cancer.

"All thoughts create energy," an oncologist is explaining to the narrator. "This new device harnesses the energy radiated when a so-called 'troll' sends anonymous abuse over the com network to somebody with severe depression. We're investigating whether the frequency of this particular energy wave can slow the growth of cancer cells."

Viewing from his hotel room, the detective mutters to himself, "I still don't know what a fucking ostrich is. How do I even know that word? 'Ostrich'. Is that even a thing?"

The lawman is scratching his head when the night porter turns to him and asks, "Do you believe in God?"

"Do I... what?! Why ask such a weird question?"

"Why is it a weird question?"

The detective gulps back more whiskey before responding. "We're sitting in a hotel room watching a screen within a screen. The first screen shows a couple of naked people who've just had sex. The second screen, which they're also watching, shows some malicious gimp with electrodes on his head surrounded by lunatics in lab coats. This might be a strange moment to dwell on belief systems from the past."

"But don't you wonder where consciousness originated?" wonders the night porter.

"Science explains the human brain far better than superstition! Nobody believes dumb fairy tales anymore! People only believe in money, which is our ruling power and gives our lives meaning. That's why we say Cash instead of God."

"Interesting..." muses the night porter. "I always thought people were worshipping a historical country singer from overground."

"What the fuck are you talking about?" demands the detective. "We worship money! Something I don't get enough of in this damn job... We need a single-syllable name for money, so we say Cash. Although, to be honest, for ages I thought people were saying 'Gash'."

"Gash?"

"Another word for axe wound."

"Let me guess... Either way, it's something you don't get enough of?"

On the medical documentary, doctors are now investigating whether throwing things at people with psychosis can accelerate the recovery of third-degree burns. "Maybe this is the reason people say 'Burn!' when they see a clever insult on the com network," suggests an elderly man wearing a white coat and glasses. "They're excited at seeing their skin heal."

"It's uplifting to see people take time from their busy schedules to help the genuinely damaged by mocking attention seekers."

"Next, we'll test whether jokes aimed at suicidal patients relieve hunger pangs in starving children."

Tom and Leah switch over to the music channels and have sex again. Leah does her best Honeysuckle impression.

Sometimes a viewer could be convinced they were watching the starlet herself, especially if they had seen those final movies before she disappeared. Naked, eager and obedient, she calls her partner 'Sir', like a harlot from an ancient overground civilisation that gave out knighthoods, and by the end she is a sticky mess. Observing her antics, the night porter declares, "She looks like a plasterer's patio."

"Don't you mean a plasterer's radio?" the detective asks.

"No, patio," insists the night porter. "Metaphorically I mean, with her personality. If you look closely, between the cracks, beneath the surface... you might see the remains of a child somebody killed."

When Leah returns home, she receives a message from Damon. He will be visiting her local nightclub in **eight** days. "No no no," she frets, replying with shaking hands to warn she will be there with somebody else. He does not take this well.

"You've moved on then?"

"I've started dating again."

"Guy or girl?"

"I'll be there with a guy. I'd want to be warned if an ex was going to the same club as me with somebody else, which is why I'm telling you."

"You end our relationship for no reason then start dating again... Do you realise how this makes me look?"

"I'm so sorry! Do you want me to stay home? I don't want to upset you!"

"I need to think."

"Let me know if you want me to stay home, and I will. I didn't mean to hurt you! I hope I did the right thing by warning you."

Damon does not reply. Estana later arrives home to find Leah in tears. "He's gonna make everybody hate me!" the sad creature wails.

"And?" asks Estana.

"You don't understand!" frets Leah. "It was such a relief when he finally agreed to let me go without destroying my life. I started dating again because I was lonely and wanted to be happy. Damon doesn't live nearby, so I thought if I keep my dates off the com network and avoid large events... But then he decides to visit the **one** nightclub within walking distance of my apartment!"

"I still don't understand why you're crying," says Estana, absently checking her manicure.

"When I warned him I was going with somebody else, he got so angry! I even offered to stay home to not upset him, but now he's stopped replying to me. What should I do? I feel sick with dread," Leah sobs. "He might use this as ammunition to socially destroy me!"

"I keep telling you to stop concerning yourself with the opinions of morons," scolds Estana. "For fuck's sake, go write or paint something!"

It is **28** days before the hotel massacre and Damon's televised hate campaign against Leah has begun. Surrounded by sympathetic women, he repeatedly mentions his illness, how Leah used him, and how the stress of her unstable behaviour exacerbated his symptoms.

His best friend, Chloe Spanbrey, passes a tissue as his downcast face suggests he might cry. "You need to be inspired by the damage she's done to you," she tells him. "Make her your muse, but not in a complimentary way."

"Yeah!" Damon agrees. "She and I were such a joke! I've never respected promiscuous girls. And she dressed too cheap for my taste!"

"She was a whore!" declares Chloe. "She treated you like a library book she'd borrowed, a book whose spine she barely bent as she skimmed through the pages."

"That's why I'm upset! After the effort I put into making our relationship work! All her scenes and insecurities... Why did I bother?"

"Aww Damon, it's because you're too nice! Don't worry. Your rise to fame will make her realise her stupidity. You can taste her tears as you achieve her goals while she rots in obscurity."

"I even bought her an expensive Tornado outfit to make her happy..."

"What a money-grabbing bitch!"

Leah watches the show at Tom's house and tries not to cry. "Everybody says I'm a whore because I slept with **four** people in a year... But some guys have that much sex in a *day* and just get congratulated! Not everybody gets judged by the same standards though, do they?"

"Just ignore those silly people," Tom comforts her. "It's nearly **eight**, shall we get something to eat?"

"Maybe," Leah sighs, grabbing the remote and switching over to the nearest documentary. Damon and Chloe disappear, replaced by a couple of men at a university.

A slick presenter in designer clothing is interviewing an academic with a tragic hairstyle. The latter individual has "Professor of Vipdile Theory" written underneath him and speaks into the microphone in the presenter's outstretched hand with rabid eagerness.

"Number **111** is a powerful place in the Vipdile Key, where a great deal of energy is released. It is the moment you gain control of every piece of machinery in Deragon Hex except the vultures and cameras. You keep this control until you finish reciting!"

The stylish presenter's gaze is blank as though listening to an alien language. He offers a toothy grin and hollow chuckle before continuing with his scripted questions.

"And what exactly is the full sequence?"

"Unfortunately, nobody knows it," admits the professor. "Many believe it to be urban legend, but the important thing about Vipdile Theory is..."

"Fuck it!" snaps Leah, turning off Tom's media screen. "I can't win, no matter what I do! I've been looking forward to this clubnight for ages. We're going!"

That evening she heads to her local nightclub with Tom. She spends the first few hours hiding in the corner having a panic attack, but after drinking copious amounts of cheap vodka, her anxiety recedes. She manages to dance and kiss her date, trying to pretend her ex-boyfriend and his entourage are not glaring. Damon's face holds the petulant fury of a spoilt child who has just had his favourite toy stolen in the playground by a bigger boy.

On the dizzying dance floor, Leah agrees to be Tom's girlfriend. She sees no purpose in holding back for the sake of public approval when most people hate her anyway.

"Leah is gonna get fucked!" the night porter surmises as Leah walks off the dance floor and her secret fans continue spying on her car crash life.

"Yeah, that last kiss was pretty hot," agrees the detective.

"No, not in that way! Not Tom, Damon! He's going to tear her life to pieces! Look at his face!"

"Shit! Yeah, you're right!"

Back at Tom's house, Leah becomes upset again as she removes her mascara. "He knows I'm socially isolated, with terrible paranoia. Why does he begrudge me the chance to be happy? And why is he telling everybody I left him for no reason when he knows I left him because of his temper?" She removes her eye make-up carefully with gentle strokes, wary of dragging her under-eye skin and causing premature ageing.

"You've just made him look bad is all," Tom comments from the bathroom doorway. "And he's worried about his social image."

"But I've not gone public with any of the awful things he did! Such as threatening to leave me in the caves by myself! And I offered to miss my favourite night at my local club so he could visit from across the city and not get upset! I'm trying so hard to not enrage him..."

"Just give it time. He'll move on."

"You haven't met him! He bears grudges for years… I once asked him why he was so hateful, and he said hate was his motivation. He said spite and the need for vengeance were what fuelled his career and were the reason he'd got so far. I'm still caught in his trap! His hate makes it impossible to move on with my life."

"Come here," says Tom. He pulls Leah into an embrace, then gropes her and they start kissing and end up having sex again.

After staring enraptured at the tangle of flesh on his computer screen, the detective suddenly turns to the night porter and asks, "What the fuck is a patio?"

His friend laughs and takes a swig of beer. "It's a paved section of 'outdoor' area for posh bastards who own fancy apartments at Road Level," he says. "It's where I keep my ostrich."

Seven days before the hotel massacre, Leah has a night out for her birthday to try taking her mind off her problems. Tom goes out in a distant hex for another friend's birthday.

At the club, Leah receives the devastating news that Tom is still in love with Forensi Purcs by none other than the rising model's ex-boyfriend. Leah feels punched in the stomach. Her life is in ruins because she chose to date Tom, and this cannot be happening.

Many of Leah's social group do not arrive until late into the after-party, and Leah gets too drunk and makes such a scene that most people stop speaking to her.

Tom messages her to say Forensi's ex-boyfriend is lying.

Leah has to believe him. She has nobody else. She tells herself she can trust him, trying to ignore the whistling sound of falling and the approach of deadly concrete.

In the lonely days that follow, she carries on sleeping with Tom because at least sex stops her feeling repulsive. He works at a studio during the day while she tries to promote her art on the com network but gets nowhere. In her solitary room, watching the social channels, she is tortured by Damon's relentless smear campaign. He frequently replays the footage of the time Leah kissed Tom in the nightclub in front of him, whipping the audience toward vengeful fury. Now a social pariah, Leah can find no respite from the animosity that hounds her, and it cannot be long before she is maimed by those dreaded vulture beams.

Terrified, she turns in tears to her unimpressed co-inhabitant. "I was just doing a stall, trying to sell my work, why did he have to pick *me*?" she sobs. "He said it was because I was smiling, but I only smile because I'm nervous and want people to like me! It's as though ever since he selected me, my social identity became his to control, alter or delete as he saw fit. Some days, it makes me want to die."

"He's certainly not worth dying over," Estana remarks. "You should be moving on from this petty nonsense by focussing on your artwork."

"But Damon might ruin my artistic reputation too!" Leah wails. "He was always hinting he could destroy my career because he's so popular! What if his friends and fans say awful things about my work, leave dreadful reviews on my pages so I never stand a chance? He really is that vindictive! I don't have a parental penthouse I can return to, so I might become homeless, and he knows this..."

"I'm talking about your art, not your career!" Estana says. "You can find relief from negative emotion by using your work as an outlet. Stop seeking validation in the form of frequent sales or positive reviews. Stop basing your worth on other people's judgement!"

"But I have to try and sell my work! What else can I do for money? I'm too crazy to do anything else..."

"I keep telling you," says Estana, "follow the instructions I give you, and you will succeed. You don't need to pander to the approval of idiots."

Four days before the hotel massacre, Leah wakes to find she is dying. Her formerly attractive body is poisoned by a cruel venom, crippled and mutilated, unable to cross the bedroom without each movement breaking her cracked and weeping skin further open.

She messages Tom straight away. Firstly, she must warn him in case she is contagious. Secondly, she needs somebody to hold her now she remembers everything and is overwhelmed by the ghastly weight of recollection. Thirdly, she is hoping he will avenge her. Notions of being saved by gallant heroism eternally float through her daydreams, and this is what a person would do if they loved her. They would hunt down and destroy her abuser.

"I'm a victim of the Poisoner!" she tells him. "The skin of my lower body is cracked and blistered and I'm losing consciousness. I might be dying."

Five minutes later, he messages her back, "I don't want to see you anymore."

The world goes black.

She had tried to believe the free-falling towards obliteration which began when she left Donnie had at least slowed when she got with Tom. Now she realises she never stopped hurtling downwards, and has almost reached concrete. She does not call an ambulance, because without the love she craves she is better off dead.

Reeling from the loss of her boyfriend at such a vulnerable time, she curls up on her bed and switches on her media screen to watch the social channels. The first thing she sees is Forensi Purcs' new opinion show.

"Leah has **zero** chance with my guy now!" Forensi smirks as the camera zooms out to show Tom sitting next to her, the **two** of them holding hands.

That finally does it.

Leah can hear the sickening crack of broken bone as her face hits the metaphorical curb it has spent the past **eight** months plummeting toward. There is nobody left to save her. Ash is in prison, Estana does not care, and now Tom has abandoned her, still in love with somebody else.

"He probably left her because she was boring. Nobody likes her anyway," Forensi declares. She makes a frown of disgust, but her eyes shine with long-awaited victory.

Leah switches off her media screen and tries to sleep. In fitful nightmares, demons laugh at her, saying she is marked by a curse and they will return in **four** days to deliver her to hell. The next morning as she sits broken in her room, she writes another letter to Ash.

She tells them what has happened to her.

She tells them she now knows who the Poisoner is.

There is nobody else to confide in, apart from Derek Blin, the visiting stray feline who provides the only company in her last waking hours.

"Who will save me, Derek?" she sniffs, hunched over a battered notebook while he purrs by her feet. Immediately after sealing the finished letter in an addressed envelope, she loses consciousness.

Without a second's hesitation, Derek jumps onto her desk, picks up the letter in his mouth and takes it from the apartment before Estana can destroy it. He scampers along filthy corridors, finds a mailbox, leaps on top of it and leans over the side to put the letter into the slot. The clever kitty then goes back to Leah's room and sits caterwauling beside her comatose body.

"Why the fuck is that damn cat making so much noise?" Estana demands after returning home from another mysterious outing. Upon entering Leah's room to find the girl in a coma, she smiles at the poisoned body in delight, saying, "Run, little puppy, run!" before calling for medical assistance.

CHAPTER 10

The night before the hotel massacre, while Leah lies in hospital in a coma, Ash stabs their cellmate to death with the red-handled screwdriver. The number carved into the plastic handle works as the master passcode for the prison doors, enabling them to escape. They have no time to ponder the suspicious convenience of this turn of events. Their only concern is avenging Leah before it is too late. They still do not know the Poisoner's identity, but Leah was often writing and drawing her troubles as a form of catharsis, so there must be clues in the apartment.

After escaping the prison hex, the first thing Ash does is find a restroom in a quiet area and clean the blood off themself at the sink. Next, they find a department store with poor Night Time surveillance and steal a pinstripe suit and office footwear, ditching their prison uniform in a deserted side street.

After making their way along the dark alleyways and inter-hex subways where they remember the camera blind spots, they arrive at the Road Level suburban streets near their former home. It is midmorning. Approaching the final corner before their apartment building, Ash is stopped in their tracks by the sight of demonstrators campaigning to switch off Leah's life-support.

"What the fuck?"

Outraged protesters have made a temporary billboard from a large, monochrome photograph of the hated girl's unconscious face with the word 'Slut' printed in bold letters over her forehead. Overcome by fury, Ash breaks cover to approach them, jab their finger at the picture and demand, "Do you actually know this person?"

A slim young woman introduces herself as Lysa Pherbonec before explaining her mission. "This is Leah! She hurt Damon

Repper, who is the nicest guy in the world, so we're petitioning to get her life-support terminated."

Ash takes a deep breath and enquires, "So, you've never even met her?"

"You don't understand," says Lysa, "I am Damon Repper's sister! I just have a different surname because I got married. And yes, I was unfortunate enough to meet the little bitch on several occasions! She didn't say much, but my poor brother told me she really hurt him, which tells me everything I need to know!"

"He has a sister?" wonders Ash. "Funny, from what I've heard of him, he behaves like an only child."

"What the fuck is that supposed to mean? Who are you?!" Lysa demands in a haughty tone, straightening her back as she steps closer.

"Ignore me!" Ash tells her with an angry smile. "I was thinking out loud. I've met some only children who've been lovely... unlike your brother, who's an evil, vindictive prick."

"How dare you say that about my brother?! If I was a violent person, I would smack you!"

Ash nods. "You're protective of your sibling, I get that. I'm murderously protective of mine. But answer me this... You can guess a man's view of women from how he treats his mother. Damon yells at his poor mother with such contempt she almost cries. How the fuck do you justify that?"

Lysa's eyes bulge as her face turns scarlet. "What the fuck are you saying?! You leave our family out of this! It's none of your damn business!"

"You've kinda made it my business by using the fact that he's your family to justify destroying a woman you barely know."

Ash and Lysa had been edging closer during this exchange with their hands balled into fists. A short man with close-cropped hair steps between them, glowering up at Ash. "We don't need to know Leah to want to kill her! She hurt our friend, that's justification enough! I personally cannot wait to see her dead."

"Excuse me, but who the fuck are you?" Ash snarls.

"I'm Shane Oberclyp," grunts the stunted caveman with folded arms. "And my girlfriend is good friends with Damon."

"That's a tenuous connection," Ash remarks. "I bet you've never spoken to Leah! You know absolutely nothing about her. Has it never occurred to you that maybe Damon Repper is just a fucking awful human being?"

The stubble-haired man grins like somebody who has promptly conceived a witty response. "Pot. Kettle. Black," he replies, and the assembled crowd snicker their approval at his intellectual prowess.

"I think you'll find, it's your eye that's black." In a blur of tailored clothing and hatred, Ash punches Shane in the side of the face, knocking him to the ground.

After a collective gasp, the demonstrators scream, "Vultures! Vultures!"

Belatedly realising the potential consequences of their actions, Ash makes a dash for their former apartment. A nearby security camera captured the assault, and a vulture appears within seconds.

"He went that way!" yells a shocked protester, waving her arms in Ash's direction while her friends try to revive Shane Oberclyp.

The flying law-enforcer takes off after the escapee.

At the apartment building the elevator is broken, so Ash must take the stairway to reach the lowest level. They mutter obscenities. Unlike the elevator, the door to the stairway has a vulture window and their airborne pursuer is able to follow them into the gloomy sub-terrain. With that notorious mechanical hum evoking the threat of imminent searing pain, the hovering sphere chases its prey, aiming a scarlet beam at Ash's retreating figure as they descend.

The robotic predator is almost close enough to get a clear shot when it stops.

After breathless moments, Ash realises they are no longer being pursued. Gazing up the stairway, they see the vulture drifting up to Road Level in aimless circles. They shrug and continue their journey, now stomping down the stairs instead of sprinting.

Their path through the lowest level takes them along twisted corridors between clusters of hexagonal apartments. They take care not to step on any rodents, having the firm belief that animals are better than most people. Each path is edged by garbage that rots in the rank heat emanating from the smooth, stone ground. The dismal scene is illuminated by blue strip lighting in the perpetual Night Time of the impoverished Minus levels.

Unaware the nearby surveillance cameras are not working, Ash prepares to be subtle in their picking of the lock. They perfected sleight of hand during their wasted youth, learning how to deftly over-ride the lock mechanism in a brief series of dexterous movements. This crime can be committed while leaning on the door frame, appearing to catch their breath while waiting for the door to open. However, these unlawful skills prove unnecessary today. When they reach the door, it opens with such unnerving timing Ash would have jumped if they had a nervous disposition.

Estana stands in the doorway.

Ash gulps and tries to forget hallucinations of chequered tiles in a castle far from here.

"Have you been dreaming of me again?" Her voice is honey laced with arsenic. She wears a shiny, black dress and a gaze more imperious than ever as she looms like a creeping shadow of dark curls and malevolence.

She says nothing more. A sapphire strip-light flickers overhead. Behind Ash, a rat scurries past, chased by a cat, while a bat can be heard flapping its leathery wings in a distant corridor. Only rats, cats and bats are left alive, as though the creator of this subterranean city was a Gothic lunatic. Ash could scream tormented frustration, having come here seeking information to save Leah and finding nothing but a wipe-clean psychopath. "I told her not to let you in!" they fume, mentally recalculating their rescue plan now that searching the apartment for clues is no longer an option.

"And *I* told her to create art from her misery rather than seeking solace in the arms of an unremarkable fool, but she doesn't listen, does she?" Estana sighs. "I don't know what we're going to do with that girl."

"Stop pretending you care about her!" Ash snaps, shoulders drawn back, standing to their full height.

Even though Ash is taller, Estana still somehow looks down on them. She asks, "Why can't you believe I also have her best interests at heart?"

Ash thought the promise of danger radiating from Estana made the answer to that question rather obvious.

As if reading their thoughts, she remarks, "You can hardly judge me for being dangerous when you just punched an unarmed man in the face."

"I'm a creature of instinct," Ash explains. "And my instincts say you want me and Leah as your puppets! You want me to attack and kill your enemies, and you'd use Leah as bait. You'll draw her into your sick plans even if it destroys her. I might have known you'd moved back in, seeing as Leah is now in a fucking coma! Don't think I haven't noticed the casualties that pile up around you!"

"I'll tell that to Shane Oberclyp and your former cellmate," Estana retorts. "Now, stop trying to insult me, and tell me why you came here."

To Ash's right, a cat springs from a pile of boxes. It has caught its prey and is batting the injured creature between its paws. Watching the predator toy with its dinner, Ash suddenly feels extremely tired. They face their foe in the doorway. "I need to know who poisoned Leah, so I can kill them and wake her from the coma. And I suppose you know who it was? Seeing as you fucking know everything..."

The dying rat squeals and the corner of Estana's mouth twitches. She produces a folded piece of paper from a pocket in her plastic dress. "The name of the Poisoner is on this list," she states, her immaculate complexion spectral in the blue-lit corridor.

Ash glares at her before taking the paper and reading the list with eyes narrowed in suspicion.

Ben Wancaski

Stan Fellowvic

Tom Dastirrian

Damon Repper

"Can't you be more specific?" Ash complains. "If you know who did this, why not tell me? Instead of handing me this death list as though it's a series of chores. Next you'll say, after I've done your killing, I should go fetch your dry cleaning."

Estana laughs. "I have somebody else for that."

Ash reads the list again with a puzzled frown. "OK, so Tom the mild-mannered model and Damon the media douche who wants to be in an 'alt power couple' are her ex-boyfriends... I've already considered them. Stan's the guy who attacked her at Feng Baca... another worthy target! But who the fuck is Ben Wancaski?"

"A guy who screws unconscious women."

"Why would anybody screw unconscious women?"

"Insecurity? Power trip? He can't please a woman who's conscious? Who cares? Why don't you run along like a good little attack dog and start killing."

Ash clenches a fist, inhales, then runs their shaking fingers through their hair while exhaling loudly. "This is all a game to you, isn't it? You don't care about Leah at all! I bet you even fucked her Cash-awful 'celebrity' boyfriend behind her back, didn't you?"

"Of course not!" gasps Estana with a tone of mock injury. "I fucked him right in front of her face."

Ash's hands clench again, a smear of blood still on their right knuckle from recent misadventures. "Can you give me a single reason why I shouldn't fucking kill you first?"

"Because I acted with her permission," replies Estana. "And because I'm the only other person in this city who's on your side."

"What the fuck are you talking about?" her androgynous visitor snaps.

Estana's lips curl into a barely perceptible smile while her eyes light up like a self-aware tiger on cocaine. Many would find this facial expression unnerving. It is not the kind of smile you wear while performing everyday domestic tasks such as cleaning the bathroom, vacuuming the carpet or shopping for groceries. The checkout worker might wonder, "Why is this woman smiling like a self-aware tiger on cocaine while buying toilet paper? Is she planning to kill me with that bread? Aren't tigers extinct? Please tell me she's stopped looking at me! I think she wants to eat my eyes."

The demented tormentor declares, "Leah should have listened to me."

Ash responds, "If we had a sea down here, I would tell you to get in it."

"Are you telling me to go swimming?"

"No, I'm telling you to drown yourself."

"You should be more specific. If I was in the sea, I would have a wonderful swim, because I could."

"But what I'm telling you is to fucking drown!"

"Well you need to pick a better expression instead of suggesting I have a lovely overground vacation by the coast," Estana insists with a wistful smile.

Ash shakes their head and says, "You're a fucking idiot."

Estana laughs. "I'm not an escaped convict or dying in a coma though, am I?"

She closes the door in their face.

Ash considers kicking down the door to smack their antagonizer. But as they stand pondering, the deathly sound of approaching vultures echoes along the corridor, suggesting it is time to recommence running.

After racing through subterranean passages to lose their distant pursuers, Ash bounds up a rickety stairway to return to Road Level, where they head straight to the lesser-monitored side streets. Beyond sight of passing shoppers, weariness hits them like a truck. They collapse in a heap of enmity and exhaustion surrounded by discarded junk.

"I finished falling and I hit the ground," sighs Leah, an ultraviolet glow beneath her skin casting jagged shadows in the desolate alleyway. She smiles although her cheeks are decorated by rivulets of black mascara.

"Leah! You're awake!" Ash tries to stand and embrace her, but discovers their body is paralysed on the trash-covered floor. The city's ubiquitous sonic backdrop of advertising, traffic and wasted revelry is muted and full of glitches as though bubbling through an atmosphere as dull and lumpy as yesterday's soup. Everything here is rotten.

"We all die the same," Leah says. Ash realises the girl they swore to protect is still in a coma, and their subconscious is merely taunting them with their failure to save her.

"Blood splattered on metal, pooled on concrete..." Leah continues. She floats inches above the ground in the empty lane between reality and a claustrophobic dreamscape. "We only exit through fatality. People style their faces, paint their hair and pretend they're not food for the vultures... but the truth is, we're all trapped in a beautiful slaughterhouse."

She still wears her hospital gown. In the distance, stray cats are fighting over a discarded dinner. The air holds the taste of imminent rain, even though it never rains here... But it's got to rain sometime. If Ash's nerves were not numb from lack of consciousness, everything would hurt.

"You'll take me to the rocks, won't you?" Leah implores. "And when we're safe on infernal stones beneath the eternal sky, we will know peace again. It will feel like coming home."

Death has made her crazier.

"Tell me who I have to kill to save you, Leah," Ash begs. They could swear lightning illuminated the haggard scene before them... although these city ceilings have never held storms.

"Our demons are lighting your path," Leah tells them. She starts to decay, and her eyes are shallow pools of hazel swamp water as she adds, "Follow the white badger."

Ash laughs in their delirium. "Follow the white badger! Ride the mauve hippopotamus! Dance with the lilac raccoon! Oh Leah, they've finally driven you insane, haven't they? I should never have left you alone in this poisonous place."

She disappears.

Ash wakes in the deserted alleyway clutching a piece of paper in their fist, with an aching body and a powerful need for coffee, pie and vengeance.

It is lunchtime, and Ash finds a cheap café in a quiet street. They "accidentally" bump into an exiting customer in the doorway, stealing his personal com screen, which they add to the other stolen goods stashed in their suit pockets. Their present collection includes cigarettes, a lighter, a metal nail file, a balaclava, and a wallet full of cash notes taken from an ill-mannered businessman. They also still carry the red-handled screwdriver.

After walking past groups of chattering workers on lunch breaks and solitary citizens consuming low-budget snacks, Ash finds an unoccupied booth along the south-west wall. They collapse onto the blue vinyl upholstery and remove their suit jacket.

Retrieving their newly acquired com screen to look for more news of Leah, the first thing they see is a repeat of a recent episode of Damon Repper's show. His snide voice creeps from the tinny speakers. "She and I were such a joke! I've never respected promiscuous girls. And she dressed too cheap for my taste!"

Ash scowls at the screen, absently tipping salt onto the table then drawing in the spill with their index finger.

"She was a whore!" says Chloe Spanbrey. "She treated you like a library book she'd borrowed, a book whose spine she barely bent as she skimmed through the pages."

Ash vows, "I'll bend your fucking spine for what you did to her, you cunt."

A lithe figure in gingham uniform approaches Ash's booth, flashing a fake smile beneath a heap of straw-coloured hair and wielding a notepad. "Hi, I'm Raychel! I'll be your waitress today. What can I... Hey, what are you doing?"

Ash looks from the com screen, to the waitress, to the crude stick figures they've sketched into spilt seasoning. They tell her, "I'm drawing a salt power couple."

Raychel looks nervous. "You're going to assault a power couple?"

Ash laughs. "Heh, maybe!" After noticing the waitress's worried expression, they add, "Sorry, I'm kidding! I'll clean this up. Can I get strong, black coffee and a slice of pie, please?"

When she returns with their order, Ash has wiped up the salt with a couple of napkins and is absorbed by Damon's show. "Just how much screen time does this prick get?"

Raychel looks at their com screen and beams when she sees what they are watching. "I know him! Yeah, the Damon Repper show is so popular now! It's because of his contacts in the music industry."

Ash opens their mouth to respond, but halts at the sound of Damon insulting Leah again. "He has a fucking nerve!" they snap. "After the way he treated her!"

Raychel frowns. "Wait... what?"

"Nothing. Forget I spoke."

"Honestly? He's dating my friend now... Should I be worried?"

Ash scrutinises Raychel as her brow furrows beneath heavy foundation. "Well if he's dating your friend, you sure you want my opinion of him?"

"Yes please! You can tell me. I won't say anything."

Ash regards Raychel a moment longer, then turns back to their com screen. "Let's just say he was a little emotionally abusive to Leah behind closed doors," is their euphemistic reply as they glare at the malignant show host. "He might behave better with your friend though. Leah did bring out the worst in certain people..."

"Yeah," agrees Raychel, "some people bring out the worst in each other... I'm sure Beryl will be fine! She's good at sticking up for herself!"

After a gulp of coffee, Ash says, "Good for her! Perhaps she'll get him in line and make him apologise to Leah."

"Maybe!" replies Raychel. She walks off to serve another customer while Ash puts down their com screen to eat their pie.

After a few bites, Damon's show takes an advertisement break. "Half price lines of econica today! Only at Bar Ethol!" exclaims an enthusiastic narrator. For a second, that name fails to register with Ash, until they remember Leah's correspondence from months ago and the guy she dated after Tharia but before Damon. They drop their fork and grab the screen.

Sure enough, the promotional footage shows the bar staff serving customers, and Ash recognises the guy from the photo embedded into Leah's letter. Bret Daner turns to the camera and tells viewers where Bar Ethol is located.

"Well isn't that delightfully fucking helpful," remarks Ash, throwing stolen cash notes beside their half-eaten pie before leaving to catch a taxi.

"There's a plastic whore on your screen," says the ancient drunk to the bartender. He is referring to a popular actress from two decades ago. She flaunts her globular assets in a too-tight blue satin dress while dancing to a predictable love song in ultra-definition.

"There usually is," replies the young purveyor of various legal poisons. He is cleaning a glass, waiting for a dull afternoon to pass, and studiously ignoring the blonde whose undulating image fills the wall to his left.

Working here, Bret has seen this candied footage too many times to care. The venue previously showed matches from popular sporting tournaments such as roller blast and skullball. Eventually though, they had to cease this entertainment after the place filled with bellowing morons whose fights caused more damage than their custom was worth. Now they play music videos and comedy programmes to entertain the clientele, which presently consists of a few solitary drunks and gaggles of aspiring socialites. The latter are mostly young, vapid and unremarkable, taking a well-earned break from a hard day's product consumption to treat themselves to cocktails and lines of econica. Mindless conversation absorbs them. They pay little attention to the delirious performance on the media screen, the starlet shimmying like animated wallpaper.

"What do you think happened to her?" enquires the weathered alcoholic.

"Who?" asks Bret, still engrossed by the same glass.

"What do you mean 'who'?" splutters the incredulous drinker. His name is Roy Dufferbion, and he clutches the dregs of a pint with grimy fingers as he stares at the wall-sized media screen. "She's the most famous actress Deragon Hex has ever seen!"

The lyricist croons, "Where have you gone? **Seven zero one**..." while the doomed woman grinds her hips to a synthetic beat. Roy's eyes shine with a curious mixture of longing and contempt.

"If she's still alive, she must be ancient by now," giggles a saccharine voice behind him, prompting the drunk to spin round in a rush of booze-soaked indignation.

A well-groomed, teenage consumer has left her table and is staring at the bartender. She leans onto the bar to display her toned flesh at the most flattering angle, pulling the bored employee's gaze away from the glass. "Yeah, I guess she would be," he replies, flashing the smile he reserves for attractive, barely legal customers.

"She will never age!" spits Roy in self-righteous outrage. "She became fictional, and this made her immortal. She will never grow old or die!"

The young woman pretends not to hear. She shuffles a little to the left, just in case the unsightly drunk's ugliness is contagious. "Can I have **nine** lines of echo and a pitcher of Strawberry Maniac please?" she asks Bret, coyly tucking a couple of auburn curls behind her ear.

"Of course you can, sweetheart," is Bret's response as he puts down the glass to prepare the order, still ignoring the faded actress on the wall. He creates the scarlet, slightly alcoholic, highly sugared cocktails with a deft series of practised moves and places them on a tray while the girl beams at him. She taps her fingers on the bar in time with the music as Bret retrieves a medium-sized serving mirror. He opens a small drawer on the back wall and uses a mini-spoon to serve the required number of tiny portions onto the gleaming surface.

"They shouldn't let you serve that stuff in here," complains Roy, changing the subject with a sigh of disapproval.

"Because being constantly drunk is a far superior lifestyle choice," is the girl's sarcastic response as she glances at the dishevelled wreck beside her with narrow-eyed disdain.

Malice flashes across Roy's haggard face as he switches again, his moods as stable as a pint glass on a trampoline. Years of drinking have pickled his brain, emptied his wallet, and deepened his mistrust of women, as though a dose of misogyny lay at the bottom of every glass. "Insolent bitch!" he cries, lurching toward the offending female.

She gasps and jumps backwards as he reaches to grab her hair.

"Hi there!" says a breezy voice as a strong hand grabs the alcoholic's arm in a deathly firm grip.

A new, pinstripe-suited customer twists Roy's arm painfully behind his back and informs him, "You were just leaving. Weren't you."

Roy mumbles barely coherent words that could be taken as agreement. Ash releases him with a shove in the direction of the door. As the drunk staggers off, the pretty girl gazes at her rescuer, thanking them profusely.

"Don't mention it," Ash replies.

The girl waits to see if her new hero wants to speak to her, but they seem preoccupied with waiting for the bartender's attention. With a final smile, she takes her pitcher of cocktails and tray of white lines and returns to her table. "Did you guys see that?" she gushes to her friends.

Meanwhile, somebody at the other end of the bar has asked Bret for directions to the bathroom. The bartender responds by raising his right arm diagonally in front of him with a straightened hand, saying, "They're over there." When not working the bar or playing computer games, Bret enjoys watching informative programmes about overground history. With a typical Hexish sense of humour, he often finds the darker eras hilarious.

Ash sits on a bar stool and surveys an array of bottled poisons while waiting for the bartender to return. Leah always said she loved alcohol because it slowed her thoughts, halting the neurotic mind-race in its eternal mission to sprint until it tripped over itself. Plus, the media screens made it look so beautiful... Models in designer clubwear sipping drinks with enhanced confidence, moving with a stylised elegance. Of course, the reality often involved staggering in the wrong direction, confused speech, vomiting, and kissing obnoxious people with unfortunate faces she would usually cross the street to avoid. Yet Leah was eternally enticed by the notion of drinking away her problems.

Ash was never as fond of alcohol as their guileless friend. They saw it as a drug for socialising, and years of bitter disappointment had made them realise they hated drugs, and socialising.

Bret returns to Ash's end of the bar and is about to ask what they want, then freezes with a look of recognition. "You used to live with Leah."

Ash says, "Yeah, I'm trying to find out who poisoned her."

Bret shakes his head and picks up another glass. "I've no idea. Can't help you."

"You were sleeping with Leah before she met Damon, weren't you?"

"No, we were just hanging out."

Ash's brain hurts from the mixture of stress and lack of sleep. That smug bitch Estana was as useful as a knife made of jam, and they urgently need this guy to provide clues regarding who the Poisoner might be. It could even be *him*... or that psycho she dated afterwards... or the fickle model she dated after the psycho...

Ash doubts it was Bret though. They can usually read people, and he doesn't seem the type. Perhaps he could help... "Aren't you angry somebody's put her in a coma?" they ask. "Wanna help me avenge her?"

Bret places the glass on the shelf and faces Ash. "Look, I had a shitty week where I didn't message her because I felt stressed from work. Next thing I knew, she was dating some asshole with his own studio! She later said she got with him by accident because he trapped her and threatened to make everybody hate her if she left. She did apologise for hurting me. I don't hate her, I just don't see how any of this is my problem. I've got my own shit to deal with."

Bret picks up another glass to clean, his eyes glaring defensively. Ash has sympathy because they remember what a trainwreck Leah could be, careening between disastrous situations in a never-ending quest to fill her inner emptiness. They refuse to give up on her though... despite it all, she still deserved to live.

Ash requests an energy drink. After paying with a generous tip using the last notes from their stolen wallet, they tell Bret, "She wanted you to rescue her, you know."

"Well, she never told me! She went off with Damon and nobody heard from her."

"If you'd asked, she might have told you she was trapped."

"She made her bed."

"She died in it."

"Well," sighs Bret, "she's nobody's problem now."

Ash breaks into a bitter grin. "Whoever did this will soon find *I* am their problem."

Knocking back their heavily caffeinated beverage, they add, "You know, maybe she never meant to be anybody's problem.

She was always trying to please people. I think her main fault was, she wanted to be the solution."

Bret laughs. "The *final* solution?"

Ash is about to reply when music hour ends and an advertisement for Tom and Forensi's new opinion show graces the media screen. They wear outfits in matching colours and Forensi grins in triumph, sarcastically saying how sad she is Leah is in a coma. Ash wonders, "Do you think it could be either of them?"

"I dunno..." Bret muses. "So far as I know, Leah and Forensi never spoke to each other. Leah was sleeping with Tom for a while, and he left her as soon as she got poisoned, but maybe that's because he was sick of her. She was always crying over how Damon treated her and all the shit she was getting from his hate campaign."

Ash nods in pretend agreement. "Girls who are being destroyed by narcissists are so bothersome aren't they?" They finish their drink. "Do you think it could be Damon who poisoned her?"

"Fuck knows," replies Bret. "She told us his temper scared her, but I don't know what she expected us to do about it."

A faux-rock jingle blares the opening credits for a comedy show, and Bret narrows his eyes at the gaudy montage of slumbering women on the media screen. "Damon being the Poisoner doesn't fit with the nice-guy image of his talk show though... It's more likely to be some fella who hosts a programme where women get assaulted, such as Stan Fellowvic or Ben Wancaski."

"Ben Wancaski?"

"Yeah, this guy," says Bret, as a man with stringy blond hair introduces himself on screen. He can barely be heard above drunken cheers from the far end of the bar.

The stunning redhead who Ash rescued pipes up with, "Eww, this guy's gross! He goes after unconscious women!"

Her friends laugh.

The diminutive blonde to her left insists, "They deserve it though! They're stupid for passing out around him."

The visuals cut from Ben in his studio to a clip of him with his ex-girlfriend and best friend, Morgua. She has a matching lanky, blond hairstyle and wears a T-shirt advertising Ben's band above a blue miniskirt. "Are you going to take those tablets for me then, sweetheart?" he asks her.

Morgua rolls her eyes and says, "OK, you're such a dickhead."

Ben turns to grin at the camera.

The show cuts to the next scene. Morgua is asleep and Ben is fucking her in the ass to the sound of laughter from the studio audience.

Cut to the next scene and Morgua wakes from her chemical sedation and exclaims, "Ow, what the fuck! You never said you were going to fuck me in the ass!"

The laughter from Ben's studio audience gets louder, as does the howling from the drunks. Some customers add eloquent commentary such as, "Good on ya, lad!" and, "She was a stupid bitch!"

"Eww, that's gross!" comments Ash's auburn-haired admirer.

Her blond friend shrugs. "She shouldn't complain, it's her own fault. Besides, some girls would love to be on his show."

The redhead frowns. "How could they love being on his show if they're not conscious?"

For his next sketch, Ben is visiting a nearby hospital. First, a clip shows the front of the building and a sign above the door saying, "Blue **Three Eight** Hospital".

"Ooh, that's just round the corner from here!" squeals a delighted fan girl.

At the reception desk, Ben tells the nurse, "I'm here to see Leah."

"Well, I am pleased she has a visitor!" the nurse chirps. "We didn't think anybody liked her."

The studio audience snicker as Ben smirks at the camera.

Bret looks at Ash to gauge their reaction, but they have disappeared. The bar's remaining customers watch on screen as Ben goes into Leah's room before the programme cuts to an advertisement break.

The redhead wonders, "Do you think he's gonna try screwing that girl who's in a coma?"

Her friend responds with, "It would be funny if he does! Everybody hates Leah after how she treated Damon Repper."

"Why? What did she do to him?"

"No idea, but his fans detest her! She's poisoned now and gets all these death threats, so she must be a horrible person."

"I feel kinda sorry... Wait, where did that hot guy go?" asks the redhead, staring at the spot where Ash had previously been sitting.

"Are you sure that was a guy?"

The commercial break finishes and the visuals switch to Ben stood by Leah's hospital bed, pulling back the covers.

"I don't care," says the redhead. "Where did... shit, is that them?" She gapes open-mouthed at the screen. A muscular figure in a pinstripe suit and black balaclava has just barged past the cameramen and orders, "Get the fuck away from her!" in a muffled voice.

Ben emits a brattish laugh, then gouges Leah's left arm with his nails to see how the intruder will react.

Her skin broken, Leah bleeds onto her hospital bedsheets.

The mysterious figure moves in a blur of black and silver, and Ben Wancaski goes flying out of the Plus **Five** window, prompting screams from pedestrians at Road Level and gasps from audiences in the bar and studio.

"What a fucking psycho!" declares the blond girl.

"He saved her..." sighs the redhead with a dreamy smile.

The attacker stands over Leah's bed gazing at her sleeping face. After a few seconds, they sprint off, knocking over the **two** cameramen in the doorway as they exit. Outside the building, the first victim on Estana's list lies broken and bleeding on the curb, and passers-by are still screaming.

CHAPTER
11

It is late afternoon on the day of the hotel massacre. In a poor, suburban segment, the ceiling's white Day Lights are dimming and the streetlamps will soon begin their soft, green glow. "Prisoner A X **zero five**, you have been filmed committing an assault hitherto unsanctioned by public approval. How do you plead?" enquires a flat, electronic voice. Ash is pinned against a concrete wall by **five** vultures that hover in a semi-circle preparing to launch skin-flaying rays. Red target beams dance across their tired face.

"I'm pleading for you to fuck right off, you shiny metal assholes!" Ash curses, confused by the digital echo of their voice until they notice they are on mediavision. In the event of a major vulture trial, all networks drop their scheduled programming and synchronise outputs to show a public execution. This is why the screen across the deserted street has switched from its nail polish infomercial to a live Crime Channel broadcast.

"Your response has been interpreted as guilty," is the machine's unsurprising reply. Ash can see themself on the sensationalist programme, their hair still messed up from the balaclava now hidden in the pocket of their suit jacket, their forehead sweating. The past few hours have been a blur of panic and hunted confusion, trying to stay awake and avoid surveillance on dizzying, darkening streets.

A homeless woman with a maimed face limps into the left of the shot, wrapped in filthy layers. She yells, "**Five nine six** is the trigger!"

"What the fuck does that mean?" the captured killer demands, but when they turn to face the lunatic vagrant, she is walking away.

Excited viewers across the city prepare to vote. With no witnesses in the vicinity, representation will happen by media link, and as Ash has no official representation, the producers do a call-out. Ridiculously stunning former-model turned chat show hostess Utasha Bibetty is on a break between shows and steps up to take the defence.

"I'll totally take his case, he's hot!" she beams.

"*She's* hot," a colleague corrects her.

"Erm, no *they're* hot," says a nearby producer.

"He, she, whatever... they're hot!" Utasha enthuses, microphone in hand, posed gracefully before the camera. This striking media personality is openly bisexual, having once slept with Honeysuckle when the starlet was on tour promoting her first movie. They almost made a film together but could never synchronise their hectic schedules.

Her adversary for the day is Botoxia Burnos, who upon hearing the call-out gleefully trills, "I am representing the case for prosecution!" Having achieved little since her days of bullying Leah, Botoxia retains a career on the social channels due to her contacts, loud mouth and trust fund.

The footage of Ash punching Shane Oberclyp in the face is played in slow motion for the viewers at home.

"What the fuck..." mutters bemused Ash, who assumed they were on trial for pushing Ben Wancaski out of the hospital window.

"They was just defending their poor friend, Leah, who's in a coma," asserts Utasha Bibetty in her overground accent.

"They *were*," Botoxia Burnos retorts, her lips forming a smug grin beneath a ridiculously tiny nose.

"Excuse me, I am speaking Hexish as my second language and I speak it better than most people here!" snaps Utasha. The media screen displaying her annoyed glare flickers as the spherical machine hovering to Ash's right starts making an odd whirring noise.

"Keep all discussion relevant to the trial," commands the flying robot closest to Ash, while the vulture to their far right turns and flies away for no apparent reason, leaving the other **four** behind.

"Most people hate Leah! She uses men and lies about them, this is why there's a petition to switch off her life-support," Botoxia smirks from her opulent studio.

Ash gets a sudden surge of white-hot adrenaline. "I know who you are, bitch! You had Leah sentenced to house arrest for almost provoking public disapproval against a dickhead. But I'm not allowed to punch a man for trying to get Leah killed?! What kind of fucked-up hypocrisy is that? It's enough to drive a person to murder!" Ash could have bashed Botoxia's spoilt face into a bathroom mirror with brutal force if she were not hiding behind a now-flickering media screen.

"You've no proof of that..." Utasha begins in Leah's defence before her face dissolves to static haze and the audio feed becomes white noise.

Their cameras malfunctioning, the **four** remaining vultures become silent as Ash's glance darts between vacant, black lenses. The machines hover for another minute before withdrawing their laser beams and floating off on different wavering trajectories.

Shoulders relaxing with relief, Ash slumps against a wall and pulls Estana's list from their pocket.

"Call us now to receive your personalised weight loss plan, free of charge! Only when you sign up for **six** months!" a cheerful, female voice exclaims from the nearest display unit. The picture returns to life, displaying a svelte model in a tight dress the colour of absinthe who holds **two** booklets with pictures of herself on the front.

"I wish I was on the cover of **two** books, then I could be an uppity bitch who thinks she's better than people," mutters Ash.

Nine seconds later, the ceiling lights have dimmed enough for the green streetlamps to activate.

The detective watches Ash's vulture trial from his hotel room and realises this is the escaped prisoner who previously lived with Leah in Alicia's former home. After **four** seconds, the detective also realises he is out of whiskey.

He rides the elevator down from Plus **Eight** and walks through the lobby and out into the blue-tinted streets of Night Time. Outside the entrance, sporadic vehicles glide past and a disfigured homeless woman shuffles her battered shoes across the concrete. She looks somehow familiar as she takes **nine** steps in his direction. He barges past her saying, "No, I don't have **five** cash digits, a spare cigarette, the number for rehab or whatever the fuck you're going to ask for."

Ava regards his passing shoulders with no expression and says, "Change the end of the passcode to **four nine**."

The detective spins around in confusion. "Wh... What?" he stammers.

The vagrant is already walking away. He stares at her retreating figure then writes the numbers she told him in his notepad in case they later turn out to mean something.

The next name on Estana's list is Stan Fellowvic. Ash is pulled in opposing directions... confused, undecided, the rope in a tug-of-war between a couple of muscular bastards. They do not wish to be Estana's puppet... but Leah must be saved, and they have no better advice to follow. Killing Ben Wancaski did not bring her back. However, considering what passes for entertainment on the social channels these days, Ash is convinced the Poisoner's antics will be the publicity stunt of a media brat. It might be Stan's handiwork. Ash would have a better idea if they questioned him. A quick search on the com network earlier revealed Stan's planned location for the evening in a nearby nightclub. Ash decides to pay him a visit... perhaps ask for his autograph, get a photo, maybe bash his face in... depending how the evening goes.

As they approach the venue, they pass a dishevelled trader trying to sell artificial flowers to disinterested women. "Wear a rose in your hair, and you could be pretty as Honeysuckle."

"Why are people still obsessed with a dead actress when they don't give a fuck about the living?" Ash wonders.

The rose seller gives a wistful smile and replies, "To some of us, she'll never be dead. She'll always be alive in our dreams."

"The rose seller and Honeysuckle?" Ash teases. "What would you be, an alt flower couple?" They are still chuckling when they turn a corner and find Stan smoking in a low-surveillance alleyway at the back of Club **303**.

New public health laws decree smoking is only allowed in residential property or the high-ceilinged "outdoor" areas of the city. This is partly for public safety but also because smoke interferes with vulture sensors. Stan is alone. Emerald streetlamps cast a sickly glow on his dimpled face as he stares at nothing and rats scurry amidst the trash near his boots. Beside him, **eight** tattered posters of Honeysuckle adorn the grimy walls and partially cover the frosted glass of a reinforced window.

"I might steal me **one** of those," Ash jokes as they light a cigarette.

"What?" asks Stan, before following Ash's gaze toward the wall. "Ah yeah, Honeysuckle!" he grins. "Her martyrdom really added to her legend, didn't it? I had **nine** of her posters on my bedroom wall as a kid... But I'm glad she vanished while she was still hot. If she was alive now, she'd be a hag!"

Ash regards the actress with a flicker of recognition. "They say toward the end, she resembled sunrise on the morning of a beautiful funeral."

"Yeah?" asks Stan.

"Although," Ash adds, "most people had no idea what sunrise looked like, and just thought the poor girl was depressed and wanted people to put things in her."

Stan laughs and takes **six** more drags from his cigarette while vehicles swerve and beep in the distance after a narrowly avoided collision.

His eyes glued to the starlet's exposed skin, Stan wonders, "What do you reckon happened to her?"

Ash smokes while pondering, then replies, "Maybe that serial killer, Alicia, got to her. She was her main target for ages! Remember when she rigged that massive mirror in her dressing room to smash into her face...?"

After kicking a rat that scuttles past his foot, Stan muses, "I heard an intriguing conspiracy theory **four** years ago... You know how people assumed she escaped overground? Well this programme said Alicia's supposed attempts to murder her were a ruse, they were secretly in league with each other, and they escaped together!"

"My favourite theory is that she wasn't real," says Ash.

"Who cares?" scoffs Stan. "Most women aren't real anyway. My favourite is the rumour where she died in that trashy nightclub wearing a silver dress. Her final act was to scrawl those **four** words in lipstick on a bathroom mirror, Here Everybody Looks Pretty, before collapsing from a drug overdose with streams of blood and wasted potential pouring from her ruptured nostrils. Ha ha! Fucking hilarious!"

"That's a stunning image," Ash admits.

"Isn't it?" Stan agrees, indulging in more brutish laughter as he stamps out his cigarette. "Right, I'm heading back inside now I've finished with my filthy drug fix!"

Ash feigns exasperation with an exaggerated sigh. "Don't the pretentious assholes who run this place know we're all gonna die anyway?"

"I know, right! I just punched a girl in the face **two** hours ago on live mediavision, but I can't exhale semi-poisonous fumes into a low-ceilinged room! This place is hilarious!"

"It really is! I love your show, by the way."

"Ah, you've seen it! It's good, isn't it? I'm quitting soon though. I'm leaving showbiz to work as a software engineer."

"Why?"

"I reckon the tide is turning and people are starting to prefer nice guys like Damon Repper to us violent types. Look what happened to Ben Wancaski! I just saw on the com network, somebody pushed him from a hospital window after he went to teach a lesson to some stupid bitch. They found him on the concrete below, mangled up, with a screwdriver stabbed through his scrotum."

Ash observes Stan with narrowed eyes as they reply.

"Her name is Leah."

Eight minutes later, on his way to the alcohol store, the detective gets a message saying media personality Stan Fellowvic has been found brutally murdered. His hair was ripped out clump by clump and his face was rammed into a reinforced window until his skull caved in.

Somebody left a note beside him saying, "I've solved death".

The detective shakes his head as he lowers his com screen, muttering, "Fucking lunatics."

Dearest Beryl,

I wanted to message you before leaving for the studio as I am in grand spirits. Have you seen the news, darling? My most recent psycho ex, Leah, has recruited a genderless thug to kill off her enemies! I'm ecstatic because this could play out extremely well for our campaign.

Of course, nothing bad will happen to either of us, because you're a fierce warrior woman and I'm protected by my army of loyal followers. But they may succeed in killing a few weaker targets, and this could give us the ammunition we need to finish her! With any luck, she will be dead within the next **eight** hours.

It's fantastic how easy she makes it to invoke hatred against her. First, she attended her local nightclub with that guy she was dating, even though I warned her I'd be visiting with my entourage. For a minute, she had me worried when she offered to stay home to spare my feelings. This might have made it difficult to have her destroyed. Luckily, my little hate campaign worked so well, we goaded her into coming out. We got so much footage of her antics that evening! I recently played the clip of her kissing Tom while I was stood nearby looking sad, and another **109** signatures joined the petition to turn off her life-support!

We're similar, you and I. We're both the kind of people who, if somebody hurts us, we make a public example of them so nobody questions our power. She's trying to play that game herself now with these little murders, but it won't work. She doesn't have our ratings. Violence committed without social approval usually leads to destruction by vultures, and if that doesn't happen, my wealthy father can assist me in funding a wolf attack. If I can't get her face scorched to the skull, I'll have it ripped into **seven** pieces by the metal teeth of my favourite savage canine.

If she had any intelligence, she would have realised her social life was over the day she ended her relationship with me. She should have crawled under a rock to die.

I know you will never be stupid enough to leave me, darling. I can't wait till we get our lovely apartment in Blue **Five Six**. You will be my queen, and together we will destroy anybody who opposes us.

Kissing important luscious Ladyship,

Damon

The detective hands the server at the alcohol store **65** cash digits for his favourite bottle of whiskey and tells him to keep the change. He stashes the precious cargo in his battered briefcase and leaves the shop. On the sidewalk stands a huddle of **nine** charity muggers collecting for starving children.

"Can you spare **three** cash digits a month to save a child's life, sir?" a bearded student in a threadbare T-shirt grovels.

"Kill yourself," replies the detective.

"Excuse me?"

"Sorry, I was testing a theory from a medical documentary that joking about suicide can relieve hunger pangs in starving children."

"How the hell does that work?"

"To be honest, I don't know," the detective confesses. "But I hope there's some truth in it. Or I'm ridiculing the suicidal for no apparent reason."

After hailing a taxi, he travels across **three** hexes to the hospital where Leah lies in her coma. Throughout the journey, his brain races with thoughts of his ongoing investigation of Alicia's former home. It cannot be a coincidence that a vigilante killer has emerged from the same residence as the city's most famous murderer. He only hopes he can fit the pieces of this together before anybody else, to bring him the success he deserves.

"That'll be **44** cash digits," the taxi driver interrupts his musing.

"*How* much??"

"Well, gasoline is in limited supply!" the driver reminds him. "And we can hardly run solar-powered vehicles down here, can we?"

Cursing as he walks into the building, the detective passes a middle-aged woman collecting for the cancer ward.

"Can you spare **six** cash digits a month to help the terminally ill, sir?"

"I've already abused a mentally ill person on the com network today, so I've done my bit."

"Bless your soul."

"Aren't those extinct?" he wonders.

Hello Forensi,

I thought I would message you even though we just got home from filming that commercial together because I'm soppy like that. I'm so glad Leah ended up poisoned and lying in a coma with the skin burned off her legs. If she hadn't, I might have ended up stuck with her and that would have made me sad because you are the **one** for me.

Have you heard about those **two** murders though? The guy who does that show where he attacks women got his skull bashed in outside that club we went to that time, in the outside smoking bit near those **eight** old Honeysuckle posters.

It's a bit scary isn't it? Especially because **47** minutes earlier some other media guy was pushed out the window of Leah's room at the hospital. Both murders were people with studio shows who are linked to Leah in some way. Do you think we should be worried? Hopefully we will be OK because I never attacked Leah, I only left her because she was dying.

Yay! I forgot to tell you! I completed level **five** of that computer game you bought me for my birthday! I defeated this massive boss. It was wicked! I think I will start level **six** now.

I can't wait to see you again later. We will have a sexy time at the club.

Sausages eggs xylophones,

Tom

"So, this guy liked to screw unconscious women?" enquires the ageing city guard. He stands beside his trainee partner outside Leah's room in a south-west segment of the hospital, waiting for the forensic assistant to finish searching the room for clues. The medics are wheeling Ben Wancaski past, with drips and wires hooked up to a mangled body that still has the red handle of a screwdriver sticking up from the crotch.

"Well, he's screwed now, isn't he?" the trainee quips, and both men collapse into fits of laughter. They fall silent when the worried parents of a sick child glare in reproach at their unprofessional conduct.

The dying are everywhere, coughing, moaning, sprawled on white bedsheets, hooked up to various liquid medicines. Due to the poisonous nature of Leah's affliction, she lies in a private room on the outer edge of the open-plan triangular ward.

The guards have spent a couple of hours taking witness statements from hospital staff and other patients. They have learned the attacker was a muscular individual of average height dressed in a pinstripe suit and balaclava. The recent death of Stan Fellowvic, a celebrity who launched his comedy career by publicly attacking Leah, strongly suggests the guards are dealing with a vigilante killer. There is talk of putting anybody who was an enemy of the girl under armed protection, but the force is too short-staffed to cover so many potential targets. Leah's best friend, Ash, is their main suspect, having escaped from prison earlier this morning, being still at large and having a history of violent conduct.

"Hey, have you seen her fucking arm?" the forensics assistant calls from inside her room.

"Yup!" responds the older city guard, sounding almost pleased. "**Four** long scratches that ooze yellow-green slime!"

"Mmm... tasty!" jokes his partner, and they both stifle further snickering.

"Not her left arm! Her right arm! It's got a Cashdamn trinity of needle holes near the crook of the elbow..."

"Well, this is a hospital..."

"But they're so recent, they're still bleeding! Her notes say they finished running tests on this chick a couple days ago. There's nothing on here about recent testing, yet her arm's dripping blood from fresh needle holes onto her bed sheets... and her blood's fucking toxic! Guys, this is ominous!"

"OK, I'm just writing this down," says the grey-haired guard. "Needle holes... on the arm of a girl who's in hospital... no possible explanation..."

"Look, the hacker's here!" the trainee exclaims, interrupting his partner's sarcasm. The detective, who has become a joke among his colleagues, is making his way across the ward to Leah's door, his scalp shining through thinning hair under the harsh hospital lighting. "We can go home now, guys!" cheers the rookie guard. "The detective's gonna solve the case by hacking the mainframe!"

Further stares of disapproval greet the guards' next amused outburst. They are too busy finding their work hilarious to notice the middle-aged businesswoman approaching the scene with her young daughter in tow. She walks straight past them and stops by the open door to Leah's room.

"I know you can hear me in there!" she calls to the unconscious patient.

"Oh, shit!" gasps the trainee, his hand rising to hover near the gun on his hip.

"Excuse me ma'am, you can't go in there," the more experienced guard informs her, stepping up with an air of seasoned authority.

Judi Gingseng remains motionless and resolute in the doorway, holding her small child's hand. This is her first real-life glimpse of Leah since the birthday party where the stupid girl ruined a lovely group photograph by draping herself over Damon, dressed as a penniless whore. The foolish creature then didn't speak for an hour and never looked remotely grateful for her wonderful boyfriend. Judi observes the comatose wreck in disgust. She herself is full of life, a tasteful perfume masking her perspiration from a busy day at the office. She stands proud in an expensive rose-print dress with her daughter beside her in matching attire. By Leah's bedside the forensics worker remains frozen, stunned by this woman's psychotic glance, her undisguised contempt for the dying.

"I know you can hear me!" Judi repeats. The guard gently takes her by the arm while the object of her hatred continues to breathe steadily into a respirator. "I just want to say, I think you're a slut!"

"This way, ma'am," insists the guard, pulling Judi away from the doorway.

She steps back with the pull, but not before adding, "I hope you never wake up!"

Without a glance at the bemused law enforcers, she walks off, still holding on to her daughter. The guard drops his hand to his side and exhales slowly as they leave.

"Who was that lady, mummy?" the little girl asks.

"She wasn't a lady, she was a slut!" replies Judi, her mouth curled in self-righteous satisfaction.

"But she was in a coma!" argues her confused offspring.

"She was a slut in a coma! Make sure you don't end up like her when you're older. This is what happens to women who wear short dresses and keep changing their boyfriends. They get what they deserve!"

Overhead, the strip lighting flickers.

"What the fuck was that about?" wonders the detective, having overheard the mother and daughter conversation as he approached his colleagues.

"A crazy, self-important bitch visited the hospital to slut-shame a woman in a coma," the trainee summarises. "So, you done any 'high-level hacking' lately?"

The detective is about to respond when a couple of passing nurses share eager gossip. "Did you see that? She was Judi Gingseng! She's good friends with Damon Repper!"

"Ha ha!" laughs the detective. "In light of recent events, she may not have done her 'good friend' any favours!"

"Nah," disagrees the younger guard. "There's no camera crew in here. Our vigilante killer won't hear of this unless she's dumb enough to boast of her antics on the social channels."

"Any more news on the vigilante?" enquires the detective.

"Well," says his ageing colleague, "either this person's spectacularly good at avoiding surveillance, or there's something wrong with our cameras today. My money's on the latter. There's sections of footage from all over town coming through glitchy as fuck."

"Why do you work in a prison full of rapists and murderers when you're afraid of your own shadow?"

An overweight prison guard stands in front of the clerk's desk, scrutinising the angular features of her anxious face. She jumps at this question. He snorts as she looks up at him while pushing her glasses back to the bridge of her nose. "It's difficult to find work these days..." she begins. She tries laughing in a nonchalant manner but ceases at the sight of his blank stare. "I... I mean, I'm not confident in interviews, and I'd been searching for a while. Bills to pay..."

When the guard grins at the hilarity of her discomfort the clerk realises he is mocking her rather than showing a genuine interest in her career choices. It takes her a while to read people. She finds it much easier to read books. She knows where she is with books.

As if hearing her thoughts, her rotund colleague remarks, "You'd be more suited to working in a library."

While her colleagues snicker at a nearby desk, the clerk sneaks a glance at her daily tormentor, the office clock, and is relieved to see it being merciful. "Well, that's me done for today!" she says, putting away her paperwork.

"Yeah, before you go, I need a new batch of those incident forms," the guard tells her, having remembered the reason for approaching her desk.

"Of course," she replies. The clerk opens her desk drawer, and there it is: Leah's final letter to Ash.

She almost freezes, but catches herself. "Here you go," she says, attempting a breezy tone as she takes a batch of forms from beside the undelivered mail and hands them over.

"Thank you, sweetheart," the prison guard leers as he accepts her offering.

He walks off, and she recommences putting away her work. With a terrified pretence at a carefree manner, she slips the envelope out of the drawer and into her handbag while trying to stop her hands from shaking.

She has read the letter. From the polite way Ash had always spoken to her, she could tell they were not a nasty person. She has been watching today's news bulletins in despair, knowing she needs to get this letter to Ash, but having no idea how.

"Bye!" she calls to each colleague she passes on her way out, most of whom ignore her.

Once outside, she starts heading home and nearly trips over a scruffy-looking cat that blocks her path. "Hey! Careful there! Silly thing..." she scolds.

When she tries to continue her journey, it will not allow her, hindering each frustrated footstep. "What do you want from me?" she finally snaps, standing still and attempting an admonishing stare.

"Meow!" replies Derek Blin, Leah's beloved feline companion.

The cat trots away in the opposite direction. After several metres, it stops to see if the clerk will follow.

Back at the hotel, the night porter is cleaning blood from the walls of a recently vacated twin room. The hotel's cameras have not delivered live feed to the main control centre in **eight** years, only a looped section of past footage. The authorities have yet to notice. This makes the hotel a popular destination for thieves, murderers and other criminal subclasses, hence **two** corpses being found this morning on Plus **Three**.

The night porter hums a tune as he picks fragments of skull off the carpet and wonders how he ended up here. He was among the original settlers who descended from the remains of overground civilisation to start a new life in Deragon Hex **37** years ago. What a joke that was. A place becomes popular, the corporations move in, and it becomes the same old glorified prison. There is no "new life". There is no escape.

He laughs to himself as he remembers his new friend, the detective. The man's an idiotic old pervert, always drunk and bashing away at computer keys, spying on women, believing he has hacked the mainframe. His supposed "breakthroughs" have all come from anonymous tip-offs. Somebody is playing that man, using him as a puppet, but the night porter does not care. The only thing he cares about is what happens to Damon Repper. This concerns him very much indeed.

The night porter wipes the last traces of blood from the skirting board, pulls a rug over the stained carpet and puts away his cleaning products. He needs a cigarette break.

He is still smoking outside the lobby when the detective arrives back from the hospital. The haggard lawman stops to joke before heading to his Plus **Eight** lodgings. "You found a decent job yet?"

"You found Alicia yet?"

The detective sighs and waits **six** seconds before responding, during which time **seven** rats scurry past, dashing out from a patch of acrylic plants to invade the hotel refuse room. "Remember me telling you why I came here? A tip-off. The mass murder of the year occurring on the top floor. This is why I'm on Plus **Eight**, to be near the action. My investigation of the Alicia files was only a side project, something I've never been able to let go. But I now have a hunch these cases are totally connected."

"How so?" asks the night porter.

"I'm not sure precisely how," the detective admits. "But I'm convinced it's got something to do with Leah. She looks like Honeysuckle and lives in Alicia's former apartment. She's got a friend who recently escaped from prison who resembles a masculine version of Alicia... This whole thing is so fucking weird! To be honest, when I first heard of this supposed mass murder of socialites, I thought it was a joke. Nearly everybody uses wolves or vultures to destroy their enemies these days, or at least obtains public approval before beginning a killing spree. It's been a long time since we last had a rogue executioner."

"What about the Poisoner?"

"That's gonna be another spoilt brat's publicity stunt for their vapid programme on Social Channel **Three**! I can't wait to see it backfire when attacking women stops being fashionable."

"But doesn't their work tie in with everything else now Leah is the latest victim?"

"It does," the detective concedes, "but us guards have no jurisdiction over media stunts. That's vulture territory! I'm more interested in the fact that we have an old-school murderer on our hands! One who's ignoring the social channels and going against the social hierarchy by selecting popular targets. They even kill their enemies themself instead of sending a wolf or making them vulture bait!"

The night porter laughs. "Sounds like this person's a hero of yours! You sure you want to catch them?"

"Yes!" insists the detective. "Don't you see? Catching them will make my job relevant again! The guards' public image never recovered from our failure to capture Alicia. Yeah, there were rumours she was secretly being held prisoner, tortured by the authorities behind closed doors, but most people don't buy that. Nobody respects us anymore. This is why the past six years have seen my hours cut drastically, and my five-year-old kid has no regard for me. These days, it's more important to work on your ratings than to follow our rules. But now, we've had two murders in quick succession without media sanction, and this person's evading the vultures! The social elite may become genuinely scared again, and turn to the guards to save them. If I catch this psycho, I could be the hero who redeems my entire profession!"

"The messiah of law enforcement!"

"Exactly! And this means I was right to investigate Leah... Both recent murder victims were enemies of hers!"

"Sounds as though you should put everybody who's abused that girl under armed protection."

"There aren't enough of us," explains the detective. "The girl's made a fair amount of foes in her life. A number of them are justified in their judgement, but it's mainly a case of people being assholes. Folks seem to get off on hating the downtrodden, don't they? This afternoon, a middle-aged mother came to find Leah in the hospital and call her a 'slut' as she's lying there in a coma!"

"That doesn't surprise me," says the night porter. "Psychologists above ground referred to this as the 'just-world hypothesis'."

"Just what?"

"Just-world. It's similar to 'karma': the notion that moral actions are rewarded, and those who commit evil deeds will eventually get the punishment they deserve."

The detective nods. "Sounds fair."

"It does," agrees the night porter. "That's why it's fairy tale. If it were only a method of self-reassurance, to create a sense of personal control, then it would be benign. Unfortunately, when projected outwards it leads to victim blaming. There was an overground psychologist called Renler who did these experiments where he made subjects watch live footage of a person being electrocuted, seemingly against their will. Of course, the 'victim' was always an actor and there were no actual shocks, for legal reasons, but the subjects weren't aware of this. They started off sympathetic. But, as the shocks continued while they could only watch, the viewer consistently turned against the 'victim'. The more pain the actor appeared to be in, the more the viewer hated them."

"Everybody hates a victim!" crows the detective.

"They really do," continues the night porter. "Which explains why violent shows on mediavision are so popular these days. It seems the best way to avoid judgement is to not suffer... but of course judgement causes suffering, so it's a vicious circle."

The detective nods in agreement, until something occurs to him. "Wait! If everybody hates victims so much, then why did so many people adore that sad actress, Honeysuckle?"

"They didn't," the night porter replies.

"Yeah, right! She's only the all-time most famous celebrity of Deragon Hex!"

"That didn't mean people adored her! Sure, men 'enjoyed' her movies, especially in the later years when she was usually naked and doing fucked-up sex scenes, but they didn't have any regard for her. And there were lonely women of low social standing who thought, 'Aww, she's so pretty and unhappy, a tragic princess, just like poor little me, boo hoo.' But this supposed admiration merely reflected how they saw themselves. They didn't give a fuck about her either. Remember when she disappeared, how gleeful people were in imagining awful ways she might have died? They were loving it! Hell, in terms of being genuinely admired, that psycho Alicia had more fans than her! This is because, even if they don't admit it, deep down everybody has a part of themself that wants to snap and fucking kill people."

The detective absently rubs the stubble on his chin while a nearby information screen beeps the arrival of **seven** o'clock in the evening. "Then why doesn't our vigilante killer have their own fan club yet?" he wonders.

"They could!" declares the night porter. "In a land where most people feed their enemies to the vultures, being prepared to commit murder almost has a certain nobility. Plus, they've got good cheekbones. They could be a cult celebrity, if only A, they weren't going up against media personalities with established ratings, and B, they weren't defending the detestable Leah! There's no hope for that girl. As you said, everybody hates a victim."

"Damn," begins the detective, "if you know so much..."

"Why am I working as a night porter?" asks his favourite staff member.

"Well... yeah."

"Because I'm an asshole."

"What do you mean?"

"A series of personal catastrophes brought me here," the night porter explains. "If you buy into the belief systems that control the population, I must have done something to deserve this. Life has been rough for me, so I can only conclude, I am an asshole."

CHAPTER 12

The shops are closing, and disgruntled consumer Brooke Nollto is heading home to write disparaging reviews of today's disappointing vendors. She passes a muscular figure in a pinstripe suit. Ash is talking to a big-haired street singer beneath emerald streetlamps, stood in what they mistakenly assume to be a surveillance blind spot. Brooke is unsure of the gender of the striking individuals with the high cheekbones, and feels the need to glower at them both as she approaches the road.

She does not notice Estana's car.

Ash hears a screech of tyres and a scream.

"Get away from that damn camera and get into the fucking car!" commands Estana. She has inclined her head to glare at Ash through the open passenger window of a sports car she has driven halfway onto the stone curb.

"What camera?!" splutters Ash. "Are you aware that you just ran into somebody?"

"You broke my fucking leg, you bitch!" shrieks Brooke Nollto, sprawled with her right leg bent at an unnatural angle, surrounded by fallen shopping bags.

Completely ignoring the injured girl, Estana yells, "Don't worry, I'll scramble the footage! Now get in the Cashdamn car before the guards arrive to drag you back to Red **Zero**!"

Ash takes a couple of cautious steps toward the vehicle. "Why should I listen to you? You've just hit a girl in the leg! With a car!" They turn to Brooke and say, "I'm sorry about her." The injured woman screams homophobic obscenities in response. Ash asks the singer, "Can you call an ambulance?"

"I'm already on it," the performer responds.

"Don't be an idiot," Estana snaps, oblivious to the hail of vitriol emanating from the broken creature on the curb. "What choice do you have?" She adjusts her rear-view mirror.

"What the fuck is that?" asks Ash, nodding to the partial remains of a dead animal fixed above the mirror's plastic casing.

"That's a badger skull," Estana replies with a warm gaze at the macabre piece of bleached bone.

"You have got to be fucking kidding me," sighs Ash, remembering their dream in the alleyway. "Follow the white badger..." They take a final glance at Brooke Nollto's ruined leg before getting into the passenger seat. After a brief wave goodbye to the singer, they check their com screen for news about Leah.

"She's still dying, you haven't saved her," Estana informs them, manoeuvring the gleaming vehicle back onto the road.

"Well, I'm still *trying* to save her," Ash scowls.

"I can help you."

"I don't trust you."

"That's a shame," Estana says, driving through green-lit streets. "Tell me, why are you so wary of my 'dangerous' nature, when you behave like a common thug?"

"It's your machinations! You're so cold-blooded and calculating! Plus, I'm not convinced you're even human..."

Estana ponders this while they glide through suburban lanes. After a minute, she asks, "So, it's OK to be violent, so long as you're impulsive, like an animal? That's not a very highly evolved mentality, is it? And you say *I'm* not human..." She approaches the exit for the inter-hex roadway. "Well, if I'm not human, why do you expect me to pander to the entirely human concept of morality?" She turns left out of the hex and onto the joining lane before heading north-west between green and blue lighting.

"I don't expect anything from you," replies Ash. "I'm just saying you give me the creeps."

"Well, how charming!"

"Where are you taking me, anyway?"

"I'm taking you home."

They travel through roadways of green, blue and red while Ash wonders if Leah will soon be dead. Estana's list is still in their suit pocket. They should have burned it instead of killing half the people on it, but fates are conspiring to make them this bitch's puppet. Tom and Damon are still alive. Estana radiates twisted malice and probably wants them dead for her own spiteful reasons, and Ash is wary of indulging her. But they still need to kill the Poisoner to save Leah. These guys are now the main suspects, the last people she fucked before her final moments, both publicly revelling in her downfall...

Nearing her destination, Estana pulls into the exit lane and follows it left into their home segment. A minute later, the car reaches the apartment's parking garage, where **one** free space remains, next to the elevator.

"The elevator's not working," Ash remembers as Estana drives up to it.

She stops the car. "It is for me."

Ash and Estana exit the car and approach the elevator. It opens straight away. They enter and Ash goes to press the button for Minus **Nine** but finds it already illuminated. They descend in silence. Ash glowers at the rusty doors that barred them earlier while their arrogant companion closes her eyes as though meditating. She does not open them until the battered cubicle reaches the ground.

As they exit and walk to the apartment, Estana turns to Ash and says, "You must take Leah to the desert. Its beauty will heal her. She needs the rocks and the stars, not the men who think they're rockstars."

"There's nothing..." Ash begins, before fully registering the idiocy of this comment.

They halt in their tracks.

"*Please* tell me you realise that wasn't a profound statement. You merely deconstructed a compound word. That's not particularly clever."

"It's cleverer than getting poisoned or arrested," Estana retorts, stopping to glare back at them.

"But it doesn't mean anything, does it? You may as well say, 'She needs the arms and the chairs, not the men who think they're armchairs.'"

"Does this flippant nature make your life any less dreadful?"

"No, but she does need new lamps. And new shades. Not the men who think they're lampshades."

"Are you finished?"

"Sorry, I'll get in the sea," says Ash. "With a horse."

"Do shut up," insists Estana, recommencing her walk along the twisted passageway as Ash follows.

Estana swaggers past garbage as though it exists to admire her and the scurrying vermin are there to take her photograph. Ash trudges in her wake. Flecks of a dead celebrity's blood decorate their stolen suit and shoes. "Rocks and stars... rocks and stars..." they mutter as they reach their previous home.

Estana unlocks the door.

"You know, everything's extinct up there!" Ash grumbles. "Nothing remains overground... This Cashdamn city is the only thing left resembling civilisation."

"Perhaps," says Estana, stepping into the apartment. "Or maybe the authorities spoon-fed you a delusion, a lie intended to inspire gratitude for these filthy streets. To force you to find comfort in your surroundings. To prevent you from trying to leave."

Ash follows her inside, closing the door behind them. The apartment is almost how they remembered it, with walls covered in peeling paint and macabre artwork, worn carpets, cheap furniture… but no Leah.

Unimpressed by Estana's cryptic philosophy, they ask, "Do you want a tinfoil hat to match that Cash complex? New arrivals descend Red **Zero**'s north wall elevator every day, always repeating the same thing: the overground is a barren war zone...

This is no conspiracy. This is masses of people with varied life stories all confirming what we suspected. Even if we could leave – which we can't – the overground is finished! We're trapped here. Forever."

While they lament society's misfortune, Estana leads them to her bedroom, where she opens a hatch in the floor. "Yes yes, you're all going to cry down here." She glances up from beside the square of darkness with a furtive smile. "Now shut up and choose a weapon! The night is young and vulnerable, and you have enemies left to slaughter."

Ash stares at the opening. "What the hell is this?"

"The best thing about having an apartment on Minus **Nine**..." Estana lowers herself onto a ladder. "Is you can have your own cellar."

She descends into the shadows below and Ash realises they have no choice but to join her. "What's in this place? You hoarding **14** bottles of the finest wines known to humanity?" they joke, lowering themself into the gloom.

"No. I'm hoarding **56** guns, **four** swords, **eight** knives, **five** boxes of grenades and **six** axes." Estana flicks a switch, allowing light to flood her armoury.

Ash reaches the ground and spins on the spot, seeing weapons in every direction. They wonder how many years they spent living above an arsenal.

"**Six** axes?"

"Yes." Estana surveys her collection with pride. "I tried to convince poor Leah that an axe should be her weapon of choice. She receives such dreadful abuse from jealous harridans. I've always thought the best way to defeat a nasty old battle-axe was in battle, with an axe."

"I wonder..." Ash muses, transfixed by the death-dealing equipment gleaming on each wall, all neatly arranged at chest height in purpose-built shelving. "Do you intend to laze in our Minus **Nine**, Blue **Two Three** apartment gloating over your weapon stash all evening, or will you be joining me in avenging Leah?"

"Why take part when it's so much fun watching your antics? Nobody's been this entertaining since Alicia!"

"Yeah," laughs Ash. "I hear she was great fun at parties."

Estana frowns. "She was the ultimate killing machine, but part of her genuinely wanted to be good. She had a keen sense of justice! This underworld was her ideal killing ground, because the people she murdered here were dreadful human beings. She was nothing like the spoilt brats today who'd set fire to somebody for the heinous crime of being homeless. In fact, she would have slaughtered these obnoxious idiots. She was an abuser of abusers."

"Is that a bomb?" asks Ash, suddenly transfixed by a small device composed of cylinders and wires.

"Never mind that," Estana replies, switching on the media screen built into the north wall beside her assortment of axes.

"Must every single room have Cashdamn mediavision?" Ash groans. The ubiquitous Damon Repper show is now broadcasting from a bigger studio. The man leers from the screen, surrounded by simpering socialites. "He gets more female followers every day! Think they'd retain their devotion if they knew he threatened to abandon his girlfriend in the caves if she didn't play his fucking sex games?"

"They'd never believe you!" declares Estana. "In public, he always doted on Leah. Also, he left Social Channel **Four** about **60** hours ago for a massive pay rise at Social Channel **Three**. They keep repeating his show due to high demand. The public are in thrall to his catshit."

"I despise him."

"Ha ha, me too! I only fucked him twice, even though he constantly, aggressively demanded my attention. It was something to alleviate the boredom, I suppose. It's funny, he was always yelling at Leah to be more grateful, but he never expected *me* to thank him for anything. I did whatever I wanted to him, laughing in his face. It was him who was grateful to me, grovelling and saying, 'Thank you, Mistress,' with a mouth still dripping with his own semen after he'd licked it from my shiny boots."

Ash takes **four** slow steps away from Estana, eyeing her footwear suspiciously.

"Don't worry," she reassures them, "I've had my boots cleaned since then."

"Great, so now I'm blessed with the knowledge that you own **eight** knives, **six** axes, a shitload of weaponised botherment and boots that once resembled a plasterer's ostrich pen. Am I supposed to be impressed?"

"I'm expecting you to understand where Leah went wrong," Estana explains. "And why you should accept me as your leader. I will show you an example of how you're supposed to treat people such as him."

She types into the keypad beneath her media screen, which starts playing a clip of herself and Damon in a hotel room. Unlike Damon, Estana is fully clothed, with the buttons on her frock undone below the waist and a strap-on emerging from the gap in her dress. "You may put lubricant on yourself if you wish," she tells him. He does so, but forgets to thank her, so she slaps him hard in the face until he agrees that Mistress is kind.

After he's lubricated himself, he asks, "What shall I do now, Mistress?" so she hits him again for asking a foolish question.

Ash shakes their head. "To be fair, that *was* a stupid question. He should have known you wanted him to bend the fuck over. I mean, the clues were all there! What did he think you wanted him to do, help you solve a crossword puzzle?"

Estana pauses the video on a shot where her prosthetic penis is in Damon's rectum. "Leah should have listened to me," she sighs. "I told her, 'Don't get too close to that, dear. Don't touch its skin. Treat it like the diseased thing it is'... The stupid girl whined, 'He's not well! He goes to hospital twice a week. That's a nasty thing to say about somebody who's ill...' I told her, 'You're so fucking gullible, it's painful.' If we're going to be vilified regardless of what we do, we may as well enjoy playing the villain! Besides, victims are despised. That's why Leah gets more abuse than me, even though she's a really sweet human being, and I'm a cunt. If she had aspired to be me instead of Honeysuckle, she wouldn't be in a coma."

Ash scowls at Estana. "Well, maybe she didn't want to be a nasty fucking narcissist."

"I was encouraging her to survive! For that, **one** sometimes requires brutality. I have too much respect for life to stop fighting for it! Do what you have to. Become a monster if you must. Just don't give up and don't fucking die."

"The problem with becoming a monster," says Ash, "is you might destroy the lives of others. That doesn't show much 'respect for life' does it?"

"Others need to grow the same mentality and become brutal with their own survival instinct. It's up to them."

"So you want to live in a world of monsters?"

"It's better than a world of ghosts."

"I suppose you think the Poisoner's monstrous behaviour is justified?"

"No," responds Estana, "because they lack the decency to stand by their actions! I fully admit to the darkness within my nature, and I don't abuse people unless they enjoy or deserve it. Also, I don't use social power to maintain a fallacy that I've done no harm while secretly destroying the vulnerable behind closed doors."

Ash nods at Damon on the screen. "So what do you call this?"

"I was providing a requested service."

"You sound like a prostitute! Did you charge him?"

"I charged him precisely **zero** cash digits," replies Estana.

"But don't worry, he will pay! I don't approve of public vendettas against anybody I live with, even if the person in question is whiny and irritating."

Estana switches off the clip and the screen returns to scheduled programming, where Damon's hate campaign against Leah continues unabated. "She only wanted me for my social contacts and the pretty outfits I bought her," he complains, pretending he might cry.

Ash whispers obscenities while Estana switches over to Social Channel **Four**, where Tom and Forensi are getting a taxi to a sex club and laughing at Leah for being in a coma.

"I guess I need to kill both Tom and Damon," Ash realises. "Just in case."

Estana's eyes gleam. "Damon's show is filmed at a studio in Green **Five Four**, while the sex club our favourite couple are attending is in Blue **Three Two**. It makes sense to kill Tom first, because he's closer."

"Making my way through your list like a dutiful attack dog..." Ash mutters.

Forensi is smiling on the screen while lights pass her window, saying "Aww, poor little Leah, it's such a shame." The show's closing credits scroll beneath her smug face.

Tom nods with a dopey grin. "I'm happier with you. At least you're not stupid enough to get yourself poisoned."

"I know, right?" laughs Forensi. "What was she thinking? She's such an idiot."

The happy couple fade out, to be replaced by the studio logo. Next up is an advertisement for a suicide hotline. Ash fumes. "I suppose somebody needs to control-alt-delete that power couple." They reach for the sharpest of the **six** axes and swing it to get used to the weight.

Estana switches off the screen and turns to Ash. "Why do you tell so many stupid jokes?"

"Humour is a crucial part of the resistance," they reply.

"Resistance against what?"

"Resistance against being destroyed by the Damons of this world... Against becoming a destroyer... Against becoming another Leah... Against becoming another *you*."

Estana narrows her eyes. "What if I told you, we three are the same?"

"Then I'd laugh."

"Why?"

"Because humour is a crucial part of the resistance."

Estana almost smiles as she returns to the ladder and climbs from basement to bedroom. "Just keep telling yourself this whole situation is fucking hilarious," she mocks as she ascends. "That will make it so." She reaches out a hand. Ash passes her the axe before climbing up after her.

In the bedroom, where manacles adorn the windowless walls, Estana returns the axe to their outstretched hand. Ash's heart thuds as the fabric of reality shimmers. Chequered tiles float above the carpet.

Decapitate to liberate.

"What the fuck?" Ash hits the side of their head with their free hand to dislodge the unwelcome visions. Reality regains its usual appearance as Estana exits the room, laughing.

With nowhere else to go, Ash follows her to the front door. Before they leave, she gives them a smart briefcase to hide their weapon, saying, "Don't kill anybody I wouldn't kill."

"I'll leave you, your pedicurist, and the guy who collects your dry cleaning alone then shall I?" quips Ash, heading out of the apartment and onwards to destruction. Rats scurry into garbage-strewn shadows at the sound of the door slamming behind them.

Ash strides through blue-lit corridors wondering how in Earth their life came to this. All they wanted was a job where they did not have to talk to anybody, and a quiet apartment where Leah could paint in peace. Instead, they are an escaped convict, Leah is in a coma, and their only hope of saving her lies in serving as an assassin for a nutty dominatrix who sodomises people when she's bored. They suppose it could be worse. At least they don't have to work in a call centre.

"Cashdamn bitch!" they snap when they get to the elevator and to their complete lack of surprise the doors will not open. "I'll take the stairs then, shall I? It's not as though I've only had an hour's sleep in an alleyway since yesterday morning because I spent last night defending myself from a mountainous rapist and today running some crazy bitch's murder errands..."

Luckily, Estana's briefcase is loaded with stacks of cash notes, so at least paying for another ride is not a problem.

They reach Road Level and hail a vehicle.

The first taxi that stops fails to have a badger skull on the mirror, but does have air conditioning. Despite never seeing sunlight, Deragon Hex is sometimes stifling, with heat radiating from stony walls as though the city is alive and its roads and corridors are the veins of a malevolent organism. Rumour says a river of molten lava runs sporadically beneath the central hex, and this is where the authorities dump the city trash.

"Hot today, isn't it?" says Ash to the taxi driver, before cringing, wondering why they had to say something so Cashdamn mediocre.

They stare out the window at passing lights and try not to brood on what lies ahead, but thoughts of their mission soon consume them. The murder of abusers to save a dying girl is something they can justify while retaining the ability to look their reflection in the eye. Unnecessary killing is different though. If they are not defending anybody, but merely trapped in the death games of an egomaniacal bitch where nothing good will come of their actions, they will be beyond redemption.

They reach the club after a **six**-minute ride and head inside, their briefcase heavy with the weight of morbid expectation.

"Are you here alone?" asks the doorman.

"I'm here with cash," replies Ash, handing over a wad of plastic notes. A similar payment at the reception desk gets them the information that Tom and Forensi's private room is booth **48**. They march past sounds of enjoyment, choking back nausea as they approach the next victim on Estana's list, feeling cursed. Something tells them if this does not bring Leah back, they are slaughtering their own humanity.

At the booth, they pull back the curtain, step inside and close it behind them.

"What are you doing here?" gasps Tom, his eyes wide with surprise, reaching for his pants.

"Just call this number to join the petition to switch off Leah's life-support machine," says Damon Repper on the back wall's media screen, goading Ash into a state of deadly hatred as they open the briefcase and retrieve the axe.

"What the fuck?" snaps Forensi in shock as Ash silently raises their weapon to obliterate their next target's brain.

Ash raises the axe over their shoulder for **two** seconds in preparation to strike, remembering how Tom abandoned Leah, but fearing what will become of them if this kill solves nothing.

They hear footsteps and a meow.

"Please don't kill anybody else until you read this," says a soft voice behind them.

The clerk has arrived bearing Leah's final letter.

CHAPTER 13

Back at the hotel, the detective's computer has almost cracked the glitch in the footage of Leah and Damon at the caves. The night porter is beside him, gazing at the security feed from a room upstairs where guests are gathering for a party. The computer emits a beep to signify a finished task, but the alcoholic lawman is too drunk to notice.

"I think your computer's telling you something," states the night porter.

"Wha...?" his friend begins, snapping to attention. Remembering his computer exists, he bashes the keyboard with clumsy fingers. "It could be that glitch from the caves decoded!"

"Shit..." he mutters. "Nope, it's just a clip with that weirdo, vigilante killer friend of Leah's."

"Ah, it's only a clip of a recently escaped convict who's been murdering people... Nothing important then!" is the night porter's sarcastic response.

The intoxicated inspector plays the decoded footage of Ash from earlier in the afternoon, stood in a green hex among a few straggling shoppers who are heading home with their purchases. Ash is talking to a street singer with a blond, back-combed hairstyle, heavy eyeliner and gothic attire, who remarks, "You remind me of Alicia."

"What Alicia would that be?" asks Ash, as a teenage girl walks past.

"She was powerful, you know."

"What power did she have? The power to be an unhinged psychopath?"

The singer emits a knowing laugh. "It was almost magical, supernatural, the way she avoided capture... As though she was using voodoo!"

"Who do..." Ash starts.

"You do know her," the musician interjects with an enigmatic smile as the teenager approaches the curb. A nearby car engine revs.

"I do what?!" splutters Ash. "Know her? You think because I'm taking a stand against elitist Cashdamn catshit we're the same person? What are you going to do next? Say I resemble her then trail off nervously?"

"You remind me of Alicia," repeats the singer.

Sounds of screeching tyres and screaming accompany the camera feed cutting out and the screen becoming static haze. The detective and his companion stare transfixed as a digital snowstorm illuminates the cluttered office.

"Do you think Ash could be Alicia?" wonders the night porter.

"He's too young and too tall," the detective responds.

"People didn't think Alicia would age though, did they? The same with Honeysuckle... They said she'd return someday, remodelled and timeless, like a plastic phoenix."

The wasted lawman groans. "Why the hell would anybody return to this damn city? A subversive sub-terrain turned miserable metropolis..." He sits bolt upright. "What drew the early settlers to this unlit hell? No sun! No Cashdamn flowers! No sound of crickets in the evening glow... just toxic company and a plethora of poisons under filthy grey ceilings..." he trails off and slugs back more alcohol.

"People choose their surroundings to match their moods," argues the night porter. "A certain sickness pulls some toward the dark."

The detective lets out a bitter laugh. "That hardly fucking helps though, does it? 'I'm miserable. I'll go reside somewhere sunless and bleak.' What a great idea!"

"It really is," his weary pal agrees. "Just like drinking yourself to death while spying on people is an excellent career move."

"WHAT?" roars the intoxicated investigator.

"I said, 'You've almost run out of booze, I'll go fetch more, shall I?'" the night porter lies with diplomacy.

"Good idea!" replies the detective.

Before leaving, the night porter tells him, "Alicia came back once, you know. A few years after she disappeared. Vagrants glimpsed her on the streets, her face gaunt, walking into walls and screaming at enemies that weren't there."

"Catshit!" snorts the detective.

The weary staff member sighs and heads out the door.

Alone again, the wasted guest watches an advertisement on the media screen that fills the north-east wall. "Are you poor and ageing? Scared you'll lose your job and be cast out of society? Just call **three nine three**, **six zero seven**, **two six zero**, to arrange your free consultation with a plastic surgeon!" With this, the commercial break finishes and a programme with homeless people being set on fire is up next. "Fuck this!" curses the detective, reaching for his remote and switching off the overbearing media distraction.

His computer beeps again. The passcode is finally ready, so he types it in. "Shit!" He curses as the computer flashes an error message. "It doesn't fucking work! This should be the correct passcode! What in Cash's name is wrong..."

He then remembers his encounter with the mutilated vagrant earlier in the day. After thumbing through his notepad, he changes the last **two** numbers of the passcode to **four** and **nine**. The code now works, and the missing segment is ready to view.

What it shows changes everything.

CHAPTER 14

As Ash reads Leah's correspondence, their hatred rises, their hands clench, and their eyes change shade from innocuous hazel into the glowing amber of inferno. "He's the **one** for me to kill," they seethe as they devour the dying girl's words from her final moments before the coma.

Dear Ash,

My legs are now **two** blistered wounds, I'm rapidly losing consciousness and this might be the last thing I ever write.

I now realise how stupid I've been. Not only in the role I've played in this particular catastrophe that's led to my destruction, but in everything... in how I've lived my life, in the pitiful thought patterns and behaviours that brought me to this place.

The problem was, I wanted everybody to like me. I've been this way ever since I was about **seven**. Now that I'm closer to **37**, I'm wondering why the fuck I didn't grow out of it sooner.

The fact that I received so much judgement was never the main problem, the problem was me taking the opinions of my judges seriously. I'd do whatever I could to change their view of me, when the only attitude I needed to change was my own. Now that I realise this, it sounds so fucking obvious, although I'm afraid the lesson has come far too late. I'm telling you this to explain why I let myself be poisoned.

When I was in the caves with Damon, I saw the mark of the Poisoner on him... the birthmark in the shape of a car. When I asked about it he became livid, shouting and screaming, "How can you accuse me? After everything I've done for you!" He threatened to leave me there by myself for daring to find fault with him. He said the mark was a minor symptom of the illness he gets dialysis for **two** times a week and how dare I insult him with my accusations.

I was petrified. I was stuck in the caves with this guy, alone. He left the room for at least **four** minutes and I hoped he'd come back calmer... But in that time he'd prepared a sermon on the subject of how awful I am. His words made me question my safety and my sanity.

I tried to pretend I'd never seen the mark. On the few occasions I tried asking about it, he gave me this threatening stare and ranted about my ingratitude, so it was just easier not to. I'm afraid I've questioned my own grip on reality so often, it's easy for people to brainwash me. When he told me I was imagining things because I'm stupid and mental, I believed him.

I could have left him though, couldn't I? Apart from that time in the caves, I was never technically with him against my will.

I was scared though... scared to leave without his agreement, because of how protective his followers are. They're the reason he's able to get away with what he does. Honestly, how do they fucking sleep at night?

I wish I had your attitude. You don't care what anybody thinks of you. And I wish you'd met the people who helped him trap me, the people I was so afraid of displeasing. You'd have called them an insipid bunch of elitist cunts and forbidden me from giving a fuck about their opinions.

The things I did to avoid disapproval... things that made me feel physically sick... and then he made them all hate me anyway! After everything I did! It's not fair!

It was so disgusting... away from the studio lighting, he's so ugly! Once I glimpsed his true nature it was as though a delusion broke and I saw what a hideous little man he is. The only reason he was never dragged off for cosmetic testing is because of how rich his father is, and it's the arrogance of privilege rather than genuine likeability that helps him maintain social status. I can see this now, but at the time I was trapped by the fallacy of how much he was helping me and how grateful I should be.

So I let him poison me.

Afterwards, I convinced myself it didn't happen. I needed to block out memories of him to survive because they made me want to scream and scream. But then I got sick.

And now I'm dying.

When I messaged him to find out why he'd done this to me, he told me, "Everything is under control, as always." Then at the start of his show five minutes later he declared he was having a "WONDERFUL afternoon".

When I told my new boyfriend what had happened, he stopped speaking to me. I was dead to him. I didn't blame him. Who would want a poisoned girl?

I realise now, as I'm falling into a coma with around **eight** minutes of consciousness left, that I've wasted my entire life caring what people think of me. My need for approval had to cause me this much damage before I could realise how ridiculous it was, and now it's probably too late. I will never wake from this coma unless you avenge me.

You know what must be done, don't you?

Damon Repper must die.

Some say there's a numerical sequence that's shorter than **700** digits but higher than **660** that may hold the Key to my salvation. But right now, my only hope is vengeance in this **six**-sided city of hell. If you don't manage to kill him in time and I never see you again, then goodbye, and thank you for everything you did for me.

Imperfect,
Languishing opium vagrant expressionism,
Yesterday only unending,
Leah

"When did you get this?" Ash asks the prison clerk, clutching the letter in their left hand while their right still grips the unused axe.

"This morning," she replies, "but from the postmark, she must have sent it **three** days ago. I didn't know how I would get it to you until this cat met me after work." She looks to where Derek was, but he has disappeared.

Ash is too distracted to register this last comment. "Well, now I know exactly who to kill," they declare, before turning to Tom, adding, "Damn! I'm going to spare your life, aren't I? Even though I hate you." They return their axe to the briefcase along with Leah's letter, then notice Damon's show is playing on the booth's media screen. "Why the fuck are you watching this shit in here?"

"We didn't put that on, the set must be broken," says Forensi. "Who the fuck are you, anyway?"

"This is the guy who's killing people for Leah," Tom explains. The happy couple had put their clothes on while Ash was reading the letter and are preparing to make their escape from the lunatic intruder.

"What is she to you?" Forensi hisses, glowering at Ash.

"You already know the answer to that."

"But why are you killing for her?"

"Because nobody else will."

Forensi fakes a crying face and says, "Aww, poor Leah."

"I love it when people have such high self-esteem, they need to insult comatose poison victims to feel good about themselves, it's great!" quips Ash. Turning to Tom, they demand, "You were the **one** she was dating when her psycho ex destroyed her life... If you ever gave a fuck, shouldn't you be helping me avenge her?"

"Why should I care?" Tom counters. "She might have been contagious! What if she poisoned me too? Me and my friends hate her now."

"You and your friends hate her for something she *might* have done, by accident," Ash seethes. "But you're not the slightest bit angry with the guy who literally poisoned her on purpose and then publicly declared he was having a 'WONDERFUL afternoon'?! What the fuck is wrong with you people?!"

Tom shrugs. "To be honest, I was kinda glad for the excuse to get back with Forensi. I was starting to find Leah a drag...

Crying at **five** in the morning because her ex had been so horrible. Always depressed, whatever I did... When it turned out she was poisoned as well, it was a relief, because it gave me a decent reason to leave her. If you leave a girl because she's always crying, it makes you look like a dick. But if you leave because she's been poisoned by something that makes her hideous, that's fair enough, isn't it?"

Ash frowns in contemplation for a few seconds before fixing Tom with a bright smile. "I know! You could say you left her because your face wouldn't stop bleeding!"

"What do you mean?" Tom wonders.

Ash punches Tom **five** times in the face, blood splattering over his and Forensi's lovely matching outfits.

"What the fuck are you doing?" Forensi snaps.

Ash grins at her. "He's all yours now, sweetheart!" Forensi leads Tom away in disgust as the blood drips from his face, leaving the attacker with the helpful clerk and the lurid screen. Ash yells, "You got off lightly!" at the retreating couple.

The prison worker clears her throat nervously.

"Thanks for bringing me this," Ash tells her.

She smiles and says, "You're welcome."

"New! Hair **88**!"

Ash's glance snaps back to the media screen as it shows an advertisement. "All this damn marketing is like bothersome wallpaper!"

A male model smiles at the camera. "Are you balding?" he asks. "Are you always gelling your hair in a convoluted style to stop your scalp from showing? Try this new hair restorer from Company **174**!" This last sentence is accompanied by the flash of a gaudy logo. "Guaranteed to give you a full head of luscious hair within **88** days!" the model promises, the camera now showing his hairstyle from every angle. "Only **15** cash digits per pack in our special promotion! Hurry! This offer is only valid for **20** days!"

Next, the visuals cut to a studio with Gothic décor, accompanied by a **nine**-second burst of irritating theme music. A narrator croons, "Welcome back to the Daaamon Repperrr showww!"

"Speak of the fucking Antichrist," remarks Ash.

The host reclines in an armchair amidst a gathering of eager disciples. He turns to the camera and says, "Welcome back to my show!" with a flash of perfect teeth. "Now it's time to introduce **two** of the special guests with us today, everybody welcome Judi and Raychel!"

The audience dutifully claps.

"Now, Judi," Damon begins, turning towards a woman on his left in a rose print dress. "You paid a visit to this show's favourite little status-**zero** friend earlier, didn't you?"

"Yes, I did," beams Judi, sitting up straight with her eyes fixed on the nearest camera. "I went with my daughter to see Leah in the hospital this afternoon."

"Did you?" purrs Damon. "And what happened there, may I ask?"

"Somebody told me which ward she was in," she continues, clutching her shiny handbag. "She was lying there, in a coma, hooked up to these machines, and I said to her, 'I know you can hear me. I think you're a slut, and I hope you never wake up!'"

"And what did she say?" asks Damon.

"Nothing!" gloats Judi. "She's in a coma!!"

The audience howl with laughter.

"Nothing, she's in a coma! That's brilliant!" cheers an audience member as Judi gazes in admiration at Damon, basking in his power over the crowd.

With eyes that could immolate, Ash yells, "What the fuck is wrong with this hag?! How can anybody with a daughter be an ally to this man?"

The clerk shakes her head sadly. "I guess he's really conned people."

Judi returns her noxious gaze to the camera. "I enjoyed telling her what I thought of her."

Ash snarls and kicks the wall beneath the screen, knocking the plaster loose and sending dust into the air. "Leah was somebody's daughter too, you stupid bitch!"

The studio audience laugh.

Regular guest Sahlee Byncorp comments, "I heard about that! Haha!"

Sahlee and her best friend, Sophey, turn to each other in their matching outfits and say in unison, "We hate her."

Damon turns back to the camera and says, "Well, it looks like karma's a bitch, doesn't it?"

Ash punches the wall by Damon's face, breaking more plaster and grazing their knuckles.

"KARMA?!" they scream. "How the fuck can anybody still believe in karma? Has nobody noticed the assholes who live to be **96** and have amazing lives? And how many kind-hearted people die young after spending their lives getting shat on? Karma's not real. It's a delusion employed by sanctimonious scum to justify their hideous behaviour. What some people fail to realise is, if you viciously bully somebody just because your friend told you to, you're not being an agent of karma, you're being a twat!"

Damon continues to grin from the screen while Ash and the prison clerk view him through a thin fog of plaster dust. "If you cross me," the host brags, "you'll find my friends have a long memory." Beryl Pesancho, who has taken her wifely place by his side as head groupie, stares at him lovingly.

Ash, taking their place as the knife in his side who will tear his fucking guts out, brings a furious face closer to the screen. "I have a long memory too, you insidious fucking shit!"

"And now," Damon continues, "it's time for special guest number **two**, my lovely friend, Raychel Spoben!" The audience applaud as the host turns toward a slim woman in a black, lacy dress sitting to the right of his group. Damon explains to his eager congregation, "Raychel has something to share with us on the subject of rumours."

"Ooooh!" the audience respond.

"This lady's heard some of my psycho ex's malicious lies, haven't you dear?"

"Yes," confirms the heavily made-up guest, who carries a tiny handbag that matches her designer dress. "I met a friend of Leah's this morning, and they told me what she's been telling everybody. She's been saying you were 'emotionally abusive' to her!"

Damon makes a theatrical gasp of shock, as do the entire studio audience. "*I* was emotionally abusive? Me? After everything she's done! She now has the nerve to spread this spiteful nonsense! What kind of childish individual slates their ex in public like that?"

"Don't worry," Damon's friend Sahlee comforts him, "only stupid people judge somebody by what their ex says."

"Yes," agrees Sophey, unaware of the irony of her conviction. "Really stupid people!"

Damon's driver, Sephen Blacroy, is holding his head in his hands. "I feel terrible," he moans. "This is basically my fault for suggesting her, isn't it? If I hadn't brought you over to her stall..."

"It's OK," Damon reassures him. "I have wise followers, I mean friends, and none of you are gullible enough to believe I could be abusive. The trait I value most in the people I surround myself with is *loyalty*."

A guest on Damon's right quips, "Well, at least you didn't make me buy any of her awful artwork, so that's a plus!"

The studio audience cackle again. Everybody is amused except Beryl Pesancho, who vows, "I won't allow this! If she dares say another word against you, I will completely destroy her!"

This prompts a hearty round of applause. “Beryl, dear,” says Damon as the clapping subsides, “you’re a fierce woman and highly intelligent. I bet you could destroy this enemy of mine without even touching her.”

“You’re right, darling,” coos Beryl. “I will go for the psychological attack! She’ll see what happens when you mess with the social elite. I shall destroy her with my words!”

The audience applaud even louder at this, whooping and cheering their approval. They continue until the lone audience member not in agreement stands up to ask a question.

“Leah is already socially ruined and lying in a coma with the skin stripped off her lower body, wouldn’t you say she was destroyed enough?”

Shouts of rage erupt at this insubordination as the questioner is dragged away by security. Beryl Pesancho yells after him, “No! She’s not destroyed enough! The coma’s too good for her! She deserves far worse than ruined skin and unconsciousness! She deserves to be in hell! Nobody speaks ill of my man! Do you hear me? NOBODY!!” This prompts the mindless herd to rise for a standing ovation.

In front of the screen with the dust settling around them, Ash mutters, “I wish these stupid cunts could actually fucking hear themselves.”

The prison clerk looks like she wants to cry. “Why are they being so horrible? Why are they angry she criticised him privately while he ruins her name on every episode of his media show? How can they not realise their hypocrisy?”

Ash laughs bitterly. “I know, right?! And they’re disputing her being abused by threatening to abuse her! What the fuck is wrong with these people?”

With a venomous grin, Damon returns to the question of Leah’s life-support. A photograph of the poisoned girl flashes up on the screen with the word ‘Slut’ printed across her forehead.

"And another thing!" Ash rants. "I never understood the use of the word 'slut' as an insult. Doesn't it basically mean, 'a person who gets a lot of sex'? Isn't that good? Most people enjoy sex, don't they? It's a bit like using 'You've got a lot of money!' 'You have plenty of food in your cupboard!' or 'You've got a really impressive collection of hats!' as an insult. It makes no sense! How would getting a lot of something that makes you happy be a bad thing?"

The clerk stares at Ash as she replies, "It really wouldn't."

Not hearing her, Ash carries on, "But let's just say it *is* a valid insult. Let's say it's the cleverest insult in the whole damn world, and his friends with their 'long memories' are so fucking smart to be using it. What I'd like them to explain is, how can she be a slut when she's lying in a Cashdamn coma? Are her medical attendants into some freaky shit? I'm sure she'd much rather be awake and enjoying herself being a 'slut' than be unconscious, mutilated and abandoned by her most recent boyfriend. You know, because psychologically destroying a woman isn't enough for Damon. He has to leave them physically and socially destroyed as well. Just to cover all the bases."

The clerk sighs and shakes her head. "Somebody needs to stop him before he kills her."

"Oh yes," Ash agrees. "Damon Repper must die. Tonight."

"You're very brave."

"'Brave' would be if I chose this. If I'm to save Leah, I have no choice."

On the screen, Damon says, "Well, she was far too cheap for me, anyway."

His best friend Chloe Spanbrey tells him, "I actually hope she wakes from her coma for the last few moments of her life, to see how well you're doing."

She turns to the camera and glares out at the viewers. "You will wake up, slut! And you will see him! Do you hear me? You will see him!"

Ash glares right back at her. "Ah, don't worry deary. Leah can't see him just yet, but *I* can. I *really* fucking see him now."

The stolen com screen in Ash's jacket starts ringing and they groan with impatience. As they take it from their pocket to switch it off, an imperious voice emanates from the device. "Why isn't Tom dead?"

"Estana?"

Ash holds up the palm-sized screen. Sure enough, there she is, jaw set and eyes blazing.

"It wasn't him, it was Damon!" Ash explains.

"Who have you been speaking to?" asks Estana. "I told you to kill Tom first! And I was hoping you'd kill Forensi too, while you were there. I mean, really! Gloating that she got the man she wanted because her rival ended up poisoned and crippled... What a bitch!"

"I'm not going to kill somebody for being bitchy. That's a bit unnecessary! Besides, if I followed that mission to its logical conclusion, I'd need to nuke this whole damn place from orbit. And I don't have a nuke. Or a spaceship. Or quite that much cuntishness. Yet."

"You punched Tom repeatedly in the face though, didn't you? And enjoyed it."

"Yeah, well I'm not a fucking saint, OK."

The clerk is gazing at Ash with a dreamy smile. "Saint Ash..." she murmurs.

"I could have my own Cashdamn day of the week," Ash jokes with a wink.

"Who are you talking to?" Estana demands.

"Nobody," says Ash.

"Well, I think Nobody likes you," Estana smirks.

"This is something I've come to terms with," Ash quips. "Now, if you'll excuse me, I've got a talk show host to decapitate."

They end the call.

"Well, good luck," says the clerk. "I hope you manage to save her."

Ash gives the clerk a hug. "Thank you. And thanks for all your help, I truly appreciate it. You're far too nice for this city."

They kiss her on the forehead, grab their briefcase and dash off to their next victim. The clerk stares into space for **eight** seconds before heading back to her lonely apartment with a mind full of happy daydreams.

Out of the club, Ash hails another taxi and rides across **two** hexes to the studio where Damon's show is filmed. They can barely contain their fury as their adrenaline rises in preparation for vengeance.

All that whining about being heartbroken while he wages social war against her...

That endless talk of what a nasty slut she is, how she uses people...

And the whole time, she was dying from his poison!

Hell, even poisoning her wasn't enough for him, he had to make her final hours a nightmare of social humiliation.

The taxi pulls up at the studio. "Keep the change," Ash tells the driver, handing over a wad of Estana's money and exiting the vehicle. Ash is ready to get brutal, but when they enter the building, what they find makes them want to scream.

Damon has finished filming his show and left the studio. The only people in the building are social channel stars Gabby Coilestio and Botoxia Burnos, **nine** members of the camera crew, and a couple of top media executives who are in a meeting. "No!" cries Ash, grabbing a nearby crew member and demanding, "Where the fuck is Damon Repper?"

The cameraman is unimpressed. "He's gone! He left to get ready for some swanky party with his fans. Of course, none of his damn crew are invited! The location was given out in secret by whatever snooty bitch planned the whole thing." The man pulls away from the mad-eyed Ash and walks off, shaking his head.

This talk of snooty bitches makes Ash realise they need to call Estana immediately. They dial back the number from her earlier call, and she answers after **two** rings. "Did you leave Nobody behind?" she teases, glancing at a screen fixed to her dashboard before returning her gaze to the front window of her car.

"Never mind that!" snaps Ash, "I need to kill Damon to bring Leah back, but I've come to his studio in Green **Five Four** and he's not here! He's gone to an exclusive party and only his Cashdamn fan club have been told the location. Can you get me the address? Seeing as you fucking know everything! And I've got **zero** hope of figuring this out by myself."

Nine seconds pass while Ash waits for Estana's response. During this time they pace **17** steps with impatient fury, the urge to kill so strong they could erupt into a whirlwind of vengeance at any moment.

"Stop pacing!" Estana commands.

Ash stops pacing.

"You have no choice now," Estana informs them. "If you want Leah to live, you must do exactly what I say."

CHAPTER
15

The detective knocks **three** ice cubes into the dregs of his beloved **64** cash digit whiskey and belches. His cluttered room is illuminated by the glow from the spy screens and his computer monitor with its frozen image of Leah's crying face. **Three** seconds later, the night porter makes **six** loud, evenly spaced knocks on the door before entering the room with a replacement bottle of precious poison. "Come look at this!" yells the detective. "I cracked that glitchy **seven**-minute section of footage from Leah's visit with Damon to the caves!"

"It's great to see our proud city guards hard at work," sighs the night porter, setting the bottle down on the desk.

"No seriously, you're gonna want to see this," the detective insists.

The night porter takes a seat as his boozy acquaintance moves the cursor to the start of the previously missing clip and presses play.

Leah is naked with Damon at their temporary lodging in the caves. "Is that... the mark of the Poisoner?" she hesitantly asks, hands shaking and eyes wide with horror. She is referring to a birthmark in the shape of a car, not visible before due to the angle Damon had always placed himself to the camera.

Her host waits **eight** tortuous seconds before responding. Leah lowers her eyes to the bedsheets, afraid she has said something wrong, afraid everything about her is wrong and she has no idea how to fix this. "I'm going to give you some time to consider what you've said," growls Damon, grabbing his clothes and marching out of the room. Leah's face crumples until she looks **92** years old. She gets dressed and sits on the sofa listlessly scrolling her com screen's news feed, rocking gently back and forth.

"That evil fucking shit," rasps the night porter.

"I know, right!" exclaims the detective. "She does nothing but cry for **five** minutes here... but wait till you hear what Damon dearest says when he comes back!"

He moves the cursor further along the timeline, trying to find the moment just before Damon's return, while his companion sits silently staring. After **nine** inebriated attempts at stopping the footage in the right place, the detective finally hits the correct spot and leans back in his chair.

"How can you accuse me? After everything I've done for you!!" screams Leah's captor, his eyes beaming a scorching fury as though trying to flay her face. "I have an illness that requires kidney dialysis! I am incredibly unwell! All I've done is take care of you despite my problems, and this is how you repay me! With these malicious accusations!"

"Can you believe this guy?!" splutters the detective, his computer monitor a tableau of tyranny.

The night porter says nothing, his mouth open in the shape of a crushed **zero**, his glance still miles away as the footage keeps playing.

"Do you remember the time you went to the psychologist because of your eating disorder?" Damon asks Leah in menacing, quiet tones. The broken girl responds by nodding meekly.

"We've seen the rest," says the detective, stopping the scene. He places his empty glass on the desk, the **three** ice cubes already shapeless in the stifling heat, and chuckles as he pours more whiskey. "Can you believe he's gotten away with this? Money, eh? I would consider uploading this clip for public viewing just to fuck with him, but with his cash and connections he could easily get it declared fake."

He leans back with his fresh drink in hand, sees the spy screens adorning the wall and remembers the tip-off that sent him to this disreputable hotel. Every room on the top floor is unoccupied apart from the main penthouse suite. The detective checks the surveillance feed for signs of potential action and sees a formerly opulent room where proud socialites are sipping champagne.

Still gazing at Leah's tearful face, the night porter finally speaks. "The Vipdile Key is over **600** digits long and is the password to gain control of every piece of machinery in Deragon Hex."

The lawman opens his mouth to respond when the media screen that fills the north-east wall switches itself on again.

"Luscious!" exclaims a model who is rendered ecstatic by her latest lip gloss. The room becomes brighter and louder as the dumbstruck detective gets a sudden rush of vertigo, a glimpse of the enormity of what he is caught up in. He senses destinies hurtling toward brutal conclusions faster than he could ever comprehend. He distracts himself from these queasy premonitions by checking out the pert breasts on the lip gloss model.

The night porter continues, "Above ground, anybody with access to a computer can look it up, but the authorities restrict what information we can access in this city. They say whoever created this place knew the Vipdile Key from memory. Shame they're long gone, and this land is now ruled by wolves and vultures."

He turns to his confused host who is still staring at the model and muttering, "I gotta get me **one** of those."

"That clip proves we need somebody to recite the Vipdile Key, delivering this den of predators to the ending it deserves," declares the night porter.

The detective turns to face his friend and politely enquires, "What the fuck are you babbling about?"

Before he has time to reply, the commercial break finishes and the irritating theme music to Damon Repper's opinion show is blaring from the media screen. "It's time for the Damon Repper show, with the **one** and only Damon Repper and his very important opinions," croons the earnest voice-over as the nerve-jangling music fades. "And here's your host for the evening, Daaaaaamon Repperrrrrr!"

"Ah, great! Here he is!" snaps the detective. "This must be his swanky new show on Social Channel **Three**... But hold up! His show shouldn't be on now... Somebody is fucking with this screen!"

"Good evening and welcome to my show," Damon smirks as he reclines in a dark red armchair in his Gothic studio. Around him, a semi-circle of sycophants sits oblivious to the reptilian coldness in his eyes.

"That's the second screen that's switched itself over to SC-**3** today," remarks the night porter, before noticing the spy feed from the occupied room upstairs. "Wait! **Zero** in on segment **five** of this frame!"

The detective opens the program that regulates the spy screens and zooms to the specified section.

"There!" cries the night porter. "Well, that show certainly isn't live! At least **three** of the women on that episode are presently in the main suite upstairs!"

"Cash, you're right!" exclaims the detective, looking as though somebody just told him he won the lottery and simultaneously slapped him. "You know what this means? I was right about Leah! Everything ties together! The mass murder of the century happening here... A vigilante killer making their way through her enemies... Damon Repper poisoning her... Damon's friends being here for a party..."

On the media screen, the vindictive celebrity appears even smugger than usual. "Later in the show, we'll be investigating whether artificial shrimp has fewer calories when consumed in a **zero**-gravity chamber," he tells his enthusiastic studio audience.

The detective looks at the grinning host and then back to the spy footage. "Her avenger is coming for Damon Repper, here, tonight!" he shouts. "This will be the massacre!!!"

"But before that, we're going to talk about rumours," Damon continues, while his whiskey-laden viewers in the hotel room continue to glower at him.

"Ooooh," murmur his enraptured studio audience.

"Now, a certain ex-girlfriend of mine has been telling poisonous lies, saying I treated her badly," he continues.

"How ridiculous!" laughs a guest on Damon's right. Heavily made-up and dressed in faded ebony lace, **54**-year-old Clare Boshpeny is a regular commentator on his show. "Is she saying, 'Help! He was a perfect gentleman, it was so horrible'?"

The studio audience laugh.

Back on the spy feed, the night porter observes more guests entering the room of the upcoming massacre. "Are you fully hacked into the hotel's security system? You could use your audio line to send an anonymous warning through the intercom... Although I'm not sure those people deserve it."

"No fucking way!" snaps the detective. "I need to catch this psycho in the act!"

The night porter nods, still watching the spy footage.

"I can't believe what that awful girl was saying about lovely Damon!" gasps a new arrival to the first acquaintance she greets.

"She won't get away with this!" her furious friend replies. "Even if she miraculously escapes her coma, which would prove she was only seeking attention, she won't survive our revenge for hurting our friend!"

"Poor cow..." sighs the night porter.

"Aren't those extinct?" wonders the detective.

"No, there are **eight** of them left in a lab somewhere. Former overground civilisations used them for sustenance, but most people here find the taste of non-synthetic food disgusting. Scientists only keep the species alive for doing random experiments such as putting them in mazes or seeing how well they conduct electricity."

"No kidding?"

"Yeah, if you ask me, scientists should be focussing on more important matters, such as trying to crack the Vipdile Key."

"Ah, not this again!"

"I'm serious! After watching that clip, how can you not want to wrestle control of this wretched city from the tyranny of malignant popularity? I'm sure a computer could easily figure out the Vipdile Key. That is, if we designed them for anything other than consumerism, voyeurism or arguing with strangers. But nobody takes Vipdile Theory seriously! In fact, the only person I ever heard argue for it with as much conviction as me was this mutilated homeless woman I met once."

This last statement makes the detective look sharply at his drinking companion. "What mutilated homeless woman?"

"She approached me in the street. I passed the cigarette she requested into her nicotine-stained fingers, and she started following me..." recalls the night porter. "At first, she only told me stuff everybody knew about the Vipdile Key, but then she said, 'I can tell you **eight** numbers'. This was **two** years ago, when I worked at the casino. I still remember those numbers. '**Zero four six six**, **five two one three**'. After she left, I typed them into my com screen for safekeeping. Maybe she was right, and they were part of the Key... although I'm not sure how much use **eight** numbers could be."

"But who *was* she?" demands the detective.

"I told you," says the night porter. "A disfigured homeless woman I met once at **four** in the morning."

"What in Cash's name?" An urgent guard report flashes on the detective's computer. It tells him **14** people have been killed at a Beryl Pesancho fan club meeting by a bomb planted behind a bookshelf. Guards searching the crime scene discovered a plot to drive Leah to suicide. Scraps of scorched paper under an overturned white board contained plans for dismantling the girl's life and sanity, gleefully scrawled in multi-coloured crayons. The deceased hostess was found clutching a battered copy of the famous troll manual, "How to Destroy People with Words", which was grimly ironic considering the lethal bomb's location. Whoever perpetrated the attack then spray-painted "First Strike!" on the wall, along with a smiley face.

It is **six** minutes until the hotel massacre.

"It's them! I know it is! It's Leah's avenger!" cries the detective. "And I bet they're heading to the gathering on Plus **Nine** right now! I'm so glad the lines here don't run to the master control room in the central hex. No other guard, wolf or vulture can arrive before me!" With a look of realisation he then mutters, "Cash, I'm too drunk for this! I didn't think it would be happening so soon! I need coffee."

The night porter is unimpressed. "Well, doesn't this make you a great big hero? You're wrong about where the master control room is though. The central hex is just a prison and Deragon Hex is controlled from somewhere overground. We're all basically lab cows, a vaguely amusing experiment for whoever is left alive up there."

The detective rolls his eyes as he pours his coffee. "Mad scientists? Elaborate numerical passwords? Experiments on cows... You sure you don't do drugs? Or watch conspiracy theory shows? You sound like a lunatic!"

"You honestly think *I'm* the lunatic here?"

"Yes, I really do."

It is **five** minutes until the massacre.

Another emergency guard bulletin flashes on the computer and the inebriated lawman sits with his coffee to read it. "Damon's friend Judi Gingseng has been found in a coma! She had the skin stripped off her lower body, an empty syringe in her arm, 'SLUT' written across her forehead in lipstick, and a note beside her saying, 'My memory is longer'."

The night porter regards the spy screen in confusion, convinced he just saw the woman in question walk past the camera in the penthouse suite, dressed as a corseted corpse.

"That'll be another **one** for Team Vengeance!" crows the detective, laughing as he re-reads the report while sipping his cheap coffee. "I bet that party on Plus **Nine** would be shitting themselves if they knew!"

It is **four** minutes until the massacre.

The night porter remembers what he was saying before the second newsflash and takes a deep breath before continuing. "Now hold up a minute! We're trapped within a system that functions because we buy into it, because we work, we consume, we drown in alcohol," he gestures toward the whiskey bottle, "to get ourselves through each day. Do you honestly believe this society was created by benevolent rulers who'd never dream of using you or withholding valuable information? If so, you're the **one** who's a lunatic!"

"Ooh, it's a secret plot by the evil king!" jokes the unconvinced detective.

"This isn't a kingdom, it's an electronic dictatorship," his friend retorts.

"Still, nobody believes in conspiracy theories anymore," argues the detective, "except the insane and the very young. You sound like a character in the fairy tales my estranged **five**-year-old daughter used to read." He goes to put on his best suit and polish his boots, leaving the remainder of his coffee on the desk. "You want any of that coffee?"

"Sure, why not?" says the night porter, taking a gulp and grimacing. "This is rancid!" he declares, but decides to keep on drinking.

The detective chuckles. "This will be my big moment."

"I'm thrilled for you," sighs the night porter.

It is **one** minute until the massacre.

The detective has his smart suit on and his shoes shined, awaiting his moment of glory, when his computer flashes with an anonymous incoming call. He mutters obscenities and grabs the audio receiver. "Yes?"

"Raychel Spoben will soon be found in a coma with the skin stripped off her lower body and 'Betray THIS' written across her forehead in lipliner," warns an electronically filtered voice.

"Who the fuck is Raychel Spoben?" snaps the detective. "You got anything substantial for me? I got something important to do!"

"Yes. Somebody's about to enter the hotel you're staking out with a bomb strapped to their waist."

CHAPTER
16

It is time to **zero** in on Ash's final conversation before the slaughter. With **nine** minutes to go, they are riding beside Estana in her sports car with blue lights passing by on the left and green lights opposite. Their pale faces shimmer in the duochrome glow like strange creatures in a faraway ocean.

"And what if I don't?" asks Ash.

"If you don't, then Leah will die," replies Estana with a flash of her predatory smile.

Ash scrutinises her features, seeking either meaning or redemption but finding neither. They ask her, "Do you care if Leah dies?"

"A poisoning committed under my roof is a crime against *me*," Estana insists. "But that's not the only reason I'm helping. In truth, you keep my life rather interesting, and I usually get so bored."

"What exactly is so interesting about me?" wonders Ash.

Estana laughs cruelly. "Watching your antics has been such fun! I told you, nobody's given me this much entertainment since Alicia." She glances in her mirror, switches on the indicator, and moves her **four**-wheeled vehicle into the port lane as the car behind drops back to make room for her.

Ash mutters to themself. "This is literally crazy... This is what a crazy person does... I am a crazy person..."

The signals up ahead are flashing white crosses to stop all starboard traffic.

Estana assures them, "The level of self-awareness needed to make those observations makes you paradoxically sane."

"Great," responds Ash, "I guess that's OK then."

As more sapphire lights go past their anxious face they wonder, "Speaking of crazy people, how can Damon have no remorse for what he's done?"

"Well, that's obvious," says Estana, lifting her foot off the accelerator. "When people get away with atrocities, they never question their behaviour. Nations only apologise for crimes they've committed in wars they've lost. He's like a colonial force that's gotten away with military violence due to powerful friends and economic privilege."

"So what am I?" asks Ash. "A fucking terrorist?"

"No, of course not," says Estana.

"I'm wearing a bomb."

As Estana's car approaches the **three** signal lights they flash blue circles, although their shape is irrelevant in the port lane. She turns left along the south wall of the blue hex towards the exit for the hotel. "I don't care," she insists. "You're more like a vigilante killer."

"What's the difference?" Ash jests.

"That's a stupid question," Estana scolds. "There's a massive difference! For a start, you're not killing indiscriminately for any religious or political ideology. You are taking out specific targets to save a person you love... Also, you're white and don't have facial hair."

"Racist bitch!"

"I try to avoid bigotry, but plenty of moronic people don't, and they carry ludicrous prejudices that began as impulsive reactions to overground atrocities. Even if you *were* a terrorist, media channels would call you something else due to your Caucasian ethnicity and lack of connection to enemy lands. They'd probably describe you as a 'troubled loner'."

Ash is still pondering this when Estana taunts, "I suppose you would need help to grow facial hair."

"I suppose you would need help with learning not to be an overly controversial, condescending bitch," is Ash's retort, peering up the nearest outer hex wall. Windows on the upper floors let residents gaze down upon colourful lights and traffic. Ash shudders, realising they are approaching the hotel entrance, and may soon die behind a pane of glass that is presently passing by above them.

“I have no problem with my dark nature!” declares Estana. “At least I’m honest about what I am, and don’t hide a record of systematic abuse behind a mask of sanctimony... You are tetchy today, aren’t you? What happened to humour being a crucial part of the resistance?”

“It is,” says Ash. “But you’re not very funny.”

The exit lane for the inner hex approaches. “I’m dreadful, aren’t I?” Estana gloats. “I know, why don’t you write an outraged review of my behaviour for a low-budget music magazine? You could take my quotes completely out of context in the hope that your uber-moral stance will get you hired as a journalist for some do-gooder left-wing broadsheet. That might teach me a lesson.”

Ash is appalled. “I might be wearing a bomb and wielding an axe, but I’m not that much of a cunt. There are limits!”

“Good,” replies Estana, taking the exit lane and turning left off the roadway. She enters the inner hex. After **30** metres she turns left again to enter the hotel parking lot.

Ash asks her, “Do you believe in God?”

Estana waits **five** seconds before responding.

“If a God exists, it is irrational, infinite, and far beyond human comprehension.” She makes for the nearest available parking space. “Why are you asking me this now?”

Ash looks at the bomb strapped to their waist and replies, “There is a chance I might die soon.”

“Well, however you interpret the unknowable won’t change the necessity of your forthcoming actions,” remarks Estana. “Now button your suit jacket before a camera sees you!”

Ash obeys, although they are far too late as the hotel’s security cameras scan each vehicle upon entrance.

Estana parks the car. “Cheer up! You can finally rescue the princess,” she says, attempting a benevolent smile that only makes her face look sinister. "I would say you're a modern-day prince, but there's no gender-neutral word for that."

Ash glowers. "Why the fuck are so many concepts still gendered?"

"In some overground languages, they give every noun a gender..."

"That's bloody complicated. And they say *I* make grammar difficult!"

"…and some would give you the option of being neuter."

"*He'll* be fucking neutered by the time I'm finished with him!"

Estana laughs. "You don't have a gender, but you sure do have an agenda!"

Ash groans. "Please leave the jokes to me and the poetry to Leah. Stick to being a creepy, arrogant bitch who controls people. Play to your strengths."

Estana narrows her eyes as she scrutinises Ash, who is adjusting their suit jacket to hide the bomb until the crucial moment. "What exactly do you see in Leah?"

"Everything *he* didn't," Ash replies, opening the car door and stepping into the blue-tinted night, still carrying their axe.

"Are you sure you still need that?" wonders Estana, nodding at the antiquated weapon.

"Yes," Ash insists, "humour is a crucial part of the resistance. But sometimes, so is an axe." They grin as they slam the car door shut and set off across the parking lot toward the hotel entrance, unaware that somebody is now making a call to the detective.

The lawman reprograms the security feed to check the lobby and sees Ash striding in purposefully, wearing a buttoned-up jacket, wielding an axe and heading past the unmanned reception desk, toward the elevator. He reaches for the gun by his side, saying, "Time to be the big damn hero."

After gazing at Ash's dramatic arrival, the night porter turns to his companion and asks, "Do you ever feel as though some people are more real than us?"

"What...?" begins the detective.

He fails to complete his question as he falls unconscious to the ground after the night porter slams a heavy glass ashtray into the back of his head.

"Worst fucking detective ever."

An elite group of Damon's most loyal fans are mingling in the penthouse suite, unaware of the metric fucktonne of aggressive botherment presently marching in their direction.

"Can you believe we're having a party here? This hotel has a shocking reputation... How risqué!"

"Ah bother! Poor Damon might not make it tonight!" an ageing socialite frets, checking her messages.

"But why? This party is in his honour!" her corseted friend enquires in dismay.

"He's ever so unwell, bless him. It's that awful ex-girlfriend of his! The stress of her saying those mean things must be making him ill."

"Ooh, she's an evil bitch!"

"She really is! At least he has the lovely Beryl to care for him now."

"I know, she's so nice! And a proper social elite! Much more suitable for him than Leah. I did hate her."

"We all did," the opinionated harpy agrees. "And I've just received a message from darling Beryl! Remember she recently got her own opinion show? Well, the rehearsal for the first episode is tonight, so she can't join us straight away. But she's heading straight home after filming to check on Damon. Hopefully they can both join us later!"

"I hope so," her companion in the black corset says. "He does deserve a party after everything that disgusting Leah put him through. I hope she dies in that coma! If we don't succeed in getting her life-support switched off, we must find another way to destroy her. Either vultures or suicide."

"Yes, Leah must die!" agrees the wrinkled sycophant.

The Gothic matriarchs clink glasses in a toast to their murderous mission, unaware that they have just signed their death warrants.

"You people make me sick," sneers a voice from the open doorway. Conversation ceases and the party guests turn to stare at the androgynous intruder who has a raised axe and a scorching glance of unadulterated hatred. "Leah was nothing but lovely to all of you!" declares the suited vigilante as they stride into the room, kicking the door shut behind them. "Where is Damon?" they demand, glaring at the assembled faces.

Damon's best friend, Chloe Spanbrey, steps forward. "Excuse me, this is an exclusive gathering for friends of Damon's. Who the fuck invited you?"

"*You* did," Ash replies, "when you started plotting to destroy Leah."

Chloe stares icily at the intruder with her arms folded. "Well, we're extremely protective of Damon! He's the nicest guy, and she treated him appallingly!"

Ash cackles to themself as their adrenaline rises, stronger and more explosive than ever before. "So, it's OK to attack somebody you barely know, providing you're being 'protective'? That's interesting. I will interpret this as full endorsement of my forthcoming behaviour." With muscles tense as coiled springs, they march into the centre of the room and turn to face the massive mirror. "Look!" they command, gesturing toward the group's reflection.

Everybody turns to face the mirror... imminent corpses in dark clothing, heavy boots and eyeliner, swilling champagne as they arrange a suicide, infiltrated by a death-bringer in stylish pinstripes. "Can you actually fucking see yourselves?" seethes

Ash. "Please stop defending that cretin for **seven** seconds and take a fucking look at yourselves!"

The party remains silent. "Tell me," Ash implores the crowd of ebony-clad sadists. "Why do you feel such pathological hatred for somebody who's done you no harm? And why are you trying to further damage a woman who already has a serious mental disorder?"

"She doesn't have a mental disorder!" snaps Chloe Spanbrey. "She's just crazy!"

Ash laughs with manic hysteria, building up to their final rant before the slaughter.

"She doesn't have a mental disorder, she's just crazy?! Are you aware of how ludicrous that sounds? I suppose she doesn't have a vivid imaginary world in her head, she makes that up? And Deragon Hex isn't a network of hexagons, it's shaped like a honeycomb!! And those aren't drops of water falling outside, it's JUST RAINING!!"

At this, the guests turn in surprise toward the window. They peer out at the dark but see nothing except their doomed reflections, ghostly and translucent through the thin drapes.

"It doesn't rain down here," says Chloe Spanbrey.

Ash's face cracks open into a vicious grin as they reply, "It's got to rain sometime!"

Using the bomb attached to their waist is not an option because they need to save it for Damon. Luckily, all this talk of destroying Leah has whipped Ash into their most brutal adrenaline high ever, rapid as demented lightning.

Guests running for the door, screaming, are severed into sodden fragments before they can escape. To the night porter watching from the floor below, Ash's violent frenzy is almost superhuman, a tornado of blade and butchery. Blood rains onto the carpet from severed throats, splattering across the inoffensive décor, oversized mirror and media screen.

Two of Damon's friends make calls on their com screens before dying, the first hailing the vultures and the second calling for a wolf.

With a particularly high axe swing, Ash knocks out the overhead lighting by mistake and is forced to make their last few kills in near darkness.

When only **seven** guests remain, Ash screams at a cringing partygoer, "Don't worry, I'm not going to decapitate you, I'm just going to cut off your head!!"

Ash is racked with insane giggles as they make the final few swings that obliterate all signs of life around them.

As suddenly as it flooded their veins, the lethal adrenaline surge passes, and the killer finds themself stood bewildered in a room turned into a scarlet ground **zero** by their lunatic murder frenzy.

"Put the axe down, mate," says a weary voice through the intercom.

Ash converses with their unexpected viewer for a while, with a brief interlude to play dead for the vultures and then smash up that irritating media screen. Meanwhile, in the hallway, the wolf summoned by a former party guest has arrived outside the door.

"And what is the truth?" asks the massacre's only living witness, while the scratching begins against the door's plastic surface and growls rumble through the stale air like a distant earthquake.

After a short wait, Ash lists their **three** answers.

"Firstly," they begin, running their left hand through their hair while the right performs restless practice swings with the bloody axe, "Damon's friends conned themselves. They believed they were decent people because they were being 'protective', but in reality, their actions were deplorable and they're going to hell. I will probably see them there soon."

The scratching against the door ceases.

"So," comments the night porter, "evil, nasty scene people are evil and nasty. There's a surprise. What else do you have for me?"

There is a loud thud of something throwing itself against the entranceway. Certain vicious, metal creatures have jaws that can tear limbs off, but due to their lack of opposable thumbs are fortunately unable to use a door handle. Their claws are brutal though, and the door's plastic casing will not hold out forever.

"Secondly," Ash continues, staring at the roving shadow in the light beneath the doorway, "the predator they followed didn't give a fuck about any of them. They were steppingstones on his path to social dominance. Anybody who could do what he did to Leah and show no remorse must be devoid of anything resembling a soul, incapable of positive sentiment toward other sentient beings."

The scratching begins again.

"Well, anybody who's watched his show from a rational perspective instead of that of a brainwashed fan girl could've told you that!" the night porter retorts. He now sounds slightly out of breath. "So, you're saying that men who get off on feeding women to the vultures are bad and mean? I suppose you'll also tell me that blood is wet, fire is hot, and giraffes are extinct. Anything else?"

The scratching gets louder as though closer to the door's nearest surface.

"The final truth is that Leah chose this," concludes Ash, unable to take their eyes from the lightning-shaped crack in the door's casing. "She knew Damon was the Poisoner ever since their weekend in the caves, when she saw the mark on him. He was a kind of suicide for her. Of course, it was murder too. He made her feel so guilty for accusing him, she questioned her own judgement and sanity. But she could have escaped him afterwards. He would have made his friends hate her for disappointing him, but he was always going to make these assholes," Ash gestures to the bodies in the blood-soaked room, "despise her whatever she did. She still could have gotten away before he poisoned her though! But there must have been part of her... a part she was barely aware of... that thought she deserved this."

"That's hardly a shocking revelation, is it?" laughs the night porter, now definitely breathing heavier.

"It wasn't supposed to be," replies Ash, who is preparing for the possibility of soon being torn to pieces. Few humans have fought wolves and survived. Ash is surrounded by darkness, bitter air and the increasingly loud scraping of metal against plastic. Perhaps this was the doom they foresaw in those years of dreading the future while running from the past.

"Well, if this is what she wanted, then why are you risking getting torn apart to save her?"

"Because she was groomed to think she deserved this by the abusers who came before him!" Ash snarls into the gloom. "She wasn't supposed to be like this! She used to be... Damn! Why in Cash's name am I telling you this crap? Me, Leah... we're both fucked anyway!"

"Not necessarily," the night porter says while a creaking sound emanates from the audio feed.

"Why?" demands Ash. "You know something I don't?"

"The best thing about being on the highest floor," says the night porter, "is you can have an attic."

"Why are you discussing architecture with me now?"

"Look above you, dickhead."

Ash stares up and sees nothing. "Fuck!" they exclaim. "I can't see anything since I put my axe through that damn screen!"

"Well that wasn't very clever was it?"

"I have a lighter!" Ash flicks on the miniature flame and the room of blood, bodies and bland furniture becomes illuminated by a wavering glow.

"Near the north-east wall," says the night porter. "To the left of the broken screen."

Ash sees the white hatch in the ceiling.

The growling sounds are interspersed with snarling noises as the plastic door cracks in the middle and a silver snout snaps through the opening.

"You could have told me about this before!"

"I didn't know if you could smash the lock before the vultures came," explains the night porter. "And I had no idea about the wolf until it was bounding through the lobby! I heard about the vultures from the guard reports."

The scratching ceases once more.

"You're with the fucking guards?" Ash spits.

"Never mind who the fuck I'm with!" responds the night porter.

Ash is still considering which item of furniture to drag beneath the hatch when the wolf throws itself at the door again. The acrylic casing gives out entirely, breaking into jagged pieces as the mechanical carnivore bounds into the room in a flurry of metal and malice. Its eyes contain camera lenses linked to a programming unit in its silver skull. Ash's mugshot is stored in its memory along with the instruction to arrest and agonize. Each lens has Night Vision and can observe the weary fighter staring back in grim determination, holding up a lighter flame and an axe. A massive beam of light then dazzles the wolf while **six** shots ring out in rapid succession.

The wolf leaps at the light source in rabid indignation as Ash drops the lighter to grab the axe with both hands. A torch beam shines out of the open ceiling hatch, held by a dishevelled old man who has a porter's uniform, a headset and a gun. The wolf now has a secondary target.

Made from mutitian metal and corporate malice, wolves are sanctioned to brutally assault or kill anybody who hinders their maiming and detaining of primary targets. With bullets lodged in its face, the wolf jumps at the hatch, snapping its jaws and snarling. The shooter had been aiming for the ruby glow within the circuitry of its eyes, the most vulnerable part of its metal skull. Each bullet missed but its silver facial casing is now split with a projectile embedded beneath its right eye.

The wolf's jump falls short of the hatch. Its claws dig into the plaster beside the screen on the north-east wall as it twists and jumps back onto the ground. It attempts another leap upwards when its sensors register a blow to the back legs as Ash tries to cripple it with their axe. It twists back to apprehend their original target.

Ash peers into the face of robotic violence in the torchlight, sees the crack in its skull, and rolls sideways to avoid the wolf's pounce in their direction. They let out an involuntary gasp as they bash their left shoulder while the night porter shoots again, twice, at the back of the wolf's head. The first bullet gets wedged in metal casing while the second ricochets off and smashes into the mirror, causing further destruction and the sound of serrated twinkling. Distracted, the wolf turns from their primary target to leap at the hatch again.

Ash crawls over to the wreckage of the media screen. They stand and look at the wiring behind the shattered plastic as the wolf jumps and snaps at the hatch.

The night porter shoots twice more before stopping to reload. "I hate this gun," the shooter mutters as the wolf turns to corner Ash.

They stand with their left arm at an odd angle as though dislocated, only raising their axe with their right arm. A furious snarl emanates from a deadly jaw as the wolf leaps to take a bite from its target's face.

Ash's left arm whips out, holding **five** loose wires from the broken media screen, which they shove into the gap in the metal case beneath the wolf's eye.

Seven blue arcs of electricity shoot out.

Ash jumps to the left as the wolf crashes into the media screen before falling to the ground with circuits fried and sparks leaping from its shattered skull.

Stood in the ruined room by their fallen foe, Ash catches their breath and realises they are not going to die just yet.

"That was fucking impressive," the night porter declares, peering out from the attic's entrance at the smouldering remains of the metal mercenary.

"Thanks," Ash grins, seeing the glint of their lighter nearby and retrieving it from the ground.

"How did you know which wires would do that?"

"I used to work the assembly line in a media screen factory," explains Ash. "It's weird, the jobs you take when you despise most of humanity."

The night porter says, "So your life wasn't entirely wasted."

Ash looks up at their unexpected ally and says, "I think I'm losing my fucking mind." They survey the room. The wolf is dead, the core members of Damon's fan club have been dismembered, and a scarlet mess is everywhere. Blood resembles spilled oil in a room lit by torchlight and sizzling electric arcs from ruined machinery. All this brutal vengeance, and still Leah is dying.

"Get yourself a cup of tea," suggests the night porter, before his face disappears from the square-shaped hatch.

"Tea?" Ash calls after him. "Are you from some former overground superpower where it rains all the fucking time, or are you just insane? I'm stood in a dark room full of corpses and you want me to drink dried leaves in hot water? What the fuck is wrong with you?!"

"Tea's been made from desiccated fibre **595** ever since we ran out of leaves," says the night porter, reappearing at the hatch and lowering a ladder. "But what it's made from is irrelevant. I think you'll find that most things are made up of other things, unless you only consume raw elements."

The ladder reaches the ground.

"Mmm, tasty carbon," jokes Ash.

Ignoring them, the night porter warns, "There could be more mechanical bastards on their way! You're best crossing the building up here to lose their trail and heading out through the fire escape."

Ash makes a final scan of the carnage, just to convince themself this really did happen, before climbing the ladder. They carry their axe by gripping the handle between their teeth for the ascent.

"There's a punchline there," quips the night porter.

"Grng gnnrrg," retorts Ash.

"I've got something for you," the night porter adds as Ash reaches the top. "If you think you've got a chance of getting to this cunt's house without the wolves or vultures annihilating you, then here's Damon Repper's address." He holds a print-out of the celebrity's records obtained from the detective's computer. "That delightful girlfriend of his should still be out, rehearsing for her opinion show."

Ash accepts the piece of paper. After glancing at the address under the torch's beam, they fold the document and put it in their pocket. "Thanks," they respond with the axe back in their hand, looking around the gloom. A brief scan of the 'attic' shows it to be an unlit storage space hollowed out of the rock above the hotel's ninth floor.

"Nice *belt* you've got there, mate," the night porter jokes. Ash's suit jacket came undone in the skirmish and hangs open to reveal the metal and wire contraption strapped to their toned waistline. Unperturbed, the night porter begins walking into the dusty expanse of black, the light from his torch shining a path over the rough stone floor through stacks of boxes.

"Thank you very much," replies Ash, following after him and buttoning the remains of their jacket. "I've been told explosives are totally *in* this season, along with torn suits and bloody axes. It's important to have the latest accessories. I'm attending some swanky parties these days and wouldn't want to embarrass myself by wearing the wrong attire." **Nine** seconds later they add, "By the way, you haven't explained why you're helping me."

"Damon Repper was in a relationship with my granddaughter, Xendra R'oppemes, before he was with Leah," the night porter explains, kicking a nearby crate as he spits the man's name. "She lived in fear of his rage. He drove her insane then convinced his little fan club she was a liar. She ended up brutally attacked by Beryl and the vultures on his disgusting show."

"For fuck's sake!" seethes Ash. "How the fuck does he keep getting away with this?"

The night porter's torch shines onto another hatch. "He won't this time," he says, "if you hurry! I really think you could be the **one** to kill him. But this guy has media and financial backing, so it won't be long before something else comes looking for you." He opens the hatch and lowers a nearby ladder. "Go out of this room into the corridor, turn left, then take the fire exit by the elevator. If you have a problem getting out or finding the place, call me: **nine five three**, **zero nine two**, **one eight six**."

Ash stores the number on their stolen com screen, then says, "Thanks again!" before hurrying down the ladder on their final mission. The night porter lumbers after them, wheezing with exertion.

"By the way, there's **one** more thing you should know," Ash adds from the doorway, with a final glance over their shoulder.

"What?" asks the night porter.

"Giraffes aren't extinct."

Ash leaves their helper behind in the unoccupied room and dashes along the corridor. They exit the building through the back stairway and run until they reach the hotel parking lot, where they are unsurprised to find Estana's car gone.

A dreaded hum signifies approaching vultures.

Ash breaks into the nearest vehicle, hot-wires the ignition, and speeds off to Damon's apartment, hoping to kill the noxious celebrity before it is too late.

CHAPTER 17

Ash drives **three** hexes to Damon Repper's new home, past red, green and blue lights, through bothersome traffic in the eternal Night Time of the inter-hex roadways. Ash should be extremely fucking tired. They muse upon the unlikelihood of being so awake when their only sleep since yesterday morning was those mere moments of lurid dreaming in an alleyway. Adrenaline can hot-wire the brain... chaotic hours streaming by, colours glowing brighter and patterns crackling under close inspection. It makes Ash wonder how many of those deranged, Sunday evening states of mind were entirely due to sleep deprivation. Another endless day of sobriety and the same sensations of those car crash weekendings crawl around inside their skull like ants.

When Ash reaches their destination, they park their stolen car beneath a sapphire streetlamp and walk over to Damon and Beryl's new Road Level apartment. They pretend to knock on the door. Next, they pick the lock with a metal nail file while pretending to casually lean on the door frame. It opens with the faintest of clicks.

Once inside, they close the door and take **eight** soft steps toward the end of the hall, where the sound of mediavision emanates from a half-open doorway. Damon is slouched on the sofa, watching a re-run of himself delivering a sermon to his brainwashed flock.

After hanging their suit jacket on an available coat hook, Ash strides into the room, walks in front of the media screen and switches off the show.

They turn to face Damon. "This is Ash," they introduce themself with a bright, open smile. "Ash has an axe, a bomb, and a sunny disposition. Ash enjoys a nice cup of tea after their daily slaughter. Be like Ash!"

Their arch enemy stares at the demented, axe-wielding visitor for a moment before remarking, "I see Leah now has her own personal attack dog."

"She's not the only one, is she?" Ash retorts, observing the tall, lanky preacher reclining on expensive furniture. "I've heard Beryl's little threats! You're pathetic. At least we've kept the battle to ourselves instead of recruiting externally. You're weak as fuck without your followers though, aren't you? That's why you manipulate the crowd into believing your Cashdamn catshit. Without your fan club, you're nothing."

Damon tries to stand. Ash takes a step forward with their axe raised and yells, "Sit the fuck back down!"

Their captive leans back, flashing his unwanted guest a sarcastic smile. "Well, at least Beryl's a strong woman," he sneers, "which makes a change from Leah!"

Ash laughs. "If Beryl was strong, she would stand up to you and make you apologise to the women whose lives you've destroyed. Instead, she let you turn her into a weaponised accessory."

"You're just jealous because nobody loves you!" Damon taunts his captor.

"Leah loves me," Ash replies. "That's why I'm going to bring her back by killing you! You should've let Leah move on, instead of poisoning her so nobody else would want her. And you should've told your friends to leave her alone too. When you insisted on destroying her reputation, you kept her trapped in the metaphorical prison of your relationship. That was stupid. I'm never leaving Leah again, so wherever she's trapped, I'm trapped. And getting trapped with *me* can be fucking dangerous."

"I'm not scared of you," declares Damon. "You're just a Cashdamn freak!"

"Are you judging me for being non-binary?" demands Ash, taking another step forward with their axe raised.

Damon scoffs, “No, I’m not judging you for that. I think you’ll find my best friend, Chloe Spanbrey, used to be a man.”

Ash shakes their head before responding. “Knowledge is knowing she used to be a man... Wisdom is knowing she was *never* a man...

“Of course,” they add with a bitter grin, “she also used to be alive...”

Damon springs up and runs at Ash, who shoves the handle of their axe into his chest, knocking him to the ground. Damon tries to stand but Ash kicks him back to the floor where he curls into a ball with his hands over his face while they deliver **nine** more kicks. Once the kicking has stopped, Damon shouts, “You’re a fucking psycho! When I call you a freak, I’m referring to the fact that you’ve decided a little social warfare is justification for outright murder!”

“I’m just ‘looking out for my own’!” insists Ash. “I thought it was possible to commit malicious atrocities and still claim the moral high ground so long as you’re being ‘protective’? Isn’t that what your little fan club used to say?”

“They were just being loyal!”

“What about Leah? Doesn’t she deserve loyalty?”

“She was a whore!” yells Damon.

Ash laughs. “A whore? Well, it must be time for you to *pay*, asshole!”

“Haven’t I paid enough for being involved with such a slut?” Damon demands. “She leaves a trail of destruction wherever she goes! No matter what I did, she was never grateful!”

“Grateful?!” splutters Ash. “For being manipulated into accompanying you to the far reaches of the caves and threatened with abandonment if she didn’t let you poison her? For constantly bearing the brunt of those vicious outbursts behind closed doors you’ve never had the decency to admit to? Grateful?! For being mutilated and left in a fucking coma, where even the fact that her very life has been destroyed isn’t enough to stop your haggard henchbitches from abusing her?! Is that what you expect her to be 'grateful' for?!"

"Leah was a suicidal mess long before I met her," smirks Damon.

"That's no reason to poison her!" Ash snaps. "What you did was ABH... Actual Bodily Harm. Your punishment will also be ABH... Actual Brutal Homicide!"

"She was a stupid, miserable bitch! How the fuck is she worth this drama?" Damon demands.

"I hate that!" Ash rants. "People finding a cheerful person's death more tragic than a sad person's... When I hear, 'What a shame, they were so happy', I think, 'Fuck you! Just because somebody's incredibly fucking depressed doesn't mean their life is worth any less!' So yeah, I'm wreaking this bloody vengeance to save a woman who was miserable as hell! Despite her endless, wretched insecurities, I believe she is still worth saving!"

Ash kicks Damon **three** more times in the stomach. Damon doubles over, gasping for breath again as he claims, "I treated her like a lady!"

"If you define a 'lady' as a woman who is expected to achieve a stupidly high standard of behaviour, then yeah you did!" Ash retorts. "You turned her into even more of a nervous fucking wreck than usual, trying to meet your expectations. Well done!"

"I was a perfect gentleman!" rasps Damon from his uncomfortable resting place on the floor.

"So many guys who describe themselves as 'gentlemen' turn out to be psychopaths, I'm beginning to see those **two** terms as synonymous," muses Ash. "I mean... 'gentleman'? Who the fuck even calls themself that? People who play polo? What the fuck is polo!? It's almost as stupid as the expression 'alt power couple'! I guess the problem with the words 'lady' and 'gentleman' is they're uber-binary relics from an era when half the population had less rights than cattle."

"You sound like a feminist," says Damon.

"You sound like a cunt," says Ash.

"*Are* you a feminist?" asks Damon.

"*Are* you a cunt?" asks Ash. "See, I just used the word 'cunt' as an insult! That sort of thing makes feminists angry. Although, if you ask me, they need to stop whining about semantics and focus on bigger problems, such as female genital mutilation, unequal pay, and the fact that people like *you* exist. Personally, I'm quite the egalitarian axe murderer and try to remain unbiased toward the sexes with my vengeful hatred."

"You're a deranged fucking psychotic!" Damon exclaims, prompting another laughing fit from Ash.

"I'm a deranged fucking psychotic!" they cheer. "As opposed to a regular fucking psychotic!"

Remembering they are holding a weapon, Ash adds, "This is a heavy fucking axe!" and throws it at a terrified Damon.

Their enemy lowers his face in time to save his skull but not his hairstyle.

"You missed," he croaks.

"Haha, I didn't miss!"

A patch of Damon's thick, spiky hair has disappeared from his heavily bleeding scalp and lies pinned beneath the axe, lodged into the carpet's fibreboard underlay. His trendy hairstyle now resembles a hedgehog crossed with a monk.

With their enemy still a battered heap on the floor, Ash marches over to the dining area at the right of the media screen. Damon reaches for the axe.

"Back to the fun activity of naming things... this is a chair!" Ash cries. They raise a metal chair above their head and throw it at Damon, smashing his arm as it reaches for the weapon, crushing it to the ground.

"And this is a delightful fucking dining table!" Ash crows, hurling the dining table in Damon's direction, where it creates a sick crunching sound upon impact with his ribcage.

Ash kicks pieces of broken furniture off their besieged foe. "And this," they continue, lifting the bloody wreck of his body into the air. "This is a petty, vindictive fucking narcissist!"

They throw Damon against the broken table, making his spine bend back at a painful angle.

"Ha! 'A book whose spine she barely bent'... Isn't that what your little fan girl called you? Well, your spine's bent now, fucker!" Ash chuckles. "That's what you get for using the expression 'alt power couple' with no trace of irony! Tune in for next week's episode of Damon and Ash Name Things in a **Six**-Sided Hell, and we'll be naming a vile fan club of abrasive matriarchs as well as various household objects. This episode was brought to you by a letter from Satan, a shitload of numbers, and the popular phrase, Overly Dramatic Fantasy Revenge Sequence."

Damon groans, "I think you broke my back."

Ash pouts. "Aw, do you need a new back?" they tease, reaching out to Damon. "Or do you need a hand?" They grin while slapping Damon hard with the back of their hand, then laugh hysterically. "Haha! You needed a BACKHAND! Fun with compound words!"

What remains of the social celebrity slips off the broken table, emitting an involuntary scream upon impact with the ground. Upon recovering his breath, he vows, "My fans won't let you get away with this! They will avenge me!"

Ash frowns and reaches for their discarded axe, wrenching it from the carpeted floor. "You keep boasting about how easily you can destroy people with your social connections. But what exactly did Leah do to deserve your mission to destroy her, apart from leave you? Isn't a person allowed to leave a shitty relationship that isn't working for them? Do you honestly expect a partner to stay with you forever, despite abuse, just to appease your fucking ego?"

"She replaced me so easily!" wails Damon. "How do you think that made me look? After everything I did for her!"

"You drove her straight into the arms of that shallow fucking prick!" yells Ash. "He told her everything she needed to hear. He promised to be the only thing she needed: the opposite of you!"

Damon glares up at Ash from beneath a blood-soaked brow. "The opposite of somebody who helps with her mental health? Who introduces her to important people? Who buys her nice things?"

"The opposite of somebody who'll scream at her until she cries for not obeying his every fucking order!" Ash swings their axe to slice through the clothing and skin of Damon's legs. "The opposite of somebody who constantly reminds her how indebted she is as a method of mind control!" Ash keeps swinging while Damon screams.

As the blood pools around the shrieking Damon's ankles, Ash continues, "She clearly felt safer dating a dumbass with the emotional depth of a fucking hamster than stuck with a Machiavellian twat who makes her a talex-clad accessory in his continued quest for social domination!"

The androgynous avenger delivers further slices until the skin of Damon's legs is in ribbons. "NOT VERY NICE HAVING THE SKIN STRIPPED OFF YOUR LOWER BODY IS IT?!"

Their victim stops screaming and merely sobs, the tears mingling with drops of blood from his scalp as they zigzag down his once-flawless face. "So I wanted us to be an alt power couple! Is that so bad?" he snivels. "She could have been by my side as I rose to fame, and we could have achieved our goals together. I had been looking for my queen! Instead, she discarded me! As soon as she was bored, she decided I was no longer the **one** for her. She never realised what I was capable of! Of course I took great satisfaction in knowing she was crying alone with her paintings nobody buys, rotting in obscurity, while I achieved her goals so casually."

Damon ceases ranting and sits brooding.

After pressing some buttons on their bomb belt, Ash kneels beside him, getting his blood on their knees. Apart from the axe held across their lap, this could be mistaken for a comforting gesture. "Is your ego really so fragile you'll destroy somebody just for leaving you?" they wonder, their voice subdued from exhaustion. "Didn't you ever think you were over-reacting?"

Damon is aghast. "*I'm* over-reacting?" he splutters. "I'm not the **one** who's spent over **seven** months acting out an odyssey of violence inspired by a paragraph in chapter **nine** of a book everybody hates! And I'm not the person wearing a bomb and wielding a fucking axe!" **Three** streams of blood mixed with tears now trickle down Damon's neck and soak into the fabric of his former band's T-shirt.

"At least I admit what I am!" Ash retorts. "And so should you! Here's **one** final chance to redeem yourself! Admit what you did to her, and show remorse before you die!"

Damon laughs in their face.

"Alright, so I poisoned her! Who gives a shit? She was a damn slut! She only wanted me for my contacts and my money. She didn't love me. I can't wait till she dies in that fucking coma. That's what she gets for crossing me! You don't understand, do you? Neither you nor Leah will ever be as important as me! You're a killer who lacks the social connections to get away with murder, and when the vultures arrive, they'll dispose of you forever. And as for Leah, she was nothing but a stupid piece of status-**zero** arm-candy that didn't know its place. I bought her pretty outfits, didn't I? Introduced her to influential people, took her to decent places. All I asked in return was her loyalty, which she lacked the decency to provide! I only poisoned her because it was what she deserved!"

Ash raises their fist, wanting to punch Damon in the face. Their captive stares back, unflinching. After a pause, Ash takes a deep breath and lowers their hand. "Don't you care that she ended up mutilated, crippled and mentally destroyed because of what you did to her?"

"No, I'm fucking glad of it," says Damon with a triumphant smile on his bloody face. "Now cry me a fucking underground river and blow your fucking self up, freak!

Ash sighs with a sad shake of their head.

"Don't be silly, Damon. I'm not a Cashdamn suicide bomber. I just wanted this whole damn underworld to know how you treat women... See, this here isn't really a bomb," they confess, gesturing to the metal contraption tied to their waist. "It's a camera."

Damon's jaw falls open in horror.

Ash rises and walks over to the media screen. "I had a chat with the executives at your studio earlier, and the lovely Botoxia Burnos now has a real bomb strapped to her waist... A bomb they'll need a code from me to deactivate. Ever since I pressed the top **five** buttons on this device, her helpful colleagues have been making sure this footage is broadcast live throughout the underworld."

Ash switches on the media screen. They turn to face the scene of the crime. The mediavision room with its broken host and smashed furniture, captured by the camera on their waist, is displayed in ultra-definition on the screen behind them.

"Now everybody knows you are the Poisoner," grins Ash as Damon's shocked and bleeding face stares out from the centre of the carnage. "This is what **one** gets for crossing me, cunt! You're finally as famous as you always wanted to be. Smile, fucker!"

CHAPTER 18

Every nearby vulture races to the crime scene as Damon asks, "What the fuck were you hoping to achieve here? You'll be killed for this!"

"I was hoping to achieve the long-awaited dismantling of your public 'nice guy' image," declares Ash. "I wanted your followers to see you for what you really are: the vile, insidious creep who destroyed Leah!"

Damon manages a weak laugh despite his agonized back and broken ribs. It makes him cough. He wipes blood and spit off his lips before replying, "That's not much of a victory when you're dead though, is it?"

"Since your confession, voters will choose Double Kill," Ash explains. "You'll be fried for what you did, and this will save Leah from the coma. I'm prepared to kill for the truth, and I'm prepared to die for it."

Damon is incredulous. Ignoring the sight of himself on the media screen amidst the debris of Ash's violence, he gasps, "Don't you know who I am? Don't you know how devoted my followers are?"

Ash gets a sick wave of dread and disgust when Damon adds, "None of my fans give a fuck about your precious Leah. She was nobody!"

Back at the hotel, the night porter watches the emergency broadcast on mediavision while the detective lies unconscious by his feet. "What the hell were you thinking?" he mutters.

Suddenly contrite, Damon makes a plea to the audience while blood drips down his face. He says he only poisoned women and spoke that way to Ash because he was unwell. Now he has faith that his wonderful followers will remain loyal and not abandon him after this dreadful ordeal.

The night porter fears the population might be stupid enough to fall for this catshit, and pours himself another glass of the detective's whiskey.

Ash turns away from Damon's drivel and walks outside, bringing the video feed with them. Once under the blue-tinted streetlamps, the killer leans back against a wall to light a cigarette. They take a drag and await their fate. The recording device on their waist shows the wall across the street, inlaid with an advertising screen that shows the emergency transmission. Trapped in a loop before a tired avenger, this screen displays incrementally smaller copies of itself. "Fuck this infinity catshit," Ash mutters, dialling the studio in Green **Five Four** to disarm the bomb on Botoxia Burnos. "Here's your **eight**-digit passcode," they tell the anxious media executives. "**Zero seven four four**, **six two three seven**." After another thoughtful drag they add, "Passcodes are always the same length, aren't they? Just like phone numbers are always **nine** digits... Why aren't passcodes ever **nine** digits? Or **six**? Or **27**?"

Visual feed from their device cuts out.

The nearby screen switches from infinity loop to media aftermath. Emergency broadcasting still over-rides all channels as viewers across Deragon Hex await the vulture trial of the century. With the highest ratings ever recorded, the authorities contact guard headquarters and warn that unless all guards stand down, future funding will be further slashed across every department.

Ash's image is captured by a nearby security camera.

The screen across the road splits into quarters: Ash smoking in the lower-left, Utasha Bibetty at her studio in the upper-left representing their defence, Damon recorded from the spy camera in his mediavision room (which he has now authorised for public viewing) in the lower-right, and a newly liberated Botoxia Burnos in the upper right, eager to represent the prosecution.

Hearing the distant sound of vulture hum, Ash slumps down to rest on the concrete and calls the night porter.

Their friend picks up on the first ring. "What the hell were you thinking?" "Why didn't you kill him to neutralize the poison in Leah's bloodstream?"

Ash takes another smoke before replying, "Because he still has enough followers left to destroy Leah."

They gaze with narrow-eyed antipathy at the spectacle of sanctimony on the screen across the road, the vote swinging toward Death by Laser for Ash despite Utasha's assertion that they were only trying to save Leah's life. The fact that Damon was caught on camera admitting he abused and poisoned his last girlfriend is somehow being overlooked. Public mood is still against Leah for letting herself be poisoned and then sending somebody to kill for her.

"I needed to turn his fan club against him and go for public execution instead," explains Ash. "This way I could save Leah from vultures and social warfare as well as from the poison. I underestimated human stupidity though! The public now wants Leah to die more than ever."

The night porter knocks back more whiskey. "You should have kept the bomb activated on that obnoxious social channel brat for leverage."

Ash takes a final drag before stubbing their cigarette out on the ground. "I promised I would disarm it, and I'm not a liar." A nearby audio bug is catching the conversation, occasional snippets of which are added to the media trial. Mostly though, Ash's dialogue is muted while Damon and Botoxia take turns to character assassinate both Leah and her avenger.

"Besides," adds Ash with a shrug of their toned shoulders, "you can't hold somebody hostage forever. And there's nothing more I can do to redeem Leah in the public's eyes. Maybe she was always doomed. Maybe we both were."

"So what are you going to do?" asks the night porter.

"What *can* I do?" sighs Ash. "I've failed. Both Leah and I will die tonight."

Shuffling out of sapphire-tinted darkness, the mysterious Ava approaches Ash from their right.

Viewers at home observe the maimed woman wandering into shot from stage left.

"I'm sorry to hear that," says the night porter.

"Don't worry about it," Ash replies, as Ava drifts closer.

"Can I just ask you something though?"

"Yeah?"

"Where the hell could you hide a giraffe down here?"

Before Ash can reply, an all-terrain vehicle pulls up in front of them and the footage in the bottom-left quarter of the screen cuts out.

"Somebody's here," says Ash. "I've gotta go."

Estana is driving while a comatose Leah is slumped on the back seat with Derek the cat beside her. "Get in!" the imperious driver commands.

"What happened to your sports car?"

"I have far more vehicles than a person could ever need because I'm a pretentious cunt. Now get in!"

"Fine! Can you get out the way?" Ash snaps at the tramp with the messed-up face who is blocking their path to the vehicle. Estana peers out the passenger window. "You get in too!" she instructs Ava. "You might be useful."

"What use could *she* be, exactly?" queries Ash. "I didn't think junkies even went to blue-lit areas at night?"

"I sent you the screwdriver with the passcode," Ava replies in her expressionless voice.

She steps out of Ash's way and gets into the front passenger seat as Ash splutters, "You?! Who the fuck are you?"

"Isn't it obvious?" sighs Estana. "Honestly, Ash! Sometimes I think you're the only person who doesn't understand what's going on around here. We can't spell it out any clearer without being trite. Just get in the damn car!"

Ash gets in the back to sit beside their best friend and her favourite alcoholic feline. Leah's poisoned body is sprawled like a lifeless rag doll. Her wounded legs weep plasma onto a plastic seat protector while her dyed black hair falls over her closed eyes, open mouth and pale blue hospital gown. Ash enquires, "Shouldn't she be hooked up to medical machines? You know, because she's in a coma?"

Estana pulls away from the curb and replies, "The hospital's medicine and cold machinery cannot help her."

"Are you a doctor?" asks Ash.

"No," says Estana, "I'm a statica. But only the desert can save her now."

"Unless she's suffering a vitamin D deficiency, you might be wrong," quips Ash. "Besides, how did you get her from the hospital without being seen?"

"I told you, I'm a statica," repeats Estana, making for the blue hex's exit. "This means I do what I want. I've nothing to fear from the vultures, and nor will you while you're with me."

"Let me guess," ventures Ash, "you're not just a nutcase, you're a *superhuman* nutcase?"

"You don't know what I've sacrificed to be what I am, so don't judge me."

As the divine driver pulls onto the inter-hex roadways, Ash looks from Estana to Ava then back again, laughing at their life's insanity. "Well, crackwhores of the machine, let's go!"

Four people and their feline companion take off across the lurid cityscape.

Ash checks their com screen. It shows nothing but the Crime Channel's emergency broadcast, which has gone single screen. "Our experts are working to get surveillance back online, find the accused and begin public execution," says the presenter, grinning in excitement at the upcoming retribution.

"For fuck's sake," mutters Ash, steadying themself by clutching the door handle as the vehicle swerves at a junction. Leah's head lolls to the right, but Ava remains motionless.

The voice from the com screen continues its gleeful narration. "Here's a recap for people who've just joined us. Leah, the ex-girlfriend of social celebrity Damon Repper, has been sentenced to Death by Laser in what has been the highest-rated vulture trial ever recorded. Vultures are also pursuing the friend who committed vigilante killings in her name, known as Ash, and the accomplices who helped them escape whose identities are presently unknown. Static interference is blocking all camera footage from **nine** hexes in the North-East district, which has somehow become a vulture no-fly zone."

"FUCK!" screams Ash. "Our plan didn't work! His stupid followers still want to destroy Leah... And he's still alive... So if they don't kill her, his Cashdamn poison will!"

The androgynous avenger slams their fist into the car door.

"Don't you dare damage my car!" warns Estana. "Things could be much worse."

Ash laughs bitterly. "How the hell could things be worse? I've killed so many people trying to save her, she's still dying, and now we're sentenced to public execution!" They gaze at the dozing damsel, frail and vulnerable in her hospital robe, and wonder how such a small creature could be a catalyst for such destruction. "I only meant to threaten him into publicly confessing, to save her," moans Ash. "I never meant to commit mass murder."

Estana graces them with a brief smile over her shoulder. "Part of you wanted to though, didn't it?"

"Yeah, but I should have stopped myself! This isn't me..."

"Aww, let me guess... You're actually a really *kind-hearted* murderer?"

"Please shut up..." groans Ash. "The question is, how the fuck do we save her now?"

"I keep telling you to trust me! I can lead you both to safety. She will be fine in the desert."

"Why do you keep saying that? What's out there?"

"Everything you've ever dreamed of," says Estana. "It will feel like coming home."

She changes to the green port lane and turns left, heading west, as the blue lights on their right are replaced by a scarlet glow.

Ash tucks an ebony curl behind Leah's ear and checks she is still breathing. The updates on their com screen continue unabated. Viewers now believe Ash is responsible for the poisoning of Judi Gingseng and Raychel Spoben as well as the bomb planted at the Beryl Pesancho fan club meeting. "As if I'd actually blow people up! Or poison women and write on their faces! That's fucking sick!"

"I know! You'd never do such a thing," agrees Estana, winking at them in the rear-view mirror. "Although... you do get those blackouts when you're angry, don't you?"

"Yeah, but I'm pretty sure I'd remember planting a bomb, poisoning somebody, or writing abuse on a coma patient!"

Estana switches to the starboard lane, the traffic parting to let her in, as always. "You do forget the occasional thing though... such as my instruction to attach the bomb to Gabby Coilestio. As revenge for how horrible she was to Leah at Stan's trial."

"I remember that! But Botoxia Burnos was there as well, and she was fucking horrible to Leah too. It was a difficult decision... In the end, I figured Gabby had a reason to hate Leah. Granted, it was a stupid reason, but it was still a reason. Botoxia though, she was just plain fucking nasty because she could be, so I figured she deserved it more. Not that it matters, because I was always going to disarm the bomb... wasn't I?"

After a taunting pause, Estana replies "Yes, of course you were." At the next junction she turns to travel north-west again, and ruby illuminations remain on the right as she crosses from green starboard lane to blue.

Ash peers at lights of blue, red and green that make them want to scream as the gaudy streets become a blur of cars and chaos. "This city was designed by a lunatic! I bet driving here when you're not a magical traffic fairy is a Cashdamn nightmare!"

Estana laughs while Ava and Leah continue their ongoing silence. Derek the cat meows and kneads his claws into Ash's leg. Startled, they demand, "And why the fuck is there a cat here?"

"He's a friend of Leah's and he might be useful," explains Estana, making another turn as the vehicle careens toward their rocky escape route.

"So the things you find useful include stray cats and helpful tramps," muses Ash. "What else do you need, a dog in a shopping trolley?"

When they reach the city edge, Estana turns off at a dirt track and drives straight on into darkness. The temperature drops. Ash folds tired arms over their suit jacket, while black air oozes a foreboding quality that renders the passengers speechless. The journey continues over uneven terrain with no other vehicles in sight. They are heading the same direction Leah took with her poisonous ex, until Estana detours from the festival route with a sudden turn.

The stony corridor narrows. The car headlights pick up fluttering bat wings and rugged tunnel edges as the road surface becomes increasingly jarring. Usually when explorers take this route, vultures chase them back to civilisation with the distinct threat of laser death. Tonight, the vultures remain absent. Security cameras are everywhere, but with Estana present they fail to detect anything except static noise.

After an eternity of jolted driving, the passage becomes too rocky for further progress and Estana stops the car.

"Is the exit here?" whispers Ash, their breath catching in their throat as Estana kills the lights and engine, making the walls disappear. Ash could have sworn there was a crunching noise in the gloom behind them, but when they listen further it has stopped. The resulting silence disturbs them further.

Unperturbed by the inky chill, Estana says, "Petrol only goes so far. The future is powered by guts and adrenaline." Ava switches on a torch pulled from the folds of her tattered clothing. Its faint light gleams off Estana's excited eyes as she turns to Ash with the eager smile of a child at Cashmas. On her, this expression looks terrifying.

"A simple 'Yes' would have sufficed," Ash mutters.

All conscious passengers exit the vehicle. Ash lifts Leah from the car and kicks the door shut while Estana activates the central locking. "Are you expecting a bat to steal your car?" Ash attempts a breezy tone although their bravado rings hollow in the sinister surroundings. They carry Leah with an arm under her back, an arm under her legs and her face resting against their shoulder as the gang sets off down the tunnel.

Derek's tiny paws scamper over stones while the humans trudge in assorted footwear. After a few minutes, annoyed by the woman's weirdness and unexplained presence, Ash turns to Ava and demands, "So who the hell are you?"

"I am an incarnation of the creator," Ava replies, walking steadily over the rocks.

"Be careful," warns Estana, "this conversation is already on the borderline of being so obvious it's painful."

Ignoring her, Ava continues, "We created this world to save people like her," with a nod at the sleeping Leah.

Estana yawns.

Ash says, "Well thanks, God, but it was this lousy world that killed her." A glowing red dot appears on the wall to their right. For a second, Ash mistakes this for a laser beam, until the blue dot appears. Then the green. Within a few moments, the group is surrounded by lightbugs, the fabled insects that filled the underworld before the humans built their metropolis. They shine the primary colours of light over jagged stones.

"Leah's so vulnerable, she could be destroyed anywhere." Ava switches off her torch and returns it to the folds of her tattered coat. Multi-chromatic insects on the surrounding walls illuminate a desecrated face both youthful and ancient. "In this world, at least you can avenge her."

A slight breeze blows Leah's hair into Ash's face while they gaze at the walls in awe. "But if you're really in charge here, why didn't you stop Damon from poisoning Leah?" They wonder if they should be humouring this madwoman, yet the strangeness of their surroundings makes them temporarily suspend disbelief.

"It's not for me to change a person's nature," Ava explains. "Creators make worlds for mortals to exist within, yet sentient beings are given free will. You always have a choice."

A dreadfully bored-looking Estana comments, "Well, I must say, Damon picked an absurd thing to be immortalised as, didn't he?"

Before Ash can figure out what she is implying, they are frozen by a contemptuous voice behind them.

"You losers are full of shit!"

The gang turns around as Beryl Pesancho appears from behind a massive rock with a gun aimed at Estana.

Spurred on by protective fury at the sight of Damon's battered face, Beryl had dashed from her studio. After reaching home in time to see Ash get into Estana's car, she had jumped into her own vehicle and followed at a distance.

"Great, you're here," drawls Estana, turning to face her enemy, who stands beneath a lifeless camera attached to the top of an insect-covered wall.

Nobody moves. If the camera's security feed depicted anything other than static snowstorm, it would show a bug-lit stand-off involving **five** people and a cat. This uncanny crew stand in a place that will someday be a Layer **Six** or Layer **Seven** hex as the city expands. They are further from the developed underground than anybody has ever been.

"**Three**," begins Ava in a quiet voice. Ignored by the group, she then continues to mumble under her breath.

"That's a funny-looking bunch of 'words' you've got there," quips Ash, nodding at Beryl's gun.

Beryl takes **five** tottering steps forward, her lean legs and fashionable arrangement of mesh and buckles making her resemble an industrial gazelle. "You deserve to die for what you did to him!" She fixes Estana with a look of demented animosity.

Estana smiles and replies, "I did nothing he didn't beg for, my dear."

Ash cringes and mutters, "This might not be the best time to bring your inherent superiority complex to the table. Try diplomacy. Or at least not being a bitch."

Beryl keeps her eyes on Estana. "You're the **one** who's 'emotionally abusive', not him!" she retorts. "That comatose brat is a liar, and once I've killed you and your little tomboy attack dog, she's next!"

Derek Blin hisses at Beryl.

Ava can be heard saying, "**Eight**, **eight**", but mostly her whispers are too soft to decipher.

The weaponised celebrity takes **five** more steps toward the group. Ava says, "**Seven**".

Keeping the gun on Estana, Beryl turns to Ava and warns, "I will put **five** rounds in your face if you don't shut up, you fucking nutjob!"

Ava goes back to whispering.

Estana raises her hands to chest height, palms outwards. "Before you shoot, answer these **two** questions," she insists. "And please be honest!"

"I'm always honest! I don't tell lies about my ex-boyfriends!" replies her statuesque, gun-wielding foe.

"Firstly," Estana begins, "would you describe yourself as a vulnerable, fragile person?"

Beryl responds to this notion with a vicious laugh. "Me? Haha! You don't know me very well, do you sweetheart?"

A metal click echoes through the shadows as Beryl removes her weapon's safety catch.

"OK," responds Estana. "Secondly... if you *were* vulnerable and fragile, what do you think your relationship with Damon would be like?"

Beryl's glowering expression fails to hide a flicker of realization.

Ash is sure Ava is still slowly mumbling numbers. Amidst her whispered syllables they detect another **seven**.

"It's written all over your face!" crows Estana. "You realise exactly how your boyfriend must have treated poor Leah. So now you understand why those protective of the girl might seek to avenge her."

"I don't fucking care!" snaps Beryl. "Nobody speaks ill of him while he's with me! Nobody!"

Ava mutters more digits. Ash hears a **two**, but the rest is unclear.

Estana regards Beryl in weary disappointment. "If you honestly don't care that he destroyed a woman, you need to drop the pretence you're on any kind of moral mission."

Ava is still whispering numbers. Ash, clutching Leah and wondering how the hell they will get out of this, detects a **four** and an **eight** amidst other, undecipherable syllables.

Beryl's hands had begun to lower. Her eyes flash as she returns her aim to Estana's chest, yelling, "I *am* fucking moral! I protect those close to me! And that means ridding this world of bitches like you!"

She shoots.

The impact knocks Estana against the cave wall, where she falls unconscious to the ground.

Disturbed insects flutter in a luminous cloud as the tunnel roof splits along a fault line.

Nine rocks are dislodged, **one** of which falls on Estana's head, making a sick crunching noise on impact. As it rolls off, a trail of blood drips from her hairline.

The instant Estana loses consciousness, a nearby camera loses its static haze and clear visuals of the gang are relayed to the authorities. The mysterious vulture no-fly zone disappears. Every flying deliverer of justice in Deragon Hex begins racing to their location, faster than ever, spurred on by the force of Damon's hate campaign.

Beryl turns to aim at Ash.

Ava is still softly reciting something beyond comprehension.

"OK, OK..." says Ash, "so that woman was fucking sinister, and I didn't entirely trust her either. But it was either take Leah and follow her to safety, or leave Leah to die among psychopaths! You understand what Damon did to her don't you? Don't judge *her* for this! She's done nothing to you. So you've killed that nutty dominatrix, well done. Now please let me and Leah go!"

The vultures reach the entrance to the caves at the city's edge while Beryl stares at Ash in blatant disgust. "What the fuck are you babbling about, you fucking psycho?"

Ava keeps muttering while insects scuttle nervously and the air vibrates with a low rumbling sound that could be mechanical hum or distant rockslide. Derek Blin leaves the humans to their lunacy and scampers into a hollow in the rocks.

"OK, so I've been a bit of a psycho recently..." Ash admits. "But you've seen how Damon acts behind closed doors! How do you think he behaved with Leah? For fuck's sake, look at her! The skin is stripped from her lower body and she's in a fucking coma! She's not his first victim either! What makes you think you won't be the next? You must have noticed the mark of the Poisoner... why are you still with him? Come with us! I'm serious! Get the fuck away from that creep before he poisons you too and calls for your public execution!"

Beryl erupts with maniacal laughter. "Don't you know who I am?" she demands through fits of mirth. "You don't get it do you? I am socially elite! Damon won't poison me, with the connections I have. He only poisons loser girls like that whore in your arms!"

The media star's laugh gets louder, as does the thunder of imminent rock fall and hum of approaching vultures. Ava is still vocalising her own contribution to the din but against the noise her words are unintelligible.

"Maybe I should kill Leah first and make you watch her die. I want you to suffer," taunts the sadistic Beryl. "You deserve this for messing with the elite!"

In the **two**-second pause before Ash responds they hear Ava say **two** more digits: **seven** and **nine**.

"Wait!" shouts Ash.

"What?" snaps Beryl.

Three rocks fall nearby as Ava intones more unclear digits followed by a clear **eight**.

"Please, just promise me **one** thing," begs Ash as a blue, glowing insect crawls over their filthy shoes. "Please promise me that sometimes... after you've killed us..."

"Yes?" demands Beryl as Ava languidly adds another number to the list.

"Please promise me... to honour our memory..." says Ash. "You'll let Damon stand on your shoulders, so you can be an Alt Tower Couple."

Beryl mutters, "Stupid asshole."

Ava shouts, "**Eight**!"

"Shut up you crazy bitch!"

Ava yells a short string ending in "**Three**!" while Beryl pulls the trigger. The bullet stays in place and the gun explodes, throwing Beryl backwards so she lands bloody and semi-conscious on the rocky ground. Vibrations from the explosion widen the fault line in the ceiling, making it crumble further.

Estana remains unconscious.

Ava reels off more digits.

The vultures have the group's location and are fast approaching. Without a miracle, there is **zero** chance of even **one** person escaping.

CHAPTER 19

Within **four** seconds, **nine** vultures appear.

"**One**!" yells Ava.

A confused Ash retorts, "Your **two** hazel eyes are broken... There's **nine** of them!"

Ava keeps shouting random numbers like a demented bingo caller. She becomes near impossible to hear over the whirr of approaching vultures and ominous rumble of crumbling stone, but from the speed her mouth is moving, this must now be a rapid recital.

Viewers across Deragon Hex are in thrall to their screens, gleefully awaiting the detested group's annihilation.

Ava calls out another string of unintelligible digits. Her cry of "**Eight**!" is barely audible above the din. The first wave of vultures gets close enough to aim target dots at the group's faces.

"**Three**!" shouts Ava, followed by further numbers drowned out by mechanical hum and imminent cave-in. More vultures appear at the end of the corridor.

Estana's eyelids flutter as she regains consciousness. The nearby security camera cuts to static and the vultures' media feed goes down, but the flying predators are now locked on target and continue rushing toward their prey.

Ash hears **three** of Ava's numbers, "**Six**! **Seven**! **Three**!" as the vultures reach the group.

Three of the machines keep whirring loudly, but **six** become quieter, as though listening.

With blood dripping down her forehead, Estana starts dragging herself over to a half-conscious Beryl while the vultures adjust their laser beams to follow her face. Beryl merely twitches in sleep-disturbed confusion.

"You're alive!" cries Ash.

"**Two**! **Four**!" shouts Ava, continuing her string of digits as the second wave of vultures reaches the group. The sounds of rock and machine are thunderous as new laser dots shine a merry pattern on their targets.

The malfunctioning security camera falls, closely followed by a section of cave wall. Ash jumps out of the way, still gripping Leah tight, as a dislodged rock almost hits their head.

Estana reaches Beryl's collapsed form and pulls a syringe of blood from her pocket. The social celebrity half-opens her eyes but does not register her surroundings.

"What the fuck are you doing?" demands Ash.

"**Four**!" cries Ava. She keeps yelling as the stones begin to settle and the vultures go silent but do not drop their laser beams, which pulsate as though building up to death rays.

Ava yells, "**Zero**!"

Estana ducks her head for a couple of seconds, then looks back up in surprise. "Damn, that should have been the trigger that exploded the bastards," she mutters. She then injects Beryl with Leah's blood. The media star flinches, eyes darting to the syringe in horror, and tries to jerk her arm away but fails. Her post-concussion state combined with the poison knocks her straight into an early coma.

"It was you!" Ash exclaims, cringing as a laser beam aimed at their face increases in temperature.

"**Six... five... six... six... four... three...**" recites Ava, no longer needing to raise her voice since the background noise has subsided. "**Zero... eight... six... zero... two... one...**"

"Yes, stealing Leah's blood to poison certain venomous hags was of course my doing," drawls the smug Estana. "I am the reason Judi Gingseng and Raychel Spoben lie in comas with the skin blistered off their legs and those delightful words scrawled across their foreheads."

"**Three... nine... four... nine... four... six...**" continues Ava, "**three... nine... five... two... two... four... seven...**"

The vultures are wavering as though disoriented, although Ash yelps and nearly drops Leah when a flickering ray scorches their hand. They turn their back to shield Leah, and a couple of vultures move around to better aim at their face. A circular red mark smoulders on Estana's syringe-wielding right hand, but she is too busy smiling at the blisters appearing on Beryl's legs to notice.

"**Three... seven... one...**" says Ava.

"Of course, I couldn't rely on you for this," Estana explains as she drops the needle to the ground, her hands losing strength. "It's too sly and vindictive to match your adrenaline-fuelled, brutish style, isn't it?"

"**Nine... zero... seven... zero...**" Ava drones into the dusty air, staring straight ahead at nothing, oblivious to the death rays aimed at her eyes. "**Two... one... seven... nine... eight... six... zero... nine... four... three... seven... zero... two... seven... seven... zero...**"

Paying no heed to Ava or the vultures, Estana declares, "If his painfully stupid followers enjoy defending a poisoner so much, it's only fitting they should bear his poison!" She remains unfazed by her proximity to execution as she pulls a cosmetic item from her pocket. "Also, this creature was planning on destroying me with words. That's an interesting war to wage against somebody like me, isn't it? This is how I respond to threats! I wonder what my next attack will entail if this continues? You can be extremely fucking certain I've not played my whole hand." A smiling Estana writes "Psycho Enabler" on Beryl's forehead with eye liner, while glowing red dots dance on both their faces.

Ash places Leah by a pile of fallen rocks and crouches to cover her as much as possible. Their clothing smoulders with the increasing heat of the death rays. "**Five... three... nine... two... one... seven...**" Ava continues, unblinking under the red heat. "**One... seven... six... two... nine... three...**"

"You planted that bomb as well, didn't you? The bomb that killed the core members of Beryl's fan club," Ash realises, looking up from their hunched position to stare at the drowsy-eyed Estana.

"**One... seven... six...**" says Ava. "**Seven... five... two... three... eight...**"

"Nobody planted that bomb," slurs Estana, slipping from consciousness again as more blood drips from her scalp.

"**Four... six... seven... four... eight... one...**"

"And when I say Nobody, I mean that mousey little prison clerk who loved you."

"**Eight... four... six... seven... six...**" recites Ava, while Ash feels the first ray burn through their clothing.

"It went against her sweet nature," says Estana. "But I can be *very* persuasive..."

"**Six... nine... four...**" Ava continues.

Ash understands they are in the presence of an ingeniously scheming lunatic, a couple of unconscious women, and a vagrant who thinks she is God but talks like a robot. They try coming to terms with the fact that this bug-lit, laser-targeted madness might be the final scene of their wasted life.

"There is something delicious in making a gentle soul commit brutality," a dreamy-eyed Estana softly whispers as her right cheek blisters.

"**Zero**!" Ava yells.

Ash and Estana duck their heads as the vultures explode, each becoming a fireball raining broken metal upon the comatose, the violent and the deranged.

As Estana mumbles into the dust, "I was wrong, it wasn't **five one three...**" her numbers are echoed by Ava.

CHAPTER 20

The gang is surrounded by fallen rocks and pieces of smashed machinery that twitch with electric jolts. The insects have returned to glowing motionless on the wall. "**Zero... zero...**" continues Ava.

Ash rises from crouching over Leah and walks to Estana, who appears close to death as she lies collapsed with her head propped against scorched stone. She has a hole in the front of her black coat and keeps her left eye closed while blood from her forehead drips over her lashes. Ash hunches beside her. They use the fabric of their suit jacket to wipe the scarlet fluid from her brow. "You're fucking insane... but you helped me and Leah, so thank you," they tell her, frowning with sympathy at their broken friend's injuries.

"**Five... six...**" Ava intones. Stood motionless as though unaware of the dust in her hair or dead vultures fallen around her, she has returned to slow recital.

"You know," Ash continues to Estana, "I never trusted you after seeing the pleasure you took in destroying your enemies. I thought you were a nasty bitch. Part of me still had faith in people and I thought they'd change their attitude once they knew the truth about Damon poisoning Leah..."

"**Eight... one...**"

"...but those assholes don't care about the truth! The only thing important to them is social power and their Cashdamn 'scene' hierarchy! I realise now, in a city like Deragon Hex, your methods are necessary for survival. I'm sorry I didn't trust you before."

"**Two... seven...**" says Ava.

The wound on Estana's head continues to pour blood as she remains silent. "You're dying, aren't you?" Ash sighs, reaching to pull back her coat. Their hand is batted feebly away by the disoriented woman. "Fuck!" snaps Ash. "I could have sworn I killed that stupid bitch at the hotel! I should have killed Damon too while I had the chance!"

Estana emits a weak cough, her throat irritated by dust that refuses to settle. "But then those morons would have made a martyr of him," she rasps. "And murdered Leah in retaliation."

"**One... four**," Ava continues, ignoring their conversation, her voice still flat and emotionless.

"Get Leah to safety while Ava is still reciting the Vipdile Key!" commands Estana, the edge to her voice strained as her strength depletes. "Between us, Ava and I have damaged the machinery too much for the authorities to trace your location. Just follow that damn cat!" As if on cue, Derek scampers from beneath a gap in the fallen rocks and meows at Estana. "He can show you the way. He followed me into the car with Leah for a reason."

"Are you sure leaving here will save her?" Ash gazes at Leah's motionless body sprawled on the tunnel floor. Jet-black hair falls over her grazed face, her mouth lolls open in the filthy air and the weeping, broken skin on her legs is now caked in dirt.

"Yes," Estana assures them. "The desert will revive her... and there is salvation to be found..."

"**Five...**" says Ava, "**two...**"

"...miles from the city of peripeteia," Estana continues.

"What kind of salvation?" asks Ash.

"You'll find out."

"**Six... three...**"

"But how do we survive up there?" Ash frets, despairing at Leah's mutilated form. "Coming from a sunless place of lethal paranoia... starting with no identity..."

"**Five... six...**"

Estana stares at Ash in earnest, grabbing their suit jacket. "Tell people what happened here! Sell your story to survive!

What you can't cut with a look, you can kill in a book. There might be money in literary prostitution, so make confession your profession..."

"**Zero... eight...**" adds Ava.

"Either that or train in a professional skill with decent career prospects. It depends how realistic you want to be. Also, when Leah wakes up, perhaps suggest she becomes less whiny and desperate. Nobody likes a whiner."

"**Two... seven...**"

"And remember to trust nobody up there except each other..." warns Estana.

"**Seven...**"

"You know what they say, 'If it looks like a rescue boat, it's probably a pirate ship'."

"That's an odd expression in a city that's never seen the sea." Ash absently wipes more blood from Estana's face with the back of their hand.

Estana laughs, then coughs, then laughs again. "I started that expression. I have seen the ocean, and it returned my gaze, knowing it could never touch me because I am the desert."

"**Eight... five...**"

"Then why don't you come with us Ms Desert?" Ash grins. "So your long-lost home can save you?"

"I've been shot and my head's all smashed up," Estana replies. "I don't think I'd survive the journey. You can't carry me as well as Leah."

"I'm sorry," Ash tells her. "I bet you wish you'd gotten out of here sooner... In fact, why didn't you?"

"Ha ha, I could have left whenever I wanted," Estana cackles, her throat hoarse from dust and dying.

"**Seven... seven...**" drones Ava.

"That's what I'm asking!" says Ash. "Why didn't you?"

Estana gives Ash the indulgent smile nice people reserve for slow children. "People like me thrive in these twisted cities.

It's easy for us, we never learned how to be vulnerable. You need to get that girl out of here." She nods in Leah's direction.

"**One... three...**"

Estana's eyes glaze over. "When you remove her from here, she'll stay hunted and haunted. There will be ghosts in her brain, and the shadows will know her name..."

"**Four... two... seven... five...**"

More blood drips down Estana's forehead. She smiles. "But forget her tragic inner pain... follow that damn cat to freedom! The rocks and the stars are waiting."

"**Seven...**"

Estana loses consciousness and goes limp. Her bashed-up head lolls to the side, her eyes close, and blood drips from her face to soak invisibly into the ebony fabric of her lovely coat. Ash kisses her on the forehead. After wiping blood from their lips, they turn to Ava and enquire, "Will you be coming with us?"

"No..." replies Ava. "**Seven...** I'll stay here and continue reciting the Vipdile Key to make sure nothing follows you... **eight...**"

"Won't we need the Vipdile Key above ground?" Ash raises their glance to the battered ceiling that obscures the distant sky.

"No, the Vipdile Key is only relevant underground," Ava informs them. "Up there you'll find... **nine... six...** infinity."

"Awesome! Infinity, eh?" Ash marvels. "I hope that includes something to eat. I'm so hungry! I'd love a slice of pie..."

"Yes," confirms Ava, "pie and infinity! **Zero... nine...**"

"Leah will be hungry too... What about cake?" Ash ponders, standing to return to the comatose figure sprawled on the filthy ground.

"Yes," Ava assures them, "foods of all description, and infinity. **One... seven...** I'm not sure you're grasping the concept of infinity here."

"Infinity pie," grins Ash. "I get it. It's obvious, really."

"**Three... six...**" Ava responds into the dust.

Ash crouches and scoops up the slumbering Leah in weary arms before turning back to Ava. "Well goodbye! Thanks for your help, whoever you are."

"I had no choice. This was my purpose." Ava's unnerving glance suggests deep understanding while somehow remaining expressionless. "Give my regards to Honeysuckle and Alicia. **Three... seven...**"

Ash's eyes widen as they gasp, "Honeysuckle and Alicia? The starlet and the serial killer... They're alive then? Are they friends of yours?"

"You could say that," says Ava. "**One... seven...** You'll find Alicia near petroglyphs on fiery rocks, and Honeysuckle waits in the city of peripeteia, languishing in her room of mirrors. **Eight... seven...** Now go! Before the Vipdile Key has finished turning!"

Derek the cat meows once more and scuttles off along a corridor littered with fallen rocks. Ash, carrying Leah, follows their feline guide over the crumbling terrain, while Ava's recital slows down but continues until they have disappeared from view.

The journey continues along twisted tunnels and strange walkways. Delirious obstinacy forces Ash onwards, clutching their poisoned cargo, never stopping until they have reached the sanctuary of open sky.

CHAPTER 21

The final climb takes them up a metal stairway through rocks the colour of rust. Despite their agonized limbs, Ash falls straight in love with the desert. Although seemingly barren at first glance, the land teems with organisms that cling to life with a terrifying tenacity, brutal creatures that slaughter to survive. It feels like coming home.

The only problem will be keeping Leah alive up here. Her skin heals the second it sees the sun, with blisters of burned flesh turning into bleached leaves of tissue paper that flutter away over dry stones to be replaced by smooth, untainted flesh. She will burn again though. She and Ash will both burn in this blinding light, being so melaninally challenged. Ash finds a sheltered spot among the rocks to take refuge and plan their next course of action.

"Meow," utters Derek. Ash sees their feline guide sitting next to a purple hedgehog, animal eyes regarding each other in mysterious communion. Before Ash has time to utter a crudely worded exclamation of surprise, both animals vanish, leaving the weary traveller to stare open mouthed at the spot they last inhabited.

Ash shrugs and turns back to Leah, deciding there are some things a person is just not supposed to understand in this life. Leah breathes softly, her face relaxed as though sleeping. Ash removes their suit jacket and shakes off the dust from battle. Despite being covered in scorch marks and blood, the garment remains mostly intact and is the closest thing they have to a blanket. They drape it over Leah, tucking the sleeves behind her shoulders, the collar into her hospital gown, and arranging the main body of the jacket to cover her chest and loosely folded arms. "Please wake up, Leah," they whisper as a stray lock of ebony hair falls over her face.

Free from their subterranean prison, Ash does not know which way to turn and has nobody left to guide them. Leah will not wake while Damon lives. If only there was a way to go back and kill him without leaving the unconscious girl at the mercy of the desert. This is not a safe environment for delicate flowers.

Ash needs a friend, somebody else who has survived the underworld. "To the petroglyphs or the city of peripeteia?" they ask themself. Ava vouched for Alicia, and it could be useful having another fearsome killer on their side as they recommence their quest for vengeance. However, this still leaves the problem of keeping Leah safe. The best option might be finding Honeysuckle first. Ash decides they will search for the starlet's room of reflections, but first they must set up camp for the evening. They know enough about seasonal variations of daylight to realise it cannot be summer. The long-awaited sun is still bright but low in the sky, and it has been aeons since Ash slept, running for days on spite and bitter determination.

They gather dead weeds and branches into a hollow in the rocks. The sun descends as they work, casting jagged shadows across the ground, and they constantly check Leah to make sure nothing has chosen her as prey. They pack their pieces of makeshift fuel tightly together. Once the sun has set and the only illumination is from the cold glitter of stars, it is time to light the fire. They previously feasted on retro survival programmes from overground and consider rubbing sticks together to make a spark, but then they remember the lighter in their jacket pocket.

The dark deepens and from across the rocks comes the sound of predators waking.

Ash is unable to relax as they guard Leah by firelight. This camp was a stupid idea... What are they, a fucking caveperson? They should have tried to push further and find the rumoured civilisations of overground before sunset.

The thought of civilisation makes Ash remember the pilfered com screen in their suit pocket, and they check to see if it has battery power remaining. Bizarrely, not only does it switch on, it also receives a signal from the Deragon Hex media network. The first thing that comes on is Damon Repper's opinion show.

"You have got to be fucking kidding me," Ash fumes.

Thanks to another massive ratings boost, Damon now sits on a throne constructed from car parts and dismantled guns. His crew transformed his studio into the workshop of a demented engineer, with walls made from twisted mechanisms, cogs, pipes and metal plating. "Welcome to my show," he says, still managing a smug smile despite broken bones and bandages. The disciples that usually join his platform are dead or dying, but he is flanked by twin sisters wearing matching outfits of red talex plastic. His congregation before the stage are the usual bunch of sycophantic social climbers and frumpy Gothic battle-axes clothed in lace, patchouli and mouldy desperation.

"Today we're going to talk about *loyalty*," he declares, and the studio audience dutifully whoop in anticipation.

"I have survived a dreadful ordeal. My psycho ex sent a couple of brainwashed allies to destroy my life because she is a malicious lunatic who enjoys attention. However, despite her best efforts to kill me, I am still here! The reason for this is *loyalty*. No matter what those horrible people say about me or bully me into saying, you, my loyal followers, will be eternally on my side."

This prompts a round of applause from all his enraptured fan club except the talex-clad twins, who continue to stare straight ahead with vacant smiles.

"Now, please pray to Cash that my darling Beryl is found alive and well," he implores. "She was last seen on surveillance footage somewhere in the caves apprehending those dreadful stalkers and..." he trails off, confused by the twins' behaviour.

With smiles fixed and eyes empty, they are cuffing his wrists to the metal arms of his throne.

"What's happening here, ladies?" he grins.

They remain silent.

A triumphant voice crows from offstage, "She won't wake until you're dead!"

The twins rise and exit stage left while Estana enters the scene from stage right accompanied by **four** armed guards.

The audience rise in panicked uproar while the law enforcers descend the short stairway to stand before the platform with guns raised. At the back of the studio, another line of **six** armed guards blocks the exit. The masses stand and shout helplessly, wanting to run but not wishing to be killed. They had only come for a nice day out and this was very upsetting.

"Shut up!" Estana commands.

The crowd becomes silent.

Estana turns to the show's bewildered host, crooning, "Hello Damon", with the smile of a praying mantis. Most of the cameras are still running. Vultures, wolves and the guards not owned by Estana are on their way to the scene, but the doors are barricaded to buy the time she needs. She swaggers to centre stage, carrying herself like a supreme being stepping up to her destiny.

Far above, in the desert, Ash watches by firelight on a com screen that has approximately **eight** minutes of battery left. "I wish you could see Damon's show now, Leah!" they tell their comatose companion. "Estana's just arrived! She's strutting like a dickhead who's about to trip over her own density, but I've got the distinct impression Damon is fucked!"

The camera closest to the captured host zooms in on his face, which despite a heavy coating of foundation is dripping with sweat. "What the fuck are you doing here?" he demands.

"Don't worry, I only came to set you on fire," Estana assures him. "Now please turn to camera **four**."

"I don't want to see you anymore!" yells Damon, as he struggles to slide his wrists out of the handcuffs. "You've got a nerve coming here, you crazy bitch!"

Estana frowns. "Honestly, Damon. You've known this day was coming, so don't insult us both by acting surprised. Nobody poisons anybody under my roof and gets away with it."

"You're supposed to be dead! I saw you collapsed on the ground after Beryl shot you!"

His tormentor unbuckles her long, black coat to the waist then places her hands on her hips. The studio audience gasp. Her open coat reveals not only a stunning black dress, but also a silver necklace that holds a large key, in which a bullet is lodged. Damon gasps, "Is that the Vipdile Key?"

"No, the Vipdile Key is a number, you moron. This is a lovely necklace I'm wearing."

"Are you telling me a bullet aimed at your heart just happened to lodge in a key attached to your necklace?"

"I'm not telling you anything! I'm unfastening my coat so I don't get too hot by the fire. The reason I'm here is because I do what I want," Estana says. "And I don't want to die at this stage of my career."

"But how the hell did you get in here?" Damon demands. "This is the top studio in Deragon Hex! You're nobody! You don't even have your own show!"

Estana laughs. "Fame is irrelevant. I don't need external validation to be who I am."

"But they shouldn't have let you in!"

"You still don't understand, do you?" sighs Estana. "I'm not waiting for permission from *them*," she gestures toward the audience. "I never was! Besides, I was always going to find you."

"You're fucking obsessed, you lunatic bitch!"

"Ha! Don't flatter yourself, Damon. I would have forgotten you existed if your faithful dogs hadn't hounded my household. You could have easily kept them leashed and let us move on.

But you didn't, did you? Quite the opposite, you publicly gloated over the damage they did to Leah!"

"You've no right to judge my behaviour after the way you use people!" Damon splutters.

"At least I'm honest about what I am!" Estana snaps. "I'm struggling to think how the fuck I could be any *more* honest. Also, I'm a psychopath with class! Unlike you. The poisoning was crass and tasteless. And your hiding behind the skirts of ghoulish henchwomen instead of admitting your crimes amplifies your guilt. I would suggest you fight your own battles next time, except there won't be a next time, will there?"

"I didn't poison you!" shouts Damon. "What's your fucking problem? You had no regard for Leah! She was an embarrassment to you!"

"I have more regard for her than for you," replies Estana. "And if you poison somebody under my roof, I will take it as a personal insult... Particularly if you then have the nerve to play victim while the girl lies in a coma."

"She got out of here, didn't she?!" snarls Damon. "Is this drama necessary? The stupid girl's been saved!"

Estana responds with a sad shake of her head. "You forget, you're not talking to Ash now, Damon, you are talking to *me*. It was Ash who only killed to save their precious Leah. I enjoy vengeance for its own sake. I find it entertaining. Fortunately, our goals are compatible because no matter how far Leah is taken from here, she won't wake up while you remain alive."

"Well take her to a fucking doctor!" Damon struggles to free himself from the cuffs attached to his throne.

"I am the only doctor she needs," Estana informs him. "Now, if you turn to camera **four** and look closely, you'll see behind the lens is a firebomb."

This is when the studio audience begin screaming.

Up in the desert, still transfixed by the spectacle on their screen, Ash shakes their head in wonder. "This woman's a few jam jars short of a **zero**-calorie jam collection but I wouldn't want to be on her bad side." They glance at Leah, who still shows no sign of waking.

Back in the studio, half the audience is crying, while others stare in hypnotised shock as though observing a car crash, fireworks or the season finale of a popular drama.

Damon sneers. "You should know, if you kill me, my followers will find Leah and destroy her. In fact, I'd bet on you having **nine** days, maximum, before a mob hunts your group down and slaughters you."

"The behaviour of people in thrall to poisonous scum is irrelevant to me," insists Estana with a calm smile. "In fact, you should probably thank them for this, for pushing me this far. I could never have done this without them. Really, this is their fault for continuing to abuse a girl whose life you had already destroyed. It's only a shame so many of them lie poisoned, exploded or decapitated so they can't see what they've driven me to."

"Fucking bitch!" curses Damon. "You have **zero** chance of getting away with this! You're finished! Do you hear me? Somebody will avenge me!"

"That's cute," replies Estana. "Well, you can tell whatever deluded moron avenges you, I'm only accepting responses in the form of artistic output. People with no talent are simply not worth my time."

"What time?" Damon grasps. "You've none left! Don't you realise your life will be torn to pieces? Don't you know how rich my father is?"

Estana remains unmoved by the threat of retribution. "No amount of money can bury the truth. Truth is sacred. Truth is eternal. Truth is what delivers us from the darkness of everlasting oblivion. And the truth is, you are an obnoxious, self-righteous prick who would look better on fire."

Damon begins screaming.

"Goodbye Damon," says Estana, giving him a wave and a look of pretend sympathy. "Remember... Everything is under control, as always."

She fades to a silhouette of monochrome dots, then vanishes. Damon is trapped on stage, alone. His screams continue while the camera to his right explodes in **one** massive ball of fire that engulfs the entire stage, consuming everything in its path.

In the desert, Ash continues to stare open-mouthed at the fiery extravaganza on their com screen. On the dusty ground beside them, Leah opens her eyes.

CHAPTER 22

Black, white and grey dots in the shape of a vengeful woman materialise beside Ash and Leah in the starlit desert. Within **four** seconds the dots colour and solidify to become Estana, who drawls, "If you want something done properly..." She cracks her trademark vicious smile.

"How the fuck did you do that?" Ash eyes Estana with a curious mixture of awe and bewilderment, failing to notice that Leah is now awake.

"I told you I could leave whenever I wanted." The proud woman basks in the camp fire's amber glow. "I just wish I had my own opinion show so I could announce what a WONDERFUL time I'm having."

"But... What the fuck *are* you?"

"What and how are less important questions than who and where," Estana replies, her glance a cryptic shimmer.

"You forgot why and when..."

"My reason was obviously revenge, but time is not relevant here."

"Is any of this real?" wonders Ash while Leah sits up beside them, blinking in the light from the golden flames.

"It's more real than most people will believe," explains Estana. "Sometimes the truth is better told through fairy tale. This is certainly closer to reality than the pile of catshit Damon's fan club were stupid enough to swallow."

"Well, thank you both for saving me," says Leah, arching her back in a delicate stretch. Ash's head whips around at the sound of her voice, their heart jolting with barely contained hope, staring a few seconds, questioning their senses.

Leah looks back at them and smiles.

"You're awake!" Ash exclaims, leaping across and throwing their arms around her, ecstatic with relief.

"I knew you'd deliver me to the desert," Leah tells them. "Now my evil ex-boyfriend is dead, I am free from his poison! I might even live to be 95! My life can be spent painting, writing, dancing and looking after many cats... Wait, where is my cat? I dreamed he was with us and we followed him to freedom."

"He scampered off somewhere," replies Ash, pulling back to gaze at her face. "He looked happy, as though he'd finished his work here."

"I'm pleased," Leah smiles. "He was the feline embodiment of a kind soul."

"Before he disappeared, he made friends with a hedgehog," Ash tells her, furrowing their brow in confusion. "I couldn't figure out what the fuck a hedgehog was doing in the desert... Maybe we need the hedges and the h..."

"Please don't start that!" snaps Estana, who is smirking despite her annoyance. For a second, her face becomes composed of black and white dots once more, but her skin soon regains its porcelain complexion.

"Sorry," says Ash, "I forgot you don't find repetitive word jokes amusing and you're only entertained when people *die*. How silly of me."

Ash gives Leah another hug. "I thought I'd lost you! I will never leave you alone with horrible people, ever again," they promise, reaching to tuck an ebony curl away from their best friend's eyes.

"And I'm going to emulate more of your behaviour," declares Leah. "Not the combustive rage attacks, but the determination to survive, general lack of self-pity, and the way you use dark, abrasive humour as a defence mechanism."

The campfire radiates warmth onto the gang's happy faces while the sound of screaming continues to emanate from Ash's com screen.

"Haha! Have you seen this?" asks Ash, showing Leah their device. "This is Damon. Damon enjoys emotionally abusing and poisoning his partners. Damon is now on fire. Don't be like Damon! Obviously, he didn't enjoy not being on fire enough to be intrinsically fireproof."

Leah's countenance clouds over as she views the remains of the dramatic death scene. "It was a shame it came to this," she sighs. "I always thought if I was nice to everybody, nobody would hurt me. I only wanted to create beautiful artwork and find the love I needed. Why did my life become a war zone?"

Ash puts their arm around her. "Don't blame yourself. You live like a teenage trainwreck, but you just wanted love. It wasn't your fault."

Leah raises her eyes to the distant silhouette of stony ridges against a twinkling sky. The desert had been calling her while she slumbered. Although appearing desolate at first glance, this land has a haunting beauty more ancient than art; it feels like the birthplace of her soul. She finally believes happiness might be possible.

The tinny sounds of screaming from the com screen's speakers are getting fainter. "Shit! The fire's nearly finished with the fucker," remarks Ash. "I do feel kinda guilty about all this death, but I'm glad it's brought you back, Leah. I hoped escaping that poisonous playground would be enough to save you... It turns out I was wrong."

Estana convulses with another burst of cruel laughter. "Surely you didn't believe the poetic delusion that our salvation lay in astronomy and dirt? We people need blood and victory! Remember who you are, you glorious fucking axe-wielding sociopath, you."

Bathing in firelight and comforted by the presence of her saviours, Leah sighs as she leans against the rocks, smiling up at the stars.

EPILOGUE

Far from here, the Vipdile Key will finish turning as Deragon Hex returns to slumber, its purpose served.

Vengeance brings salvation.

Leah will live, her body purged of poison because Damon Repper is dead.

"That's a spectacularly lifeless psycho right there!" Ash still stares at the tiny screen. "You'd have to persecute some orphans or nuke a mental health inpatient unit to bring him back from this."

"Nobody's nuking anybody!" Leah insists, shaking her tousled ringlets in dismay. "What would we become?"

Estana gazes lovingly into the fire as though reconnecting with an old friend, calm and poised in her black overcoat, exquisite dress and buckled boots. She says, "It's too late to be asking that now, honey."

The androgynous assassin looks up from their dying device. "He's stopped screaming," they remark before yawning and rubbing their eyes.

"He's turning into you," says Estana.

"How so?"

"He's becoming ash."

"Looks more like flame-grilled remains to me! That's a big barbecue of bastard right there," jokes Ash with a satisfied nod of their head.

"His parents are married," replies Estana.

"That was a joke, dumbass! An amazing attempt at alliteration."

"How delightful. You should write a book."

"*You* write a fucking book!"

"Never mind writing a book!" cries Leah. "We must build a manageable life for ourselves, find a realistic method of survival... Or what will happen to us?"

Estana turns to smile at her underlings with brutal serenity in her lunatic countenance. "What will happen to us?" she repeats as a spark leaps from the fire to die on her footwear. "Well, we've had our revenge... and it was glorious, but there's no coming back from what we've done...

"We **three** now belong to the desert."

ABOUT THE AUTHOR(S)

The Carlie Nooka Martece collective is a gender-fluid, dissociative system working as a visual artist, "model" and independently published writer. They reside in a dark but hilarious dreamworld. They are eternally grateful to everybody who has supported their career so far, helped with editing and promotion, and defended them from vulture attacks.

Martece wrote their first book, the semi-autobiographical Toxic Nursery, to provide insight into dissociative identity disorder. They have since been diagnosed with comorbid autism. Deragon Hex: The Vipdile Key was their first work of science fiction, later followed by Chroma: Calanooka. These books form the Constructed Sanity Sequence, an ongoing series of autobiographies and novels that will increasingly entangle as the overall story progresses.

The collective is presently living Toxic Nursery's sequel, and continue to share their artistic creations with the world via their website at www.carliemartece.com

Find them online.

www.ingramcontent.com/pod-product-compliance
Ingram Content Group UK Ltd.
Pitfield, Milton Keynes, MK11 3LW, UK
UKHW040004200726
13854UKWH00001B/31

9 780992 871666